# RAIN SHADOW

# RAIN SHADOW

## CATHERINE MADERA

Tres Caballos Press

Copyright 2012 by Catherine Madera
All rights reserved

Published by Tres Caballos Press
PO Box 211
Acme, WA 98220
For ordering information, or to contact the author, please visit:
www.catherinemadera.com

This is a work of fiction. In all fiction the literary perceptions and insights are based on experience, however, names, characters, places, and incidents are either products of the author's imagination or are used fictitiously. No reference to a real person is intended or should be inferred.

Cover and book design by Karen Bacon, www.karenannbacon.com
Cover photos by Chris Galbraith and Ellende, BigStockPhoto
Back cover photo by Kinetic Imagery, BigStockPhoto
Additional chapter photo by Ellende, BigStockPhoto
Editing by Dan Bettle and Karen Bacon

For permission to reprint the photo of Hero, grateful acknowledgment is made to Emily Green, www.shadesofgreenphotography.com.

ISBN 978-0-615-61384-0
Printed in the United States of America

*For my son, Nicholas*

*"We're all looking for redemption;
just afraid to say the word."*

— Pat Greene "Wave on Wave"

# PROLOGUE

The mare followed at a distance. Twiggy undergrowth as tall as the saddle horn scratched at her on either side. Overhead a canopy of branches arched toward the sky from the broad trunk of a single, enormous maple tree. The late afternoon sunshine intensified its gold-edged leaves, a gilded warning that autumn approached

The man took no notice of the narrowing trail, striding onward with a purpose that contrasted sharply with the mare's hobbling gait. The hitch in her step had deteriorated to a three-legged limp after only a few minutes of riding. When she could no longer bear his weight the man dismounted.

"Useless."

An edge in his voice made the mare's ears prick up. She flicked them back and forth. The man walked to her side, unhooked the throatlatch and slid the bit quickly from between her teeth. The mare hung her head as he snapped a lead rope to the worn halter.

"Come on, then. I don't have all day."

And so she followed him down the unfamiliar trail, stepping quickly every time he jerked on the lead, sputtering at face level spider webs.

They finally entered a small clearing surrounded by Douglas Fir trees. The grass, protected by shade, was still green and growing. Alpine strawberries, crimson from the lateness of the season, were scattered here and there like tiny gems. Their sweet fragrance hung in the still air. It was the perfect place for a cozy picnic with a lady. *Next time*, the man thought. He touched his hip, fingering the solid weight of the .357 Magnum.

Walking to the mare he pulled the latigo free, loosening the saddle. It was good leather, well worth saving. With a calloused finger he traced an imaginary triangle on the mare's forehead and dropped the lead rope.

"Go ahead; git yourself some lunch, girl." He backed up several steps.

The mare did not eat. She followed after the man, searching his body language for a familiar cue.

"Go on now!" The man raised his arms, flapping his hands at her. When she did not move he smacked her jaw with the heel of his hand.

"Good God Almighty—I said git!"

The mare faltered. Slowly she lowered her head, allowing the grass to tickle her lips as they hovered over the earth. Her eyes followed the man.

"There ya go."

He spoke soothingly, but the mare was not comforted. She watched his hand move to his hip and pull at the object hanging there.

"Ya gotta make this hard," he grunted. "Women always do."

He slipped seven rounds into the cylinder. Seven was overkill. Only'd take one round, well placed. He backed up, aimed at a spot above the mare's left eye, and pulled the trigger.

The stiff crack shattered the silence. Invisible life lurking in the bushes scurried away. The mare dropped her head, her legs buckling. Slowly, gracefully, she slumped to the ground as if laying down for a nap on a balmy day.

The man walked to her side and considered his handiwork. The mare had fallen on a small rise and gravity forced the oozing blood over her eye into a trail that ran down her neck and pooled near the shoulder. The man watched, fascinated, as the blood brightened the mare's most distinguishable feature, a large patch of rust-colored hair that stamped her otherwise grey body. It reminded him of a film in sepia tone that suddenly changes to full color.

The strange marking—now a rich magenta—had stood out as an anomaly from the moment of the mare's birth. Like an upside down ice cream cone he'd thought at the time. The "cone" began, point up, at the wither and spread into a large uneven oval that extended over the shoulder. At first the marking had been part of the mare's odd appeal. His friends were not intrigued.

"I got about as much use for them horses as I got for the friggin' camel jockeys who bred 'em." Shaking his head, the man's buddy flicked a cigarette butt in the mare's direction. He took a sip of Budweiser. "Git yourself a real horse, Hombre. This freak of nature don't fit the bill."

Over time the man had come to the same conclusion.

He pushed at her shoulder with the toe of his work boots. He'd forgotten how much blood one round could make. The man stepped aside, wiping the heavy tread of his shoes on a spongy patch of grass. He felt a twinge of guilt. The mare had been a good horse. No arguing that. She'd had the most soulful eyes he'd ever seen on a beast. She seemed to know his thoughts and wishes a split second before he expressed them. Damn uncanny. *Female intuition,* he supposed.

But he'd tired of her in the way he tired of the women who wandered in and out of his life. High maintenance all of them. He pushed the guilt aside. No sense beating a dead horse. The man smirked at his private humor.

Fact is he'd given the mare a chance to move on, too. The ad in the paper had gotten one response, a young father looking for a horse for his daughter. But the mare turned up lame. Even without the hitch in her step they'd been critical of the marking.

"The hell's that?"

"A-rabs say mark like that shows some kind of favor—a special blessing."

"They think their rag heads look good, too."

And so they had passed on his mare. By then he was saving for a new horse. A Quarter Horse this time; bred in the good ole US of A. The man was not about to spend his hard earned cash to treat a female's mystery lameness. Not his fault at all.

Satisfied the mare was gone, the man slung his saddle over a forearm in the gathering dusk and left by the way he had come.

Later, under the half light of a waxing gibbous moon, the mare stirred and staggered to her feet.

# Chapter 1

'Where Friends Meet.'

Taylor pondered the wooden signage hanging above the door of the tiny grocery store. It seemed mildly threatening. Even if a friend lurked out here in the boonies she wasn't looking for a reunion. There was only one friend on her list—her grocery list: Sara Lee.

Stepping from the safety of her car, Taylor adjusted the too-big waist of her olive green sweats. The surface of the blacktop glistened from a recent shower, glass-like in the sun that had broken gloriously through the clouds. An hour ago the world was a muted grey, indistinct. A great excuse for Salvation Army sweat pants. But it had only taken a moment for the surrounding countryside to be transformed as the sun reminded residents it was still summer. Jewel tones shimmered everywhere—emerald green pines; sapphire blue skies. Not far away the snow-capped head of Mount Baker was blinding. Pure white diamonds. Maybe instant makeovers were a specialty in Washington

State. One could hope.

She plodded toward an enormous wooden door that looked as if it was lifted from the set of *Lord of the Rings*. Though the sign promised the mundane— "groceries"—it seemed like the sort of place one might barter for the eccentric. Magic bean seeds, for instance. Once inside, Taylor made her way down wooden floors so old and worn the grain was no longer visible. Years of log truck drivers' heavy tread and farmers' rubber boots resulted in a deeply grooved surface that suggested endless toil and the spirit of the rugged lives that sought nourishment within the confines of the store. The air smelled of musty herbs.

Taylor scrunched up her toes, feeling the grit under her flip-flops, and began scanning the aisles. *Green olives, soup.... Where are frozen foods?* There was something disconcerting about an unfamiliar grocery store. Who knew what was stocked there? Especially in this part of the country. Wheat grass and bean curd were probably standard fare; regular food with preservatives could be illegal. Like smoking. Another vice she was looking forward to horrifying healthy people with. In Vista, Taylor knew exactly where to find nourishment at the store. There was no floundering about, no need to buy an off-brand. Not that Sara Lee would be considered nourishment by everyone's standards.

Finally Taylor located the frozen foods section, barely half an aisle long. She held her breath as she scanned shelves filled with orange juice, cheap ice cream, and whipped topping. There, next to a Hungry-Man fried chicken dinner, was one beautiful coconut cream pie. Un-freaking-believable.

After locating her prize, Taylor wandered around the store. Cereal might be a good idea. She located the breakfast aisle and stared at the choices, first picking up a box with chocolate in the title, then some granola with flax. Whole grain or high fructose corn syrup? Choosing a cereal shouldn't be this hard. In exasperation Taylor replaced the boxes and approached the check-out. On the way she picked up a six-pack of Corona, two limes, and a package of flour tortillas.

"What's for dinner?"

It took Taylor a moment to register the clerk's question, her attention stolen by a huge jar of pickled eggs that perched on the counter between them. She stared, mesmerized, at the pale orbs that rocked gently within a yellow, sulfurous liquid. The eyeballs of giants? Sasquatch was known to be partial to the Pacific Northwest.

"Uh, yeah. That's about it." She nodded toward the items being bagged and waited for the clerk to ask for ID. Buying alcohol felt weird, even though she'd been 21 for over a month.

"Dinner of champions." The checker chuckled, revealing a section of missing teeth. She bagged the beer without hesitation. "I'm Della. Haven't seen you around. You new in the area?"

"Yeah."

Taylor took extra time filtering through the contents of her small backpack. She wasn't particularly interested in the clerk becoming the "friend" she met when shopping. Obviously employees took the store's motto seriously.

As she drove home Taylor considered the grocery shopping experience. Another neon sign indicating she was in strange territory. In California, the closest Sara Lee coconut cream pies were down the street at a corner convenience store. The clerks there could have watched her being mugged without getting involved. They'd continue talking to each other in Hindi, or Spanish, or Chinese and calmly dial 911. If she was lucky. If, say, blood was involved.

Taylor drove east, toward the Mount Baker foothills and her brand new digs. Sure, it was far out, but the simple beauty of the place, the peaceful isolation, was irresistible. Bellingham would have been the natural choice, but Taylor felt drawn to call on the ad for a "Cozy-one bedroom house on herb farm. Find your spirit here." If there was any hope in locating her spirit, it must be at the tiny yellow house with the overgrown Honeysuckle. Taylor put down a deposit after the five-minute tour.

She drove down the drive slowly, waving at her new land lady, Rowan, digging in a field of Echinacea. *Rowan, Sage, Clover.* In one week she'd met three people named after plants. That had to be a sign of some sort. Was it good or bad things that came in threes? She couldn't remember. Rowan was eccentric, yes, but Taylor couldn't imagine the woman fell into the category of bad luck.

"What is Rowan? Like, what does it mean?" Taylor had blurted out her curiosity a few minutes after meeting the serene, grandmotherly woman—a hippy sort of grandmother with dreadlocks, long turquoise dreamcatcher earrings and a huge tattoo of a tree that grew up the length of one deeply tanned arm. Forthright was not her usual style with strangers, but the woman's open demeanor put Taylor at ease.

"Rowan is a type of tree. I chose the name when I was ten. I have a special connection to this tree; perhaps I was a Rowan in my previous life—roots deeply coiled around the earth, arms reaching for the clouds."

Her future landlady opened both hands, made deliberate fists around invisible air, then extended her arms toward the sky. Taylor gawked at the tree tattoo, fascinated with the way its leafy branches drooped into the folds of old lady skin that sagged toward Rowan's shoulders as she reached heavenward. The tattoo turned into an upside down weeping willow. Her eyes were striking, a cool vivid green like the inside of a kiwi. With her hair, eyes, and droopy tan skin, Rowan could be a cover model for *National Geographic Magazine*.

If she had been her mother, Taylor would have made a show of checking the schedule on her Blackberry at that moment. She would have told Rowan she had other "prospects." Made it seem she was already late and, "I'll call you if I'm interested." But she wasn't her mother. Not even close. The herb farm was peaceful and conveniently inconvenient for visitors—her mother, for instance.

Taylor parked her '91 Toyota and sat for a minute, watching the purple, daisy-like heads of the flowers flutter in a warm September breeze. There was no doubt she felt pulled toward this patch of earth. Her own roots longed to coil around something sheltering.

A moment later she sunk her fork into the coconut cream pie without bothering to defrost it. This was the joy of independence, no one around to tell her she couldn't have pie for dinner—*frozen* pie. Taylor finished the entire dessert, crinkled its foil tin into the trash and cracked open a beer. She walked outside and sat in a lawn chair, considering her new environment.

Across the street was an old graveyard. "Sacred Cross Cemetery," read a wooden sign. It hung crookedly from two broad posts and had a subtle green patina permanently etched into the grooves of white painted wood—moss and mildew, the state "flower."

Taylor had already wandered around the cemetery and noted the names and dates on the tombstones. Some were so old the etchings had crumbled and she could only make out the odd letter or a date. Rhododendrons and azaleas were scattered like green sentries guarding the dead. Rowan promised they were "a glimpse of paradise" when they blossomed in May.

Ian would love the cemetery Taylor thought, as she sipped the Corona. He'd love to take walks there and read the epitaphs. He would be close, his hands never far from her body; twining with her fingers, brushing against her back, finding a lock of brunette hair to coil and uncoil around an index finger. His restless, masculine energy was like an electric fence she'd touched once. She could sense the current pulsing through the fence, vibrating in some sort of dangerous other dimension. A place not meant to contact tender skin. The pull to feel that energy had been irresistible. She still remembered the jolt when her childish hand grasped the wire, still hear herself cry out.

The fact that she would choose her new home across from a cemetery probably said something important. She was a head shrinker's dream, no doubt, drawn back to the horror of that day in the same way a passerby is drawn to look at a traffic accident. Only she wasn't an innocent passerby and no matter what she did the memories seeped back into her mind at every opportunity, like a bad smell. Something dead needed to be buried.

Taylor guzzled the last of the beer and pushed the feelings down—deep down—as the warmth of a buzz mellowed the edges of memory. She might be a head shrinker's dream, but she would not cry. No drama. Just a new start in this land of plant people and strangely soothing cemeteries. And rain.

Oh, the rain was coming. Taylor could feel it in the fall chill that chased away the remnants of an Indian summer day. A record breaking summer in terms of heat Rowan had shared. The grass around the little cottage was crispy and tan, like southern California without irrigation. But it would turn green again, even in winter. The rain would demand it.

She'd left Seattle—and the rain—at 17, pulled as if by a magnet to San Diego. To life with her father, beaches kissed with eternal sun and the promise of endless summer. Nobody could stop her. Interstate 5 stretched out like a race track and she had sped toward the pot of gold waiting near the Mexican border. For three years she hadn't wasted a moment thinking about her mother, the Pacific Northwest, or the eternal, depressing rain. No grey skies allowed.

It was funny how things changed. In a way she had returned for the rain, longed for it while barreling back up I-5. As she crossed the Columbia River into Washington the first rain drops pelted her windshield. Not a serious rain, just a few welcoming drops. She had sighed deeply at the sight of them, cracked the window to smell the cool fresh moisture. Yes, she had returned for the rain. And to bury her dead.

Goose bumps prickled Taylor's skin as she rose from the chair. She heard her cell phone beeping a reminder that someone had left a message. Seeing as she knew nobody in greater Bellingham it could only be one person.

*Taylor Ann, it's your mother. I need to talk to you about the office. Two days a week you'll follow an agent, learn the ropes, and be gofer girl. I'll give you a week to get settled but the Bellingham office is expecting a call. Got it? Make sure you go for your broker's license, too. Call me so we can talk about it. I'm planning to be in Bellingham on Saturday.*

Punching a button to delete the message, Taylor sank into the lone chair and flicked on the TV. Conflicting emotions swirled like a tornado. Was this the dumbest thing she'd ever done? No, definitely not. But it still felt like a future train wreck. She was back under her mother's thumb and the subject of her charity. There were expectations now, not like when she lived with Neal and Tom. Her mom had been resolute on the phone.

"You're going nowhere, Taylor Ann. I can feel it all the way in Seattle. Get your real estate license and come work at the office. I'll help you get started. It's time to *do* something. You can't lounge on the beach for the rest of your life."

Taylor hated that her mother was right, hated to admit that by accepting the offer she needed help. Her *mother's* help. But nothing—and nobody—begged her to stay. The fine-as-sugar beaches and pounding surf no longer appealed to her. Even the sun had gotten tiring—relentless and unchanging. She felt naked in that sun, her faults accentuated for all to see. Instead, she craved the rain of the northwest; it complimented so many comforting things—fog, slouchy sweats, mugs of cocoa, blankets. Her thirsty soul would sop up that rain like a dry sponge.

One would think a good movie or two could be had on a Friday night, even with limited channels. Taylor flicked her way through an infomercial, a weather report, a TV preacher, and two sitcom reruns. She went back to the preacher.

"Jesus told a parable about talents. Know what a talent is, people? That's your abilities, your resources, your time, and your money. It's what God gave you to manage on this earth. *What are you doing with it?*"

The preacher was working himself into a frenzy. Taylor watched him loosen his tie, his red face bunched with emotion. "Most of you are waiting to get mugged by happiness, all the while burying your talents in the sand rather than investing in God's kingdom. *Do something with what God's given you!* Happiness will come when you do that." A number came up on the screen for donors to call in. Taylor shut off the TV. If God was so great and powerful, why was He always short on cash? Still, the preacher's words lingered.

*What am I doing with my talents?*

In the silence she considered the question. She had no money and very few abilities. Still, God *had* given her something. But she had proven she could not be trusted. She probably deserved to be mugged, and not by happiness.

Tears swelled behind Taylor's eyes. She felt fragile, her emotions sloppy and unmanageable. She'd accomplished a whole lot of nothing in 21 years, existing only on the good graces of others. The latest adventure—becoming a real estate agent—wasn't even her idea. It was an escape, a pathetic attempt to get on with her life. She felt the sudden urge to do a good deed, to give to someone else and atone for her own neediness, her mistakes, her squandering of God's gifts. A warm, benevolent feeling struggled to rise above the fog of alcohol and tears. But do what?

☙

# Chapter 2

It took Taylor several wrong turns to locate the animal shelter. It was tucked away on the outskirts of town, neatly hidden behind a row of self-storage units and a lumber warehouse. Parking the Corolla, Taylor noticed a field and a three-sided shelter directly behind the building. The grey-blue sky glowered overhead, threatening rain. An early autumn wind blew leaves around her feet as she walked to the door of the facility.

"Hi. I called earlier about volunteering. Taylor Reed."

The woman at the front desk was rifling through files in a cabinet. She seemed oblivious to Taylor's presence. *Liz* was the name on a plastic badge pinned to a berry-colored Carhartt vest. Just as Taylor opened her mouth to speak again, Liz looked up. She pushed a double-sided piece of paper across the desk.

"Fill this out, then I'll give you a tour. It'll be brief. I gotta pick up feral cats in an hour."

As she filled out the paperwork, Taylor snuck peeks at Liz who alternated between plucking on a computer keyboard and hobbling in and out of a doorway leading to the animals in the back. She was a wiry woman who looked like she lived her life outside. Not something you'd expect from a person obviously handicapped. Cerebral Palsy, maybe. While the left side of Liz's body looked normal, the right sagged dramatically as if continually tugged down by unseen forces.

The process seemed to begin at the corner of her mouth and continued through her shoulder, hip, and knee, pulling the joints out of alignment. Instead of parallel to each other, Liz's legs turned in, the right knee constantly brushing up against the left. She walked with a peculiar gait, her slim shoulders shrugging slightly with each step, hitching up the uncooperative side like a too-big pair of pants. Her face was small and sharp and she blinked often, the muscles in her face twitching to an inner rhythm.

Despite physical handicaps, Liz had an intimidating presence. She moved with the efficiency of someone with an important job to do; someone who disliked wasting time on small talk. Her eyes never lingered anywhere for long but continually looked for a new task to focus on. When Taylor handed the paperwork in, Liz barely glanced at her. She scanned the paper as she walked to the hallway, beckoning Taylor to follow.

"What days are you available?"

"Sunday."

Liz's left eyebrow raised, "Just Sunday?"

"Just Sunday. I live out in the county; it's a half hour drive to get here. I'm in real estate school … this is just something to fill in my free time. Help out a little." Taylor felt irritation rise. She'd expected a little gratitude. Did these people get volunteers everyday or something? Liz seemed skeptical.

"And why did you want to work here?"

No way would she tell the truth: *I drank two beers and watched a preacher on TV talk about giving back. The next show I watched was Animal Planet; it seemed like a sign.*

"I like animals?"

"I should hope so."

Liz frowned, as if Taylor had flunked some sort of test. "You know this isn't all warm and fuzzy, playing with puppies and such. You'll be doing lots of cleaning up crap."

*What is with this woman?* The knee jerk sympathy Taylor had felt for Liz evaporated.

"Speaking of which, I give you exhibit A."

They stopped in front of the first kennel. A yellow dog that looked to be a mixture of pit bull, lab, and something unknown, exploded to the front, clawing at the wire and whining like he was high on methamphetamines. From front to back, the kennel was a stinking soup of feces and water.

"Forrest here likes to make an obscene mess of his cage. Came from a filthy house where he literally slept in his own droppings. I hope you have a strong stomach."

Taylor grimaced. She'd definitely had something more warm and fuzzy in mind.

The tour continued while Liz gave running commentary on the cleaning routine, the dogs and cats available for adoption, the euthanasia schedule. Taylor was happy to find that three hound-mix puppies were included in the current lot.

"There's one more thing; a horse out back that will need its paddock cleaned while you're here."

"A horse?"

Liz nodded. "We don't have a lot of room at this facility, but a horse or two can stay here if need be. We're looking for a foster situation for this particular mare. Are you comfortable with horses?"

"When I lived in California I spent two summers at horse camp so, yeah, I like horses."

Liz made her way out of the kennel and proceeded to lead Taylor along a narrow path covered in woodchips. A light-grey horse stood alongside the metal panels of a large round pen. It pulled hay from a feeder and pricked an ear in their direction.

"Wow. I think she has the biggest, blackest eyes I've ever seen."

"Eye."

"Excuse me?"

"She has only one eye."

Liz moved to the gate, lifted the latch and gestured for Taylor to follow. The mare turned toward them, gracefully extending her neck in greeting. A low rumble rolled from somewhere deep in her throat. From the front the mare, like Liz herself, looked like two separate individuals. Her right eye, a glistening orb of dark mystery and gentle intelligence, examined the world with curiosity. In contrast, the left side of her face was a bony landscape of unnatural indentations, scars, and emptiness. The hair had been shaved and skin from around the socket neatly pulled together in a row of tidy stitches yet to be removed.

"What happened?"

"Shot."

"She lived? Isn't that impossible?"

Liz chuckled. "Nope. Seems Miss Miracle here didn't want to die. She was found up near Glacier when she wandered into someone's backyard. Vet said he'd never seen anything like it; the bullet missed her brain entirely. She lost a lot of blood, but she'll be fine. She's young and we think broke to ride. Could make somebody a nice, one-eyed horse."

Taylor moved to the mare's face. It bothered her that Liz seemed amused with the spectacular facts of the horse's personal horror story. Cradling the mare's jaw with one hand, she brushed the flies off the scarred landscape of her face. Taylor expected the horse to flinch or move off, but the mare only sighed and dropped her head.

"Who would do something like that to such a sweetheart?"

"Somebody who didn't want to treat the nasty abscess in her hoof, apparently."

Liz picked up an empty bucket, her busy demeanor suggesting it was time to collect feral cats. The horror of the horse's condition seemed to have long since mellowed to simple fact. Maybe all the wounded animals in this place existed only as case files in her mind. She was a woman who had seen everything, no doubt, and her own personal deformities were testimony to the fact that life was not fair.

Taylor wanted to linger; the mare's gentle presence drawing her to stay. She moved to the horse's side, running her hand down the crest of the mare's neck and over her shoulder. It was then that she caught sight of the marking.

"Why does she have this gnarly dark patch of hair?"

The question seemed to still Liz's impatience. She hitched up her leg and leaned against the side of the wooden shelter.

"Now *that's* interesting. If you like legends. This horse is an Arabian. Arabs say a horse with a bloody shoulder is blessed by Allah."

"Bloody shoulder?"

Liz jerked her head toward the mare. "The marking. It's called a bloody shoulder. I gotta get going but I'll give you an abbreviated version of the bloody shoulder legend on our way to the office."

Taylor hesitated, and then patted the mare's shoulder. "I'll see you again, Sweetie." The horse followed them to the gate.

"I've never been a fan of once-upon-a-time, but here we go." Liz hobbled as fast as she could, the speed of the words a mirror of her gait. Her face seemed to twitch extra fast. "Once upon a time there was a Bedouin warrior who owned a special mare he used for battle. They had a strong bond of love. The warrior was wounded badly in battle one day and fell across the neck and shoulder of his mare. For many miles the mare carried him unconscious across the desert until they reached home. When the warrior was taken from the mare's back her shoulder remained permanently stained with the master's blood. She was in foal and when the baby came it also bore the bloody shoulder marking. People believed that Allah had rewarded the mare for her courage, loyalty, and faith. The bloody shoulder was an eternal reminder of his favor."

"Huh. Cool story."

"Yeah. I gotta go. See you on Sunday then?"

"I'll be here." Taylor was lost in thought as she moved to the door. Outside, the beginning of a rain storm pelted the windows of the shelter. She heard the tinkle of car keys and the sound of Liz shrugging into a jacket.

"What's her name?"

"Name?" Liz furrowed bushy eyebrows, her mind set on the task at hand. She looked out the window as if considering the weather, her expression momentarily softening. "How about *Rain*? 'Into every life a little rain must fall,' isn't that how the saying goes? I think our girl out back has had her share of rain."

On the drive home the rain increased. The clouds overhead had churned into a threatening mass, black as soot. Raindrops beat at the windshield. Taylor turned the wipers on high speed.

## Chapter 3

A faint, roasty smell of coffee assured Taylor the double-sided paper was the right one. She pulled it from the thin stack of job applications she'd collected and brought the paper to her nose, inhaling the aroma like a scratch-and-sniff sticker. *Barista.* Sounded like a sexy Latin dance with no relation whatsoever to "coffee maker." Sure, people drank lattes in California, but in Bellingham it was an elevated activity.

*A coffee artist.* That's how the black-haired employee at Holy Grounds had described the job. Only part-time so she could devote herself to getting her agent and broker license online and learn the ropes at the real estate office. Less than twenty hours a week, plus plenty of hot drinks. Perfect.

Taylor had always wanted to be an artist of some kind. Trouble was nothing quite fit. What was she talking about—nothing came even close. Too awkward for dance, too distracted for writing, and no natural talent for music. How was it fair to be given a great love for music, but no ability to make music? Painting and drawing were definitely out. Pottery once had appeal. She had signed up for a class after watching her father's favorite old movie, *Ghost*, but operating the wheel wasn't near as easy—or sexy—in real life. The most memorable thing about the experience was her pottery instructor and his pungent old-man body odor badly masked by patchouli. His teaching mantra was constant and conspicuously aimed in her direction.

"Let the clay find its natural shape. It wants to be something; don't force it! Let it find its own life."

After six weeks her "naturally-shaped" pots sat on her dresser like ill-conceived blimps made by a kindergartner on craft day. She could relate to the pots. They didn't seem capable of finding a functional, much less beautiful, existence. Forced into service, they trudged into life sullen and unattractive. She'd put one—the best one that was *almost* a vase—in the kitchen and filled it with Black-Eyed Susans. Her father still had it. Kept out of pity, no doubt.

How many jobs had she had since high school? Babysitting, food service at a retirement home, Wal-Mart, selling tickets at a movie theater. Forget *Dirty Jobs*, her personal reality show would be called, *Desperate Jobs*.

After scratching the necessary information on the job application, Taylor hopped in her car for the thirty-minute drive to town. On the way, her eyes roamed the countryside whizzing by outside. It was a breathtaking collage of beauty, snow-capped mountains, the winding Nooksack River, pastoral scenes of dairy cows and horses. Low-lying fog hung on the surrounding hills, verdant with evergreens, as if a giant had walked through trailing cotton batting. Taylor could sit in a chair for hours on end and just absorb the beauty of the place. But work called. She forced her mind to the task at hand as she approached the outskirts of Bellingham. Of course she'd get the barista position; how hard could it be? It sounded like a desperate job, the kind people wanted when nothing else was available.

~ ~ ~

"You forgot to fill out the felony part."

Taylor blinked at "Melissa" and watched her stubby index finger stab at a blank line on the application, its silver-polished nail bitten to the quick.

"You think I'm going to molest the latte machine or something?" A burst of laughter escaped her throat before she could stop it.

Melissa's eyes widened. "This is a *border* town. You have no idea what passes through here. Ever hear of Ted Bundy? And that guy who went on a random shooting spree cross-country? Both hung out in Bellingham. Probably applied for jobs at places like this." She pressed slick purple lips together, and furrowed her twice-pierced eyebrows. Hard brown eyes stared a challenge at Taylor. "I've got a stack of applications in the back. You want to be considered, list your felonies." She shoved the paper back.

*List your felonies.*

Taylor took the paper and wrote N/A on the line without looking down. She pushed the paper back. "I don't have any."

"Well. I'll give this to the owner ... along with the other applications. Maybe she'll call you." Without saying goodbye, Melissa moved to the drive-up window where a car waited.

Taylor walked to the parking lot. *Felonious barista.* It did have a certain ring to it. Her dad would appreciate the juxtaposition of words. He cracked her up with descriptions that didn't go together: carnival worker/Ph.D; taxidermist/flamenco dancer; librarian/sport fisherman; rocket scientist/knitter. The man knew that a title can be deceiving and a person's job description doesn't accurately add up the sum of their life, or comprise a ready-made list of corresponding traits. That's the wisdom that comes from the two-word description, father/gay man. Not that her father had ever discussed his feelings or lifestyle choices with her. He wouldn't. His favorite reply when someone questioned him deeper than he wanted to go was, "I am what I am." End of conversation.

Taylor pulled her key out of the ignition and thought of her father. She missed his easy company and odd sense of humor; missed his anomalies. Like how they'd be driving along, in complete silence, and he'd suddenly offer a description to make her giggle. She made a mental note to call him and describe the "felonious baristas" that resided in northwest Washington.

Pulling a pack of cigarettes from her pocket Taylor tapped one out. It slid smoothly into her hand. Out of habit she looked around, instantly hating herself for checking for her mother's car. They weren't supposed to meet for another twenty minutes, but Ann was notorious for being early. Her work associates admired the obsessive punctuality, as if it indicated solid character or some stellar work ethic. Taylor knew better. Her mother—Ann Archer, real estate legend and Condo Queen—lived to catch someone doing something they weren't supposed to be doing.

Taylor took a long drag on the cigarette and tried to let it seep gently out of her mouth. Ian could inhale, talk, and never appear to actually exhale. The smoke simply drifted, without effort, from between his lips, hovering and then dissipating into the surrounding air. She could watch him smoke for hours.

Instead of her mother, it was Melissa who watched her with disapproval. Taylor scuffed her toe into the gravel parking lot and blew a line of smoke in the girl's direction. What was her problem anyway? She tapped cigarette ashes onto the ground and took another drag. Melissa immediately opened the door of the coffee stand and marched over. Taylor noticed something glinting in her middle, a belly button ring attached to a thin chain that anchored onto her jeans pocket. Real smart. At least if she took a swing at her Taylor would know what to grab.

"You're littering—do you mind?"

"Are you for real? I've dropped like a hundredth of an *ounce* of *ash* on the *gravel*. Biodegradable."

Melissa glared at her. "The ashes from a *cigarette* don't count as biodegradable. Not with all the toxins they leach into the soil. Toxins polluting your lungs just now, I might add." She seemed to cheer at the thought. "We protect life around here and don't appreciate you killing it."

Taylor took another drag off the cigarette. "I don't see any life." She blew smoke toward Melissa, dropped the cigarette butt, and ground it out on the gravel.

"Oh. My. God. You better get the hell out of here."

Taylor stood her ground. "Relax Al Gore. I won't leave anything that might damage the ozone" She bent and picked up the butt. "In case you hadn't realized, this is a public parking lot. I can stand here all day if I want. I'm just waiting for somebody; don't get your panties in a twist."

Melissa stared hard at Taylor, as if invoking some sort of evil spell. Just before turning on her heel she smirked and said, "I'm not sure what's going to happen with your application. With so many it's easy to misplace one … "

The crunch of gravel interrupted the girls' conversation. Without looking Taylor knew it was a silver Lexus. The car slowed to a stop as she fluffed her windbreaker, hoping any leftover smoke would evaporate. She opened the car door and slid into the passenger's seat.

"You stink."

"Nice to see you, too."

"I can't believe you're still smoking."

Her mother's eyes roamed over Taylor's face, as if looking for something she already knew wasn't there. "You realize what you're doing to your body?"

"Just drop it, okay?"

"I thought you were smarter, that's all." Her mother eased the car onto the road. "Guess the apple doesn't fall far from the tree."

Too bad she didn't have a dollar for every time she'd heard that phrase growing up. Instead of becoming an agent, she'd have invested in some serious real estate and put down roots in a tropical paradise somewhere. Taylor glanced at her mother's profile. "On the contrary, I think it fell rather far. Are we going to fight or do you want me to learn how to be a real estate agent?"

Ann smoothed down the back of her extra short black hair with one manicured hand, and then fingered the thin gold chain and delicate cross at her throat. She looked at Taylor, smiled, and winked. "I'm glad to have you back in the northwest, dear. We're going to have fun together."

"No doubt."

"Aren't you going to say hello to Minnie?"

Taylor sighed. She'd been trying to ignore the only being on earth that never disappointed her mother, the tiny, persistent black dog wiggling in the back seat.

"Come on, Twit." Taylor clapped her knees and the Miniature Pinscher launched over the armrest and into her lap, wiggling and shaking like an epileptic. "Chill, would you?" Taylor tried to cover her face as Minnie bounced in her lap. She couldn't help giggling even though the dog was quite possibly the most useless creature on earth.

Her mother beamed. "Did I tell you Minnie and I are blogging now?" She reached over to caress the dog's glossy coat.

"Do I even want to know what you're writing about?"

Ann pulled into The Olive Garden parking lot. "Don't laugh. Social networking is critical for success in nearly every business now."

"Like I said, do I want to know what you write about?"

"Minnie Musings. That's the name of the blog. Check it out for yourself. I'm encouraging all my agents to get involved with social networking." Ann turned off the car. "Bye, Min-Min. Keep the seat warm." She looked lovingly at the dog before getting out of the car. Taylor followed her into the restaurant, shaking her head.

The smell of butter and garlic greeted them inside. A hostess showed them to a small table, filled glasses with water and left menus. Ann only glanced at the entrée choices before placing the menu at the table's edge. Taylor lingered over photos of lasagna and chicken parmesan. She was tired of eating frozen pie and more than ready to hunker down over a serious meal.

"They have a great lunch special here. Light and inexpensive. I recommend the minestrone."

"I'm pretty hungry. That's not enough for me."

Ann pursed her lips as the waitress placed a steaming basket of bread sticks in the middle of the table.

"I would like the lunch special—a cup of minestrone soup and salad."

The waitress wrote it down then looked at Taylor chewing a huge bite of bread sticks. She smiled, "Those are refillable."

Taylor swallowed and smiled back, "Mmmm, so good. I could live off these things. I'd like the Tour of Italy, please."

As the waitress walked toward the kitchen Taylor steeled herself and scrutinized a family of four across the room. Ignoring her mother's gaze, she watched the father cutting his daughter's meat into small pieces. He laughed at something and touched the girl's hand.

"You've put on weight."

"Thanks for noticing." Taylor gave her mother a fake grin.

"You used to be so active and fit. Didn't you spend time on the beach in California? Surfing and such?" Her mother took a careful sip of water and patted her lips with a napkin.

"Yeah. Guess I like eating more now than I used to."

This was true. But the empty calories from her frequent dates with Corona hadn't helped, either. Taylor knew all about empty calories. Nutrition and, more importantly, keeping up one's appearance were areas of mothering never neglected by Ann Archer.

Taylor remembered the days of watching her mother carefully and mimicking her food habits—measuring out exactly ¼ cup of almonds, never eating more than a palm-sized piece of meat. Until recently, her 5'8 frame had fit perfectly into a size six. It was the one area of her life she knew didn't disappoint her mother. Now a small tummy roll and larger thighs felt most comfortable in size ten jeans. Still, that hardly qualified as obese. Taylor took another bread stick from the basket and dipped it into a fragrant puddle of cheesy red sauce.

Ann grimaced. "White bread is like glue in the intestines."

"So you've said before." Taylor continued chewing.

Her mother sighed. "Okay, you've made your point: You're an adult now and can live however you want—glue up your insides, paint tar on your lungs, whatever. But just tell me what happened in the last three years, Taylor Ann; something is very different about you."

*You have no idea.*

Taylor looked at her mother, her eyes jumping from Ann's French-manicured fingers to her perfectly arched eyebrows to the charcoal grey sweater set that hung just so on the trim frame. Her worst, desperate moments were not something sharable with such a woman, even if that woman was her own mother. Especially if that woman was Ann Archer.

"As you said, I'm an adult now. Guess I've grown up since you saw me last."

Strange how one event could define a person, mark time into solid chunks as unchangeable as stone: BA—before the abortion; AA—after the abortion.

## Chapter 4

After lunch Taylor followed her mother to the car and they drove to the office, Northcoast Realty. Because it was a Saturday, only a couple agents lingered inside. After a tour of the small space, Ann moved toward a desk in the corner. Taylor gratefully sank into the swivel chair, her stomach straining against the zipper of her jeans. She tried to focus on her mother who had remained standing and gestured to the space with one hand.

"Real estate in this down economy is all about cutting the fat." Ann smoothed the front of her size four black skirt. "A few years ago we spent much more money on advertising the traditional way—flyers and such thrown everywhere—but now it's all about niche marketing and name branding. I'm known here and in my main office as the Condo Queen because that's where I've chosen to become an expert. I encourage all my agents to find a niche and work the niche. Don't try to be good at everything. But get *great* at social marketing."

She looked pointedly at Taylor. "Remember the blog I told you about? Many of my past clients have dogs they love. This gives us something in common besides the sale of a property. I make sure to show interest in the areas we share. Some keep in touch with me through Facebook and subscribe to my blog. We become friends, in a matter of speaking. Friends look after and support each other. It's simple, really."

*Of course it's simple.*

For some people everything was simple. Her mother was such a person: make "smart" choices—cause and effect. You make the bed you want to lie in. Life was black and white and very efficient. No drama, no messy emotions. The messiest thing in Ann Archer's life had been an ill-fated marriage to a closet gay man. And the resulting unplanned daughter. But Taylor knew better than to probe *that* particular subject. As far as her mother was concerned, the whole experience had been dumped into a mental junk drawer and stored in the dark indefinitely. She had long replaced whatever dreamy and romantic girl had married Taylor's gentle, humorous father with a woman of destiny. A woman who made her own breaks in life and needed no one.

Taylor's head felt fuzzy from the food. She wished for a bed to stretch out on, but forced herself to concentrate on her mother's words.

"You're all signed up for the online real estate program, right?"

"Yeah, start Monday."

"Why not tomorrow?"

Taylor chewed her bottom lip before answering. "I have a commitment tomorrow. Plus, it's Sunday."

Her mother frowned. "How could you have a commitment in a new city where you have no friends?"

This was the way her mother operated when she got set on a course of action. Immediacy became key. Nothing should delay moving toward a worthy goal. Her goal? Operation Daughter Makeover. Apparently she'd forgotten this operation had failed in the past. Multiple times.

"I'm volunteering at a shelter on Sundays. An animal shelter."

"Whatever for?" Her mother furrowed slender brows.

"Because," Taylor squirmed in her chair, "I want to."

"Suit yourself."

Ann moved to a desk and pulled out a newspaper, clearly ready to move on. "This paper has a great article on real estate in Whatcom County. It has changed dramatically in the last five years. Useful reading material. Outside of your studies online, I'd like you to come into the office twice a week. I have an agent you can shadow and you can begin helping in the office with whatever anyone needs you to do. I'm only a phone call away if you have questions."

Ann's life revolved around her main office in Seattle where she remained the most successful condo saleswoman in the area. Northcoast Realty, the new office, opened shortly after Taylor had moved to San Diego. Though Ann's expertise was 90 miles to the south, she navigated Bellingham like she'd lived there all her life. Taylor knew she had spent hours researching the area, making acquaintances with local business people, and otherwise greasing the wheels for future sales. Sharp. If nothing else, the woman was sharp.

"Your mother's one sharp cookie."

As if reading her mind a heavy-set man with ruddy cheeks approached. He took big strides, rocking from his heels to the balls of his feet and pushing off in a manner that thrust his balding head upward with every step. It reminded Taylor of a giraffe, minus the long skinny neck.

"This must be Taylor. Beautiful, like her Mama."

Ignoring the compliments, her mother smiled without showing teeth. "Steve, this is my daughter, Taylor Ann. Your soon-to-be assistant."

"A pleasure." Steve offered a moist, meaty palm and squeezed Taylor's hand, the metal edges of a high school class ring crushing her fingers. "I've never had an assistant."

Taylor shook his hand and discreetly wiped it on her thigh. "I'll be in next week."

"Looking forward to it."

Steve grinned, revealing teeth that would have been perfect minus a small chip in front. Taylor noted a sprinkling of crumbs on his tie and what looked like an old ketchup stain. His squarish face had a strong jaw and clear blue eyes which hinted at European descent. This impression was strengthened by the blond hue in the thinning hair gelled into submission atop his head.

In another time period Steve had been handsome; before he lost his hair, acquired fifty extra pounds, and added a trembling double chin under the imposing Aryan jaw line. He carried himself with the pride of someone who'd once been somebody—a high school football star, perhaps.

Taylor immediately got the sense that Steve still clung to the glory days of his youth when looks and social status guaranteed a girl would never tell him No. Regardless of what time had done to his athletic abilities, the cocky edge in his speech suggested he still expected to score.

When they got in the car Taylor turned to her mother. "What's with Steve? He's sort of … lecherous, or something."

"Don't be dramatic. He's a little coarse in some ways. But he's a very good agent." Her mother adjusted the rear view mirror and applied lipstick in one smooth motion. "He's quite good at selling commercial property; has lots of connections in Bellingham. Just did a nice deal for us."

Taylor adjusted the seatbelt and considered the information. Despite being sharp, focused, and completely in control, her mother had almost no ability to sense an undercurrent in a person. This was probably the reason she'd married a gay man and why she remained single for the last twenty years. It wasn't for lack of male interest. She simply ignored any and all advances, as if she knew somehow that her instincts in that department couldn't be trusted.

"While we're discussing appearances," Ann looked meaningfully at Taylor, "destroy your lungs on your own time, please. No smoking around clients, in or directly outside the office, or in the car with Steve."

"When am I supposed to have a smoke?" Taylor wished she'd been born fifty years earlier when smoking was in its glory days, before it became akin to pulling out a dead rat and gnawing on it.

"You'll figure something out."

The Lexus pulled into the parking lot behind Holy Grounds and Taylor opened the door.

"Thanks for lunch, Mom."

As she got out of the car her independence evaporated. She wished, irrationally, that she could return to Seattle with her mother, not drive thirty minutes to a strange house she inhabited alone. She hesitated, then impulsively grabbed Minnie and kissed the dog on the head.

"We'll talk soon. Remember to call me with any questions."

As she closed the door Taylor watched her mother pat her legs. Minnie leapt to her lap.

Before she could unlock the car door, Taylor noticed a scrap of paper folded and shoved under one windshield wiper. She opened it and read: *You're hired. That is, if you can handle it. AND if you don't smoke on the job. Come in Monday at eight. Melissa*

So much for that "stack" of applications Melissa had referenced. Taylor smirked as she read the note. An official new beginning: job and profession, all in one day. Not to mention an Italian meal instead of frozen pie and Corona. She should be happy.

# Chapter 5

"The list of today's duties is on the white board." Liz jerked her head, indicating something beyond the door that led to the animals in back. "I'll be along in a few minutes. For now, start cleaning out Rain's paddock."

*There will be lots of cleaning up of crap.* Obviously Liz wanted to get her started on *that* first thing. Taylor walked past the rows of kennels, toward the paddock at the limits of the property. She pondered her decision to volunteer: random, that's what it was. But she'd committed herself and it did provide something to do on a Sunday besides worry. Outside of working on an Olympic gold medal for anxiety, her current list of activities included drinking beer and watching old ladies weed around the grave stones across the street. That, or catching up on the Canadian news that appeared daily on one of the three channels she could count on getting.

Rain rumbled a greeting as Taylor approached. She pushed the wheelbarrow inside the enclosure and surveyed the paddock as the mare watched. Despite a three-sided shelter, it was big enough to ride in, if you didn't mind going around and around in circles. A few scattered patches of grass remained in the corners and along the sides of the fencing, but they were nipped so close to the ground the vegetation was as brown as the earth. Rain ambled this way and that while Taylor worked, delicately plucking up stray stalks of hay with nimble lips. After filling the wheelbarrow, Taylor approached the horse and laid a hand on her back. Rain nuzzled her and sighed.

"I know how you feel." Taylor traced the horse's odd marking with a finger and sighed along with her. "I could use a friend, too."

The loneliness and anxiety she'd been fighting to keep at bay swelled inside. Without thinking she laid her head on the horse's back and breathed in the deep earthy smell. She could hear Rain's heartbeat, steady and regular.

Up close, the rust-colored marking blurred to red. It reminded Taylor of blood. She wondered, as she continued to trace the edges of hair, did suffering have a physical shape in a person's body, like a tumor? Did it take up space, or leave a vacuum? A loss might leave a specific shape on a person's soul, as surely as Rain's patch of reddish hair, the horse's skin dictating the pattern of hair and its hue, year after year. Regardless of what she'd been told at the clinic about cells and what constituted life, deep inside Taylor felt the shape of her loss.

In the stillness, Taylor could hear only the muffled thump of the horse's heartbeat and the gentle swish of her tail. She had an overwhelming desire to slip onto the mare's back and simply be supported there for awhile.

"I wish I could be like you, girl. Just move on and forget it. You don't feel sorry for yourself. I bet you never think about your eye, or how you lost it."

Taylor imagined Rain before the loss of her eye, how beautiful her face must have been—deep, dreamy eyes surrounded by dark skin that edged the pale coat. Stunning. The mare turned toward her but from Taylor's vantage point all she could see was a mass of scars and emptiness. She imagined the gentle creature following her owner trustingly into the mountains. Had she sensed what was going to happen? Been afraid? Had she known she'd fallen out of favor and would be discarded like yesterday's trash? A sob caught in her throat. Rain nudged her hip and Taylor swallowed the lump back down.

"Can I just sit on you for awhile?" Taylor moved to Rain's good side and looked deep into the mare's remaining eye. She didn't want to force herself on the horse. Rain stood quietly, waiting.

Taylor laid her arms over the mare's back and leaned into her, testing the response. Rain waited. Without thinking further, Taylor jumped once, twice, three times and threw herself over the horse's back. Shimmying her body this way and that she jerked an elbow back, jabbing the mare in the flanks. Rain shifted her weight as if trying to help. Grabbing a chunk of mane hair, Taylor finally pulled herself upright.

"It's been a long time since I rode, Sweetie. I'm sorry."

Taylor tried to relax and find some sense of balance. It occurred to her suddenly that there was no lead rope or rein connecting her to the horse. Rain could walk—or for God's sake *run*— and she couldn't do a thing about it. That might be tricky to explain to Liz. Or her mother when she didn't show up for work: *I got a concussion when I fell off a one-eyed horse I shouldn't have been riding.*

It would be smart to slide off. Pronto. Instead, Taylor continued to sit on the horse, absorbing the mare's peaceful demeanor and earthy smell. Instead of lowering her head to graze, Rain remained standing with neck upright as if she sensed any movement might throw her rider off balance. Taylor stroked the crest of her neck.

"You enjoying yourself?"

Taylor startled and Rain tensed, swinging her neck so she could see Liz leaning against the paddock gate. Taylor immediately slid to the ground and brushed at the seat of her jeans.

"I … "

"Nobody's ridden that horse. We *believed* her to be broke based on her behavior, but no one has tried her out. Was planning on getting to that myself, later." Liz's voice was even but Taylor sensed her disapproval.

"It's been a long time since I rode … something just made me want to get on her back."

Liz stared hard at Taylor, her mouth twitching. "Am I going to have to worry about monitoring your sudden impulses?"

Taylor opened and shut her mouth.

Liz didn't wait for a reply. "Because I really don't have time for that. Someone's coming to look at Rain this afternoon—possible new home. At least I can tell them she tolerates a bareback rider."

Taylor's heart beat faster. "Someone might adopt her?"

"This is a temporary shelter, not a petting zoo." Liz raised bushy eyebrows and Taylor noticed they almost met in the middle, like fuzzy caterpillars. "Animals need a permanent home, their own person to love."

Taylor felt her throat tighten. She moved back to the mare's side and brushed her fingers down Rain's face.

"You'll make sure it's a good home?"

Liz looked at her strangely. "That *is* my job. Now, if you don't mind, break time is over. Finish whatever you were doing here and come back inside. I need help clipping dog nails."

## Chapter 6

Taylor shuffled to the kitchen of her tiny house and pulled a bag out of the cabinet. She studied the back label: "Bold, intense flavor with caramel undertones." Sounded like the description on one of her father's expensive wine bottles, not an introduction to coffee beans. Coffee had never been a favorite beverage. She could not remember a time when her mother drank it and her father kept only instant in the house. Once in awhile he made a cup and it looked about as appealing as dish water. Melissa had nearly dropped of a heart attack when Taylor expressed her lack of coffee affinity on her first day at Holy Grounds.

"Coffee is the *only* drink." Melissa narrowed heavily painted eyes, the lashes layered with mascara, and studied Taylor as if she were an alien. "Do you have any sense for the sacred history of coffee?"

Taylor simply stared at the tiny diamond twinkling at the side of Melissa's nose ring. *Historian/barista/goth chick.* Her dad would love this girl.

"In the 15th century, monks in Yemen discovered that drinking coffee helped them stay awake during extended prayer. Other mystics noted they experienced new vitality by drinking coffee and in England it was believed coffee helped expel fumes from the brain."

Melissa sounded like she was reading from an encyclopedia. Taylor watched her adjust a headband that restrained a thick mane of jet black hair so dark she expected Melissa's scalp was dyed, too.

"Brewing coffee, like cultivating grapes, is an art form. One translation of the word is 'wine of the bean.' Bellingham has more places to buy coffee, per capita, than *Seattle*. We pride ourselves on loving this particular wine." Melissa slid a small grinder off the shelf behind the espresso machine. "I'll pretend I didn't hear you say you don't like coffee. We're fixing that, pronto."

A few minutes later, Melissa filled a narrow cobalt mug with inky fluid and pushed it at Taylor.

"Do you have cream … and sugar?"

"Do I have cream and sugar."

Melissa's tone was dead pan. She sighed in exasperation and gestured around the tiny space. Every shelf and cupboard was devoted to coffee accompaniments: syrups, cream of several kinds, sugar—raw, white, and organic, as well as sugar substitutes in a rainbow of colored packets. Taylor knew from the two minute tour that a small freezer was stuffed with ice cream for milk shakes. "Of course I have cream and sugar. But you don't get any. As a coffee virgin you need to first develop an appreciation for the straight-up real thing."

*Somebody takes their job way too seriously.*

Taylor looked for a hint of a smile on the girl's face, but Melissa only waited, hands on her hips. She took a sip of the beverage and choked.

"I'm not trying to grow hair on my chest, all right! I can't drink this crap."

"You'll get used to it." Melissa smirked and shook her head. "It's kind of like switching to thong underwear when you're used to briefs. Seems sorta radical at first, but eventually you'll wonder how you used anything else."

"Excuse me? You're comparing coffee drinking to underwear? We're not going to get personal, are we?" Taylor wrinkled her nose.

"With you? God, no." Melissa looked disgusted. "But put that down for now. We've got customers. Time for you to watch and learn."

For the next two hours Taylor watched Melissa expertly froth milk and draw narrow jets of espresso, dark as chocolate, from twin spouts on the machine. She eventually made her first mocha and a hazelnut latte which Melissa sipped with disdain. "Too sweet. The coffee always rules."

"Is that Latte Law or something? Will I get stoned for non-compliance?"

"Boy, you are a smart ass." Melissa stared hard at Taylor seeming to cast, once again, her own brand of curse

"Takes one to know one."

Unexpectedly, Melissa laughed out loud. "Actually, it's known as Melissa's Law. I'm the best barista at Holy Grounds. Wait and see. Nobody knows the bean like me." A smile crinkled the edges of her mouth.

Taylor bowed her head. "I am your humble apprentice."

Melissa laughed again, husky and contagious. Taylor smiled back. The girl was weird, no doubt, but maybe they'd find a way to get along.

Before she left that first day Melissa had thrust a white bag of beans in her face. "We'll break you in with a light roast Columbian coffee, virgin that you are." She also grabbed a small grinder and gave it to Taylor. "Until you get your own. Fresh ground is the only way to go."

Now Taylor considered the grinder on her kitchen counter. Seeing as coffee drinking was not a choice, she'd best get started right away. She measured half a cup of beans and pushed the button. At least the smell was good—rich and roasty. Once the coffee was brewed, Taylor doctored it with plenty of cream and sugar and sat in front of her mother's laptop. She flicked the machine on and watched the screen load with images. A smartly dressed brunette popped up promising, "In only 12 weeks, without quitting my job, I got my real estate license."

Instead of real estate, Taylor could only think of Rain and wonder if the mare would still be at the shelter when she returned on Sunday. She fought the urge to call Liz and ask her not to adopt the horse out until she had a chance to say goodbye. But how could she explain that? She'd seen the horse only twice. Hardly enough time to become attached.

Yet, listening to Liz talk to prospective adoptive owners the previous week had stirred Taylor's emotions. She felt protective of the mare. Especially when the visitor commented about Rain's appearance. It had been all Taylor could do not to stomp outside and punch the woman in the face. Fortunately, Liz had taken care of the situation. Through the small open window in the back door Taylor had watched and heard the entire conversation.

"She's a little coarse. Arabians should have some refinement, especially in the head."

Taylor watched the heavy-set blond stand back and regard Rain with a horseman's trained eye. Rain stood quietly, unaware her life was up for grabs.

"This mare survived a gunshot wound *to the head.*"

Taylor watched Liz hitch up her bad side and move toward Rain. She hadn't known the woman long, but one look at her twitching face and Taylor knew she was agitated.

"You said on the phone you were looking for a gentle mare for a pasture companion. Not a show horse."

"I am. For my stud. I'd like a foal from him. This mare is a bit clunky for my taste, but the stud should help with that. Perhaps she'll do … " The woman walked around Rain in a circle, evaluating her legs and hind end. "She does have great legs and hooves."

Liz laid a hand on Rain's back. Taylor watched her hitch up her leg once, twice, three times. "We have another interested party coming to see this horse. My job is to ensure she gets the best home possible."

"Let me know, then. I'll take her off your hands." The woman adjusted the position of a broad belt buckle that held back multiple rolls of flesh at her waistline. Taylor imagined Rain sagging under the sheer mass of the woman.

"Will do."

Liz continued to stand at Rain's side, hand lingering on the mare's back. She did not say goodbye and made no effort to help the visitor out of the round pen. Taylor wanted to sprint outside and give her a bear hug.

She considered the "interested party" Liz referred to. Would they tire of Rain, discard her again? What if they didn't feed her properly and she starved to death? Dark scenarios played over and over in Taylor's mind as she tried to focus on the computer screen and textbook open in front of her. Perhaps the shelter could keep the horse permanently, like a mascot. They could organize educational tours for people—school children, maybe—and talk about the danger of guns. Or, the challenges of living with only one eye. Her mind groped at possibilities. Perhaps the mare could give rides around the property. Yes, why couldn't that work? She'd talk to Liz about it at her next shift. If Rain was still there.

# Chapter 7

On the drive to the shelter the next Sunday, Taylor silently practiced her speech to Liz while soaking in the view outside. Thick fog hovered over the farm fields as if sent from heaven to help the last crops of the summer retain the earth's waning heat. Like a down comforter, Taylor thought, thick and cozy. In the distance the granite spires of The Twin Sisters jutted into the sky, the outline so clear and clean it looked like a fake background someone could slide in and out at will. Below the peaks, evergreen forested hills undulated across the valley floor.

Despite patches of clear cut, the scene retained a wildness that resisted domestication. As she drove, Taylor focused on the long swags of power lines held by massive poles that looked like iron giants, their huge shoulders bearing the full weight of human civilization. Though the giants, metal fists clenched around necessity, were imposing they were no match for the army of trees below that stretched as far as the eye could see. After the concrete jungle of California, the strength of the natural world before her was inspiring.

A strange truck was parked in front of the shelter when Taylor pulled into the parking lot. She glanced at her watch. Nobody but employees and volunteers should be at an animal shelter at 8:45 on a Sunday. Her heart beat faster and she nearly ran to the paddock in the back. It was empty. Taylor stopped short at the narrow gravel pathway leading to the paddock gate and stared at the enclosure. Her arms hung limply at her side.

"Morning."

Liz hobbled around the side of the building. Curly, one of the hound-mix pups, pranced at the end of a leash.

"You gave Rain to that woman?"

Taylor gritted her teeth to keep back her emotions. She would feign a migraine and beg off helping today. She could not deal with an empty paddock, and that was that.

"I'm insulted you think I would do such a thing." Liz bunched her eyebrows together. "Go look in the shelter. She's eating her hay in there today. Ground's been getting muddy so we're putting it up in the feeder now."

"Oh." Taylor exhaled and offered a smile. "I'm sorry to insult you … I was just worried about her. What are you doing with Curly?"

"If it's okay with *you*, Larry and Curly have a new home. Owners had to come early. Larry is already in the truck." Liz jerked her head toward the front of the building. "You could give Mo a little extra love. He's going to be lonely without his brothers."

"I will. After I see Rain for a minute."

Liz said nothing. Taylor watched her shake her head as she hobbled away with Curly.

"Rain." She spoke softly as she entered the paddock.

A white head poked out of the shelter and the horse nickered a greeting, stalks of hay clinging to the whiskers on her chin. Taylor approached and stroked the mare's neck. She listened to her chew and snuffle inside the feeder, searching for the best pieces of hay. The sound was overwhelmingly peaceful. Pushing the anxiety down, Taylor breathed deeply in and out. Today would be a good day. And it would start with ensuring Rain's safe keeping at the shelter.

"We'll figure something out girl, don't worry. I won't let you become entertainment for somebody's stud. I don't care how cute he is." She gave the horse a gentle pat and left her to breakfast.

Liz was just saying goodbye to a tall, thin man with sandy hair. In the back of the pickup, Taylor could hear the confused baying of Larry and Curly from inside a large crate.

"They'll have a good home," Liz nodded her head, satisfied. "The man's a hunter and doesn't mind that the dogs aren't purebred."

"Great. Um, Liz, I wanted to talk to you about something ... " Taylor shifted her weight from one foot to the other.

Liz made her way to the desk and sat down. "What is it?" She didn't make eye contact, but instead took a sip from a mug of coffee.

"It's about Rain. I've been thinking we could keep her as a mascot ... I could come up with a program for kids that is ... educational. They could ride her. It might draw people in here and we could get more, you know, donations and interest and stuff. Maybe even adopt out more dogs and cats." Taylor knew she was rambling but couldn't stop herself. The words tumbled out as Liz sipped her drink in silence. "I mean, a one-eyed horse is different and it *is* amazing she survived being shot. What about gun safety awareness?" Taylor forced herself to stop. She took a deep breath and waited for Liz to comment.

"The animals here need a person who will love and care for them long-term. A real home." Liz spoke slowly and with conviction, but her tone was kind.

For the first time, Taylor recognized something in the odd woman's features—deep compassion. It shone in her sharp blue eyes, as distinct as the Twin Sister's outline against a backdrop of open sky. A moment later the look disappeared, replaced with her usual efficiency and detachment.

"We could never offer riding here, Taylor. Do you have any idea how expensive insurance for that would be? We aren't set up to offer *awareness* education, about anything. But especially about firearms. The sheriff's department already offers gun safety classes. Anyway, in Rain's case there was no accident. Someone intended to kill her. Period."

"I just," Taylor scrambled for something else to add, to build her case. "I'm worried about her. Rain doesn't need to be any baby factory for someone." Her voice rose and cracked. "Didn't you say you have another 'interested party'? What do *they* want to use her for? Aren't you worried about that?"

"I do have an interested party. And I told you I would never let her go to that ignoramus that came in here the other day. Believe me."

"Who is this interested party, then?"

Taylor knew she sounded demanding in a situation where she had no right, but it didn't matter. Nothing mattered except fulfilling her promise to a wounded grey mare.

"The interested party is *you*." Liz's voice was quiet again, her features momentarily at peace.

Taylor's mouth dropped open. For several seconds the women stared at each other.

"I ... why would you say that?" Even as she asked the question, Taylor knew why. And she knew that the horse, for reasons that made no sense at all, was meant to be hers. Relief and inexplicable joy swelled inside.

"Because I just *know*." Liz nodded her head. "Don't you live out in the county? Do you have room for a horse?"

"I don't know ... I mean, yes, there is a small pasture, but I rent. I'd have to ask my landlady. She might say No."

Taylor felt giddy and confused with the possibilities. *She might say no. Then what?* Not only that, what would her mother say? And her father? He was paying the rent for six months so she could get on her feet. Feeding and caring for a thousand pound farm animal wasn't included in that. It all made no sense. At the same time, Taylor felt she would do anything, say anything, to have Rain.

"I've never owned a horse, Liz. I don't really know how to feed them and I haven't ridden in a long time. Only pony camps during the summer. I probably can't remember how to put a saddle on. Not that I even have one." The details of the situation dawned on her, overwhelming and impossible.

"You were sitting her pretty well the other day with *no* saddle."

"Yeah, but that was just ... I don't know."

"Look, I'm not going to force the horse on you." Liz downed the last of the coffee. "I just see something there for the two of you. I can teach you what you need to know about horse care and even give you a few basic riding lessons, if you want. Just figure out the housing situation. We'll go from there."

"You ride?"

"Surprised?"

Taylor scrambled for a politically correct reply—*You look differently-abled?* She decided to just be honest. "Yeah, a little. I thought, well, you look ... "

"Handicapped?" Liz interrupted. She drew out the word, emphasizing syllables. A dangerous smile played at the corners of her mouth. "Oh, *I ride*. Toby and I compete in competitive trail and I have my sights on my first 50-mile endurance ride in the spring. I would leave you in the dust."

Taylor watched Liz's thin lips form the word 'dust.' She suddenly felt humble. "When did you start riding?"

"At the age of eight." Liz's features began to twitch, double-time. "I love horses; they never feel sorry for me."

# Chapter 8

Taylor heard the rumble of the F350 well before it turned onto the gravel driveway. She watched Liz maneuver the big rig around the small parking area between the two houses. Liz needed no extra time to correct over-steering. She smoothly pulled up and backed a three-horse trailer around behind Rowan's house. From her porch, Taylor saw her park next to the small lean-to and turn off the engine. The sun had so far been unable to penetrate a grey, opaque sky and a fine mist made every exposed surface moist. Taylor eased into a light jacket and pulled on a new pair of rubber boots. She jogged to meet Liz.

"How do you like my fence?" She pointed proudly at the length of hotwire that encircled a one-acre pasture. "I called in sick to the office and Rowan helped me. She already had posts up from when she had a herd of goats."

Liz shrugged, "Looks good enough. Long as it's hot." She limped toward the back of the trailer to unlock the door. Taylor noticed she looked stiffer than usual but decided against saying so. Instead, she peeked through the narrow open vents along the trailer sides.

"Hi, pretty girl."

Rain shifted inside and gave a low rumbling nicker.

"Go ahead and reach through and unhook her. I'll get her out."

Taylor did as she was told and watched Liz back the mare slowly from the trailer. She handed her the lead rope. "Your horse."

Taylor stroked Rain's neck as the horse flagged her tail and snorted with excitement. "I hope you'll like it here, Rain."

Rowan had opened the door and Taylor watched her approach. They'd be a trio of single country ladies: a tree woman, a one-eyed horse, and a basket case. Perfect.

"Oh, she is a beauty." Rowan laced her leathery fingers together and her face crinkled into a smile. "A lovely lady she is, Taylor, just like you."

"Her face is kinda messed up, but that's not her fault."

Rowan studied the mare. "We are all wounded spirits. That doesn't eliminate our beauty. Rain has a most beautiful spirit."

"Yes," Taylor sighed happily, "yes, she does."

"Quit yapping and come help me with this hay." Liz's sharp voice broke the spell Rowan always seemed to cast over a conversation.

"Thanks, Rowan; thank you so much for letting me keep Rain here."

Rowan simply smiled, lost to her inner Zen, so Taylor hurried the mare into the pasture and took off her halter. Then she jumped into the bed of Liz's truck and began removing ten bales of grass hay. She stacked them in the lean-to next to a meager collection of horse supplies: a lead rope and halter, two brushes, a hoof pick, and one bucket. Liz had offered to feed Rain for three months, claiming a generous donation to the shelter provided for some extra hay. When Taylor had tried to thank her, Liz brushed it off.

"Mare deserves to have care this time around. You just be sure you don't let her down."

"I won't."

As Taylor moved hay she thought about the responsibility she was taking on. She hadn't screwed up the courage yet to tell her parents. Not only was she living on a shoe string, she was an emotional mess that didn't know a thing about horse care. Anxiety ate away at the euphoria of actually owning Rain. After stacking the bales of hay she approached Liz who was busy checking the trailer for the ride home.

"Liz?" She stuffed her hands into the jacket pockets.

"What's up?"

"I'm a little worried about caring for Rain … and I don't know much about riding or working with horses … I … "

"That's why I'm coming back in a few days," Liz interrupted. She thrust a page of notebook paper at Taylor. Feeding instructions for Rain were outlined in her neat block handwriting. "Just follow the directions for now; I'll show you horse handling basics soon. And I'll bring you an old saddle I scrounged off a friend."

"I appreciate you doing all this … you don't really even know me."

Liz cocked her head, a mysterious look on her face. "I know things about people. Anyway, I want to do a good turn for that mare. A wrong needs to be righted. You'll be home on Wednesday evening, maybe four o'clock?"

"Yeah, I'll make sure I'm here."

"Good. You'll get your first lessons on becoming a horsewoman. I think it'll suit you."

At that Liz pulled herself into the truck. Before rolling up the window she handed Taylor a manila envelope. "From the vet who saved her life. You can see the x-rays and be amazed she's alive and grazing in your back pasture."

Taylor took the envelope and absentmindedly waved to Liz as she pulled out of the driveway. Opening the brad fastener she withdrew a couple sheets of paper and x-rays of Rain's injury. Even with no medical knowledge it was easy to identify the damage to the horse's skull within the smoky outlines of the x-ray. A brief description was included: *Permanent damage to left occipital bone includes loss of eye; nerve damage; severe blood loss and dehydration.*

Under the x-rays and medical documentation of the injury Taylor found a photograph. It was a close-up of a man's hand, the fingers upturned and cradling a bullet that rested in the center of his palm. Such a small piece of destruction, Taylor thought. Considered on its own, with no knowledge of what it was intended to do, a bullet didn't appear capable of inflicting catastrophic damage. She focused on the masculine lines of the veterinarian's hand and wondered about the man behind it. His hands looked capable, strong, and kind. Saving hands.

~ ~ ~

Taylor pulled into the parking lot behind Holy Grounds five minutes before her shift began at ten. Melissa opened the stand at six and worked nearly all the early mornings. She needed afternoons free for the business classes she took at the community college. Taylor would fly solo after the morning rush and Melissa would leave at one. She'd close at three and make it home just in time to meet Liz and have her first basic horsemanship lesson. It was all she could think about.

"You forgot, didn't you?"

Melissa set two twenty-ounce coffees in the window and made change for the customer waiting outside.

"Forgot?" Oh, God—the coffee beans! Do we have enough for today?"

"Not of the good stuff. I won't use those discount beans the owner brought in. They're crap. My customers will know the difference."

"Really?"

"Really."

Melissa had her hands on her hips, fingering the ragged belt loops of ripped camouflage jeans. Silver rings glinted on every finger. "I'm doing okay for the moment so rush your ass to the Co-op and get the good stuff. Jamaican Joe's espresso roast. The *whole* beans, not ground."

"Duh." Taylor shook her head. "What am I, an idiot?"

Melissa raised her eyebrows. "*Idiot* might be a tad harsh, but you are still my humble apprentice. Now, get outta here." She waved her finger tips as if Taylor were an annoying fly and moved to take another order at the window.

After purchasing twenty pounds of bulk beans at the Co-op—"Organically grown using methods kind to the environment"—Taylor returned to Holy Grounds and stored the coffee. Her "desperate" job, though admittedly common and status-less, had turned out to be kind of fun. More fun than learning about property taxes, state law and ordinances. And the job definitely beat out driving the county with Steve and being forced to listen to endless stories arranged to showcase his prowess as an agent. The guy gave Taylor the willies. He probably found all his dates on the internet under "casual encounters."

Despite Melissa's outward appearance and brusque attitude, she was hard working, accountable, and quick with numbers. Regular customers consistently frowned when Taylor came to the window and she'd see them crane their necks for a glimpse of Melissa inside. The brassy ones simply said, "I want Melissa to make my coffee." After several such orders Taylor finally broke down and asked for help.

"Okay, Obi-Wan Kenobi, what's the secret? The Force seems to be with you."

Melissa giggled and Taylor glimpsed a momentary softness under the girl's bristly exterior.

"Normally *no one* hears my secrets. But I like you. You're growing on me, Taylor, like a bad rash."

"I feel the love."

"The secret, young Padawan, is in the tamping of the grounds. A simple thing but it makes a big difference." Melissa moved to the espresso machine and removed the stainless steel grounds container. She tapped a used disk of coffee into the trash and refilled it with freshly ground coffee.

"I do all that *and* I always make sure the grind is fresh."

"Wait, wait," Melissa gestured toward the coffee. "You have to use the tamper more then once to stuff the grains together as tightly as they'll go."

Taylor watched her take the small wooden tamper and push it into the coffee.

"See? More grounds can fit inside. Then you tamp again. When the coffee is expressed it should make its own froth on top. That's how you know the grounds are tight enough; that's how you know it's good."

Melissa flicked the switch on the machine. Twin jets of chocolaty liquid drained into a waiting shot glass. When it was finished she lifted the glass to her lips and drank it straight up. "Mmmm. The coffee is king; don't forget that, Sugar Baby."

"Yuck. I can't believe you drink that straight." Taylor wrinkled her nose.

"That's how my hair stays dark and my personality charming."

A moment later a black truck pulled up. When Taylor slid the window open an older man with a salt and pepper buzz cut greeted her. "Is Melissa here?"

Taylor stepped aside and gestured toward the back with a flourish. Melissa stuck her head out. "Tim, my man! Let Taylor make your triple white chocolate mocha today, kay? I've taught her all my secrets. You'll love it or the drink is on me."

"I suppose I could live dangerously for one day." Tim looked unconvinced.

Taylor took extra time to tamp the heck out of the coffee grounds and froth milk with precision. When she handed Tim the drink both girls waited as he sipped.

"I don't know," a teasing smile played at the edges of Tim's mouth, "I may detect a slight difference. I think I need a free one to decide for sure."

"The difference is I usually spit in yours, you rascal. Now cough up the dough!"

Tim grinned broadly and gave Melissa a five. "Keep the change, ladies."

As he drove away Taylor felt a surge of irrational pride in her achievement. She was finally an artist.

"It's all in the details, Padawan." Melissa smiled and high-fived her. "Now, you mind if I leave early?"

Taylor glanced at the clock. "It's only 11:30."

"You'll be okay, the morning rush is over."

Melissa donned a worn black leather jacket. "Peter had an important test. He couldn't give me a lift to class so I gotta walk." She crouched down and rummaged for her backpack. Taylor examined the design on the back of the jacket as it fanned over the slim hump of Melissa's shoulders. *Love Kills Slowly* was embroidered on a rose-covered banner that encircled a large pale skull stitched into the leather. Thorny rose branches hooked into the empty eye sockets of the skull. Red rhinestones winked at Taylor, scattered within the stitched petals of several crimson flowers.

"You believe that?"

Melissa straightened and smoothed her thick black mane. "Believe what?"

"That love kills slowly."

"I'll let you know."

She looked serious behind the thin smile that pulled at the corners of her mouth. "Peter and I have only been together six months. Some days it feels like dying,' though."

Taylor had yet to meet Peter but had pieced together a few details from the little Melissa had shared and bits of conversation she overheard from the girl's cell phone conversations: student at Western Washington University, last year environmental science major, treehugger. Melissa joked about the last trait—"He'd hold a candlelight vigil for discarded Christmas trees." Joking aside, Taylor detected an all too familiar admiration-bordering-on-reverence for the guy.

"He's super intelligent; not like me," she'd shared one day. "He's an agent of change. He'll, like, reverse global warming, or something. Wait and see."

Taylor snorted. "That's a load of crap you know. Plenty of scientists don't buy in to Drama King Al Gore."

Melissa's eyes narrowed. "The *truth* inconvenient for you?"

"Whatever," Taylor shook her head. "Don't let Wonder Boy spoon feed you, that's all I'm saying. Do some investigation for yourself. My

Dad told me Greenland is one place that defies the global warming scarefest Hollywood loves so much. Greenland got its name because it was a *green land* at one time. Long before man was driving cars and using hair spray to ruin the ozone. Naturally occurring warming follows naturally occurring cooling cycles. The earth has cooling *and* warming cycles."

"You must be a Republican," Melissa said in disgust.

"Republican? Hardly. But I do try to think for myself."

On the drive home Taylor pondered the conversation with Melissa. Republican, Democrat, Christian, Catholic, Agnostic, Tree-Hugger, Pro-life/Pro-choice. Labels, all of them. Labels and agendas people all too often slapped on their lives like bumper stickers with no idea whatsoever what that label looked like in practice. She thought about her senior year in California and debating with another student about abortion in speech class. Back then she'd been so sure of herself; she could not yet say in despair, *been there and done that*. The assignment had quickly turned personal.

"I just don't know how you get off telling *me* I can't make certain choices for *my* body."

"I thought you were Catholic?" Shelly, pious daughter of a local Baptist preacher, raised her eyebrows. "The pope himself condemns abortion as killing a human life. How can you be Catholic *and* Pro-choice?"

"I don't care about that pompous old fart." Anger warmed Taylor's resolve like a stove burner turned up high. She wanted to blast Shelly and her Bible into outer space. "A person has no right to tell another what to do. Free choice. God *Himself* gave us free choice. Plus, a ball of cells is hardly a human life."

"Be careful girls." Mr. Whitman, the teacher, raised his arms and pushed his palms down. "Keep it civil. This is a huge issue in our culture and worthy to explore. However, we want to be respectful of our differences."

"Of course, Mr. Whitman," Shelly nodded, her voice low and smooth as honey. Taylor wanted to punch her in the nose.

"Are you familiar with the protected status of the Bald Eagle?" Shelly turned again toward Taylor.

"Duh."

Mr. Whitman raised his eyebrows.

"I mean, yes, Miss Pomoroy." Taylor pasted a smile on her lips.

"Bald Eagles are a national treasure. It is a federal crime not only to kill or capture a bird but to take even an egg out of the nest. I wonder why ... The egg, after all, is hardly *life*; it's just a ball of cells."

"The egg will *become* a bird if left to grow." Taylor felt herself mentally backing into a corner. Noting the victorious grin on Shelly's face she added quickly, "And it's not like human beings are endangered like Bald Eagles."

"I think a human being, in God's eyes, is more of a treasure than some dumb bird."

"This debate needs to be shelved for another time, girls." Mr. Whitman looked at the clock. "Time for lunch."

On the way out Shelly elbowed Taylor as they squeezed out the door. "I still can't believe a Catholic advocates abortion."

"And I can't believe a preacher's kid is such a judgmental snob."

"I just hope you make the right choice ... should the situation present itself someday."

It had all been theory back then, when serious issues could be concluded at lunchtime.

Taylor pulled into the driveway and parked in front of her tiny home. She'd never been *against* life; she just desperately wanted choices, a way out. Like a terrified animal caught in a trap, she had gnawed off her own limb in an effort to escape.

Catholic; Republican; Democrat. All the labels faded when she became the girl in the poster. The girl who'd made the choice that placed her on a path no federally-funded procedure could magically lift her from.

૱

# Chapter 9

"Horses value congruency."

Taylor glanced quickly at Liz and adjusted her position in the saddle as Rain walked stiffly around the yard. "What do you mean?"

"Congruency means your actions match up with your emotions, with what's going on inside. Horses never lie and their own actions always match what they're feeling. They always tell the truth." Liz's hands continually knotted and unknotted a lead rope as she talked, her body moving to an internal demand for constant motion.

They'd spent the better part of an hour going over basic horse care, saddling, and safety procedures like tying a quick release knot. Bits and pieces of summer camp lessons appeared at the edges of Taylor's memory as if they'd simply needed a gentle shake to come to the surface. Now Taylor perched on Rain's back and tried to get comfortable. Rain continually hesitated, stopped, and walked on when she was prodded.

"You're not comfortable."

"I *know.*"

"You're ignoring your feelings and Rain senses it; that's why she isn't moving out nicely."

*Great, a psychic horse. Just what I need.*

"Relax. I'm remembering a girl I saw a few days ago, sitting bareback like it was the most natural thing in the world."

*That was different,* Taylor thought. Now she was on display and Liz was sure to see how unprepared she was to own a horse. She pulled the mare to a stop and turned toward Liz.

"Rain wants to know you're the leader; that you're going to take care of her and keep her safe. Horses are herd animals and they find security in solid leadership within the herd."

"I'm not a good leader. What if I mess up taking care of Rain?"

"You're going to make mistakes, Taylor," Liz's tone softened," we're not looking for perfection. This will all come to you with practice. But try to match your actions with your emotions. Think about it. We've done enough for one day."

When was the last time her actions had matched her emotions? Taylor couldn't remember. She'd been hiding her feelings for so long it had become a way of life.

"So, tell me how you started riding?" Besides being curious as heck about Liz, Taylor wanted to shift the attention. She dismounted and tied Rain. Liz didn't respond immediately. She waited for Taylor to remove the mare's headstall then picked it up and began fiddling with the bit.

"Aren't you gonna ask me the million-dollar question?"

"What's that?"

"The *'what's wrong with you,'* question." Liz's small eyes twitched.

"Do you want to tell me?"

The air between them seemed to compress and become charged with energy, the moment before a secret is revealed. Liz's shoulders slumped. "I was born with spina bifida. Do you know what that is?"

Taylor distinctly remembered a certain picture from a textbook: senior year anatomy and physiology. Hunchback babies, the spinal cord freakishly bursting from their backs like ill-conceived flowers in bloom.

"It's like a spinal cord deformity, right?"

"Pretty much," Liz nodded. She seemed surprised at Taylor's knowledge and momentarily relaxed.

"But you can walk … and ride. Is that normal?"

The twitching started again and Taylor watched Liz's defenses rise like hackles on a dog.

"I just love that word … *normal*. As if anyone is really normal, without a handicap of some sort."

"I didn't mean to insult you. I'm just curious."

"Everybody is." Liz had an edge to her voice but she hitched up her leg and continued. "The lower the injury to the spine, the more use of the legs you have. My injury was low but I was born with swelling on the brain like a lot of spina bifida cases. That causes neurological issues. In case you hadn't noticed."

"I'm sorry."

"Why would you be sorry? That's a stupid thing to say."

Taylor cringed. "You're right."

"The sorry thing would have been if my mother had thought I wasn't worth her time. Incidents of spina bifida are down because there's a test so parents can terminate a pregnancy before being burdened with a less than perfect baby. An *abnormal* baby. Good thing Hank Williams senior didn't get terminated, or John Mellencamp, or Frida Kahlo."

"Those people had spina bifida?" Taylor paused from brushing Rain's back and flanks. "For real?"

"Oh yeah. Other famous people, too: wheel chair Olympians, poets, and Pulitzer Prize winning journalists. My favorite is Buddy Winnett, a jockey. He wasn't expected to live past the age of six." Liz smoothed Rain's forelock and seemed to go to a faraway place. "He found his freedom on the back of a horse."

She suddenly looked at Taylor. "Did you know the information from the DNA of one person would stretch to the moon and back? A human being is a miracle. That's what my mother always told me; that

I'm a miracle. I think of that when people look at me like I'm some kind of science experiment gone wrong."

"Is your mother still around?"

"Nope," Liz looked away and hobbled toward a bucket. She picked it up and wiped at invisible dirt inside. "Her DNA carried a cancer handicap. She fought breast cancer, twice. Lost that battle a couple years back."

Taylor said nothing. "Sorry" could never encompass the emotion that twitched a calypso dance over Liz's sharp features. Sorry, now that she considered it, *was* a stupid thing to say.

As if the word *mother* had the power to summon its object, Taylor watched in disbelief as a silver Lexus pulled into the drive. She untied Rain and quickly put her in the pasture.

"Great … speaking of mothers … "

"I gotta go anyway. We'll get together next week."

Liz didn't give Taylor time to answer, but simply pulled herself into the truck and rumbled down the driveway. Taylor's mind raced as she watched her mother step out of the Lexus wearing a fitted powder blue jogging suit. Minnie danced at the end of a leash, a matching hoodie snuggled around her tiny body. She wiggled and whined as she watched Taylor approach.

"So, this is the place." Her mother stepped carefully off the grass with pristine white tennis shoes.

"How did you find me?"

"The address is on your information at the office. I have a GPS app on my Blackberry. Thought I'd come see where you're spending your time. Since it isn't at the office."

Taylor felt admiration mix with something close to anger. How could her mother continually stay on top of life, of people? Taylor pushed the feelings down. Congruency was overrated. So much of life demanded one's actions contradict the emotions inside.

"I've been working on the real estate course here at home, plus hours at the coffee stand."

"You need to begin spending time with Steve. He said you haven't called."

"I will. Wanna come inside?"

Taylor pointed toward her small house, desperate to get her mother safely behind closed doors where she would hopefully forget about the horse grazing outside.

Her mother pursed her lips but nodded. "I do not understand why you chose to live so far away from everything."

"It's peaceful."

"Your father's paying for it so I'll keep my feelings to myself."

*Right.* Her mother could take a lesson or two in *not* being congruent.

Once inside her mother surveyed the small space dismissively, and then gazed out the picture window into the cemetery across the street.

"That's a Catholic cemetery."

"I wouldn't know."

Actually, the *first* thing Taylor had ascertained about the place was that it was Catholic. Feigning ignorance annoyed her mother and gave her a perverse sense of delight.

"Bellingham has a couple good churches. I'd like to take you to Mass some Sunday."

Her mother spoke with the assurance of someone used to getting her way. Taylor shook her head. "I don't go to Mass anymore, Mom. That's your thing. We've talked about this."

They'd been talking about the Catholic faith since Taylor was twelve. About the time she refused to kiss the priest's ring for the sacrament of confirmation. Her mother had been incredulous. She was not used to being refused by her only daughter.

"For heaven's sake, Taylor Ann, it's just a small kiss. The priest is the representation of Jesus Christ. Imagine you're kissing him."

That was worse. Taylor would look at the twisted Jesus on the cross, his facial features arranged in agony, blood painted on his thin naked body, and recoil. Jesus didn't look kissable. She understood that it all was symbolic and that a line-up of good Catholic kids behind her would receive the same treatment. But … No. It was the first time she had refused her mother anything. She'd gone to Mass, learned Hail

Marys and completed catechism, but confirmation, if it included kissing a stern-faced guy wearing a dress, was not happening.

She'd paid penance for this decision; grounded for a month plus thirty days of badgering: how ashamed she should be for treating the embodiment of Christ in that manner, how stubborn and willful and disappointing she had become. She should at least be willing to do confession for her sins and take first communion.

Her mother eventually wore her down, along with the fear she was kept out of heaven for sure.

*O My God, I am heartily sorry for having offended thee and I detest all my sins, because I dread the loss of heaven and the pains of hell but most of all because I love thee, my God, who art all good and deserving of my love. I firmly resolve, with the help of thy grace, to confess my sins, to do penance, and to amend my life. Amen.*

It didn't escape Taylor that listed first was the fear of hell and loss of heaven, not love for God, but she didn't want to split hairs. She had put on a black skirt and trudged to Saint Catherine's like a sheep to the slaughter. A black sheep.

"Bless me, sir, for I have sinned." Taylor slumped on the stool inside the confessional and recited the mantra her mother had repeated at least three times in the car on the way to the church. The priest loomed behind the curtain, a dark and disapproving shape.

"I am not 'sir,' I am 'Father.' For that do three Hail Marys and one Our Father."

It was not a good sign to flunk one's first confession. Taylor trudged to a pew and sat down in defeat. She reached into her pocket. The rosary was pretty much the best thing about being Catholic. As a reward for agreeing to confession and first communion, Ann had taken Taylor's cheap plastic rosary and replaced it with one made of black onyx. It felt like a bribe. Taylor wondered what the priest, not to mention Jesus, would think of *that*.

Still, the rosary was the most beautiful thing Taylor owned. The smooth stones were polished impossibly glossy, the white Jesus on the dangling cross a stunning contrast in ivory. It invited her to touch it, to open her mouth and confess everything. Taylor fingered the new beads and recited the Hail Marys: *Hail Mary, full of grace! The Lord is with thee; blessed art thou amongst women and blessed is the fruit of thy womb, Jesus. Holy Mary, Mother of God, pray for us sinners, now and at the hour of our death. Amen.*

Did the Holy Mary really pray for her? Taylor thought of the prayer now as she watched her mother's face. Ann sat carefully on the denim futon that constituted the living room furniture.

"Do you still have the rosary I bought you?"

Over time her mother had ceased to bring up the confirmation debacle and seemed content that Taylor attended Mass with her. But after moving to California Taylor shed Catholic rituals along with her insulated Pacific Northwest clothing. Time to rid herself of hot, uncomfortable attire. Her father and his partner, Tom, did not attend church of any kind, especially not Catholic. "I don't take guilt trips anymore," her father had shared once, with a wink. "Those are for your mother to enjoy."

"Yeah, I have it."

She not only still owned the rosary, she held it frequently and touched the beads in reverence, silent prayers running a merry-go-round in her mind. The prayers helped her relax on sleepless nights, like counting sheep. Counting black sheep.

# CHAPTER 10

The only sounds along the trail came from the hum of insects in the warm fall air and the clopping of horse hooves. Taylor gazed at the slender backside of Liz and Toby's broad rear end in front of her. Rain followed so closely every swish of Toby's tail smacked her in the face.

"You should back off. Practice staying at least a horse length behind me," Liz instructed, without turning around. "For safety's sake."

Taylor pulled up on the reins and Rain slowed. She chomped the bit in impatience as Toby moved farther ahead. Liz continued talking.

"Rain is probably insecure, this being her first trail ride with only one eye. That's why she wants to be right on our butt. She'll have to learn to compensate for her blindness on one side and you need to be extra aware. Especially on the trail where you'll encounter all sorts of obstacles. Rain depends on you. She needs to trust you."

Liz had been a running commentary on horses and horsemanship since they'd arrived at the mountain trail head for Taylor's first time out. If all went well they'd make a weekly date of riding together until the weather turned. Taylor listened, relaxing into her saddle and the balmy scenery around her, and watched the easy sway of Liz's hips moving with Toby's stride. No wonder the woman rode every chance she could get. In the saddle it was hard to recognize any physical handicap. Taylor thought of Liz's deceased mother who had nurtured the childish Liz and introduced her to the one thing that allowed her freedom from a cumbersome body.

Liz's mother appeared saintly when Taylor considered her own parents: a mother continually disappointed and a father who simply didn't pay attention enough to know much about her. How often had she wished, irrationally, for a physical handicap like her adopted brother, Anthony? If she had cystic fibrosis would her father have a reason to invest himself in her life?

Taylor hated herself for resenting Anthony; it would be hard to find a sweeter ten-year-old boy. Abandoned to social services when he was a toddler, Anthony never knew his parents or siblings. He had especially severe lung damage from the disease and was not expected to live past the age of 15. Using his background as a nurse, her father had made it a life mission to ease the suffering of Anthony and give him some kind of life before he died—*Building tomorrows into every day*, her father liked to say, echoing the motto of the Cystic Fibrosis Foundation.

Neal also volunteered at the school, took Anthony to baseball practice whenever he was healthy enough to participate, and to Boy Scout activities. Anything that might allow the boy to "live a little." This was in between the sleepless nights and hospital trips that left Neal, Tom, and Anthony exhausted: A trio of misery and hope.

As a healthy 17-year-old girl, Taylor discovered quickly she didn't fit in to the fantasy home life she'd naively imagined would exist when she finally got the chance to spend time with her father. She'd soon found other pursuits to take up her time, including a lover engaged to be married.

A deeply private man, Taylor knew her father's involvement with the public, through Anthony's on again off again social life, was difficult. Even in a liberal state like California gossip circulated around a gay couple and their adopted boy. Taylor vacillated between hating the situation for not being "normal" and admiring and protecting her father. More than once, her feelings nearly got her in a fist fight. One situation in particular remained burned into her memory.

Not long before moving back to Washington, Taylor had accompanied her dad, Tom, and Anthony to the beach on a day the boy felt good. She'd overheard two college guys talking by the outdoor showers at a state park as she exited the bathroom.

"You see those faggots with that little boy? Probably recruiting him for their faggot lifestyle. Makes me sick."

Instead of continuing down the walkway to the beach, Taylor wrapped her towel tightly around her torso and marched herself into their faces.

"Guess what? You would have been *really* sick to see those men last night with that kid."

The guys smirked back at her, looks of disgust twisting their features.

"Yeah, that's right. Last night they were up about three hours hitting his back to loosen the gobs of phlegm so he could breathe. He threw up all over *my dad* from being suffocated by the junk in his own lungs. Good times. Don't pretend you know *anything* about 'the faggots' down there. You jerks wouldn't know about that kind of love and devotion."

People had stopped to stare by the time Taylor finished. She nearly screamed out the last words, her hands balled into fists in case she needed to use them.

"Whoa. Just chill, okay?"

One of the guys held his hands up in surrender. Taylor simply glared at him, hoping to mask her own horror at the vehement outburst, and then stalked back to the beach with tears in her eyes.

"It's okay, Honey, just another day in paradise for us. Shhhh ... "

Her dad had patted her arm when she plopped by his side. She leaned into him for a moment, feeling as if her life were an iceberg, the visible tip the only thing her father was capable of seeing. Ironic that she couldn't share her deepest pain with the one person who perhaps understood those feelings better than anyone else. But he had enough to do caring for a child that would surely die; a child no one wanted to die.

Still, her dad *had* provided a doorway of escape when she needed one. Taylor breathed in the salty smell of warm horse and smoothed the long strands of steel grey hair that fell along the crest of Rain's pale neck. He'd arranged for riding lessons after she confessed to him in California that she'd always loved horses.

Gazing at a hawk floating high above the tips of evergreen trees, Taylor felt more alive here than she'd possibly ever been, like a winter animal beginning to awaken after a long hibernation. Her dad had given her a gift neither of them realized would only be fully unwrapped at a future time. She felt grateful.

"We're coming to a pretty good sized stream here, look sharp."

Taylor was abruptly jolted from her dream world at the sound of rushing water not far ahead. Rain turned her head to the side and craned her neck, then snorted. Taylor felt her body contract as her neck stiffened.

"She'll be a little nervous. Because of the placement of their eyes, horses do not have great depth perception. And of course Rain's will be worse because she only has one eye to work with."

"Maybe I should get off." Taylor felt her stomach churn into a knot.

Ahead of her, Liz allowed Toby to sniff the water that coursed swiftly over a bed of jumbled river rock, before urging him on. The horse methodically placed his feet over and around the slick obstacle course of rockery. Liz shouted over the noise of the water, "Don't do that, you'll get all wet. Rain can do it if you just take your time. Don't panic, that's the main thing. Remember what I told you about congruency."

"Yeah, that's so helpful right now," Taylor muttered under her breath. Unhappy to lose the security of Toby's backend, Rain began dancing a nervous jig.

"She'll be fine," Liz shouted back without turning around, "just give her a kick."

Taylor watched water splash up around Toby's belly as he made his way to the dirt trail on the other side of stream. Water pulled at the horse's legs and soaked half of his tail.

Taylor could feel Rain's heart beat pounding under her calves as her own anxiety turned to terror. She sensed the mare's intense fear and as her heart began beating triple time she disappeared into an agonizingly familiar place. She tried in vain to slow her breathing as the sound of the water roared around her.

*It will be fine.*

Taylor knew what it felt like to be told all would fine when everything around her screamed otherwise. The words were not convincing. Not now, not the last time she'd heard them from a nurse while lying on a clinic recovery table, shell-shocked.

Taylor laid a shaky hand on Rain's neck, slick with sweat, as the mare continued to dance and toss her head. She willed herself to be strong, to say something comforting to the horse, but her lips remained frozen. Instead, details of that day returned in excruciating detail.

*Trauma intensifies memory.* Indeed. She remembered the clinic exam room in living color: the benign, sherbet green colored walls; the number of cotton balls that remained in a glass jar on the countertop—eleven; the spider-like pattern of water damage in a ceiling tile overhead; a *Better Homes and Gardens* magazine lying on the seat of a blue chair in one corner of the room advertising that inside one could discover an easy way to make a layer cake from scratch.

When the nurse bent over her, Taylor noted the fine lines around her eyes, counted four dark mustache hairs on the woman's upper lip, and considered the freshly applied mauve lipstick smeared on a front tooth. The woman's mouth had spoken then, her breath smelling of onion, and uttered four words of a lie. She and Rain both knew better than to trust someone who tried to convince them everything would be fine.

"Taylor!"

Opening her eyes, Taylor focused on the concerned twitching face of Liz only a few feet away.

"Are you okay?"

"I … she …," Taylor gestured at the swirling mountain stream. "We were afraid. It looks too deep."

"Just follow me step by step." Liz spoke confidently above the sound of the water. "We'll let Rain be as close as she needs. Can you do that?"

Taylor nodded, feeling like a mental patient.

Toby turned back to the stream and Taylor urged Rain to follow. Each step or two Toby stopped and Liz looked back. "Doing okay?"

"Yep."

Taylor looked down at the water rushing around Rain's legs. The mare continually turned her head to allow her eye to check the surface of the stream. Occasionally she snorted at the spray of water over the rocks.

"She'll get better at this. You both will." Liz's voice was reassuring as they plodded into the center of the stream. "Let's just stop here and stand a minute. Rain can get comfortable being in the water and hearing it rush around her."

As they waited it occurred to Taylor that nothing had actually changed in the last few minutes. She still felt vulnerable and breathless, Rain's heart still pounded, they could still both slip and fall into the icy water at any moment. The difference was someone stood by in case that should happen. She was not alone.

On the ride back to the trail head Liz remained silent as if she knew Taylor didn't want to talk or, for that matter, listen. There had been enough horsemanship lessons for one day. After untacking and loading the horses in the trailer, Liz finally spoke.

"I shouldn't have left you at that stream. I'm sorry."

"It's okay. I'm learning, right?"

"Yes you are." Liz looked concerned, "Are you afraid now?"

"I'm up for trying again. You said Rain will get used to compensating for having only one eye. Plus, I hope to become a better leader for her."

Liz nodded vigorously, "You will. Absolutely. In two weeks the

Back Country Horsemen are hosting a ten mile fall foliage poker ride at a great spot. We can squeeze a couple rides in before then to get you ready. But only if you want."

"I want."

# Chapter 11

It was interesting how much you could learn about someone just by paying attention. It took a few days of feeding time ritual, but one day Taylor realized that Rain was careful to avoid allowing anyone to surprise her on the blind side. She moved thoughtfully and precisely, so subtle an untrained eye would miss the mare's protective defenses.

Each morning the routine was the same: approach a nickering horse bobbing its head in greeting over the gate, rub her neck a few times, and then retrieve thick flakes of grass hay from the feed shed. Taylor always inhaled deeply as the hay tickled her cheeks—the smell of sunshine. Upon entering the paddock, Rain would back off a few steps and wait while Taylor dropped the food. The horse then lowered her muzzle into the hay.

There was something soothing and relaxing about listening to a horse eat. Taylor thought the snuffling sounds of chewing should be recorded onto a CD and sold as mood music, like the nature sound tracks of rain drops, thunder, and water trickling.

It was in those very aware moments of listening that Taylor first noticed Rain's injury had affected the mare beyond the physical injury and loss of vision. Even if her head was in the hay, Rain was not comfortable with Taylor standing on the blind side for more than a few seconds. If she continued to stand out of the horse's line of sight, Rain would back up one or two steps and swing her body to position Taylor within view of her seeing eye. Though the maneuver seemed relaxed, even methodical, and the mare never lifted her head, Taylor recognized meaning behind the move. A betrayal of trust had left its mark on Rain's horsy soul.

Vulnerability felt uncomfortable. Taylor got that. And so she made note of Rain's sensitivity and catered to her comfort, making sure to stand on the seeing side during their few moments of bonding each morning and evening. At those times Taylor would hum something, whatever song from the radio had stuck in her head, and scratch the mare's withers while she ate. Sometimes Rain nickered into the hay, a quiet "Thank You," or so it seemed, for accommodating an insecurity.

Noticing details were key. The horse gave Taylor an opportunity to lose awareness of herself and focus it on another. Self awareness had become painful; like spending a sunny day outside without glasses.

~ ~ ~

Morning rush had long since passed by the time Taylor arrived at Holy Grounds. A clock on the wall announced the lunch hour was about to pass, too, and she watched Melissa rummage through her backpack and pull out a plastic baggie with what looked like nuts inside.

"Time for a snack." Melissa plopped into a chair, leaned back, and put her feet up on the counter. Bare white skin peeked between red Converse sneakers and the cut, frayed bottoms of a pair of jeans. A Japanese character was tattooed on the side of one ankle.

"Those look weird," Taylor gestured toward the baggie, "what are they?"

"Sprouted almonds." Melissa popped several nuts into her mouth and chewed. After swallowing she added, "They're super good for you."

"Why would anyone want to sprout almonds?" Taylor wrinkled her nose. "I only like smoked."

"Figures," Melissa eyed Taylor's pack of cigarettes. "Not that you'd care, but the high heat involved with smoking and roasting almonds kills off nutrients. Plus there's usually added fat and chemicals for flavor. Sprouted almonds are the healthiest."

Taylor shook her head, retrieved the cigarettes, and hid them in a jacket pocket. Laughter bubbled out of her throat.

"Something funny?"

"Yeah, you're funny. You just don't look like someone who'd care much about being healthy—freakishly healthy."

"Why? Because of my piercings, tatts, wild sense of style?" Melissa grinned and fingered the large silver skull charm hanging from a choker.

"Exactly that."

"Think of me as Abby from *NCIS*. If I knew any nuns I'd take them bowling." Melissa crunched another handful of healthy nuts.

Taylor giggled again. "My Dad would love you."

"What's he like? Besides being a man of obvious good taste."

Taylor hesitated only a moment, "He's gay."

Melissa's expression remained neutral. "That always how you describe him when someone asks?"

"It's usually all people want to know."

"You ashamed of him?"

"No," Taylor's voice rose and she shook her head vigorously. "My dad might be the kindest man I know. It's just … weird to explain to people. My life has been weird. Not exactly a traditional family, you know?"

"Traditional family? I saw one of those once," Melissa snorted, "in a museum. I was raised by the son of one of my mom's many boyfriends. No traditions found in my life, sister."

"I love my dad," Taylor continued, "I just wish he were more involved in my life. I have an adopted brother who has cystic fibrosis. A bad case. Doctors say he won't make it past 15."

"And you wish you could get noticed without developing a terminal illness or breaking the law."

"How do you know that?" Taylor bit her lip, ashamed her weaknesses were so obvious. "Is that wrong?"

Melissa stared back at her for several moments, her eyes sadder and wiser than her years. "It's not wrong. Maybe by helping a sick kid nobody else wanted your dad's trying to atone for something. Like not giving you that traditional family."

"I never thought about that," Taylor stared at the milky grey sky outside the coffee shop window.

"Well, I don't know the man, but people do lots of things to atone for their choices. Like my mother giving me a car once for no reason. Personally, I'm trying to minimize the things I'll have to atone for someday. I want to make a life I'm proud of. Speaking of which, Real Estate Queen, what do you make of this?" Melissa pulled out a piece of paper that had been folded into a neat square and handed it over. Taylor unfolded it and saw two pictures of Holy Grounds. Under the photos large block letters announced *FOR SALE*.

"Wow, looks like you and I may be out of a job soon."

"Not if I have anything to do with it," Melissa's eyes narrowed and she dropped her legs from the counter top and sat up straighter. "I'm going to try to buy this place. I've been taking that business class and we both know who makes the best coffee in this town. I've got loads of ideas about marketing, getting interactive with customers on the internet—making a little coffee community!"

Melissa was talking fast and gesturing wildly as she paced the interior square of the coffee house. Taylor couldn't remember ever seeing her so animated. Suddenly she paused and looked at Taylor, a happy grin plastered across her face.

"All I need is a real estate agent to represent my financial best interests." She raised her eyebrows, "Know of anyone?"

## Chapter 12

Taylor shook a generous amount of "whitener" into the chipped purple mug. Instead of dissolving, it floated into a tiny white blimp and drifted across the surface of the coffee. If you could call it that. Taylor stabbed the clump of chalky creamer with a stir stick and watched it struggle to dissolve into the tan-colored liquid. Melissa would die from caffeine withdrawals before allowing the foul substance to touch her lips.

"Mmmm, you already know how I like it—white, but not too sweet. Kinda like my women." He winked. Taylor read the slogan on the side of the mug as Steve lifted it to his lips and took a long slug of the brew—*Real Estate Agents Do It Without Contingencies.*

Steve wiped at a trickle of coffee that dripped down the edge of the mug, making triple tan dots on the white shirt that strained to cover his engorged belly. Hair poked through the spaces between buttons.

"Guess I got a hole in my lip … Now, where was I?"

*That would be a hole in your head I think.*

It took all her effort to avoid visually broadcasting her disgust for the man. Keeping her face neutral, Taylor sank into the chair opposite Steve and pretended to be vitally interested in what he had to say. She focused on the tarnished football trophy by his computer that proudly proclaimed *State Champions 1990.*

"Like I was saying, it takes certain *interpersonal* skills to succeed as a real estate agent. You have to like people and be interested in getting them what they need."

While Steve droned on, Taylor thought of Melissa and felt a twinge of envy. What would it be like to be both good at something *and* passionate about it? Taylor could totally see Melissa owning Holy Grounds and taking the business straight to the top. Her own little coffee shop utopia. In the process Taylor had the chance to do her first real estate deal as an agent. They'd both get something important out of the experience. Instead of being excited, however, Taylor felt melancholy. Her time at the coffee stand would soon end. Working there was a temporary gig, something to fill the time and provide a little cash while waiting for real estate to take over. As she thought of Melissa's dreams, she wished to somehow be a part of them.

"Are you listening?

"Huh?"

Steve frowned then patted her knee. "You have a lot to learn, Taylor, and it's my job to teach you." He squeezed her thigh with meaty fingers. "Go call that woman who wants to see the strip mall space for rent. Let's make sure she's still planning to meet us after lunch."

Taylor rose from her chair, ignoring Steve's outstretched hand holding an empty coffee mug.

"Aaahem."

"Did you need something?"

"I think you know what I need," Steve winked. "This is a good opportunity to practice your people skills."

Taylor forced herself to remain pleasant and took the mug. She wondered if Steve had some sort of winking disease.

After Steve had consumed six soft tacos and a milk shake, they made their way to The Plaza and the small business space available for rent. Steve managed six of the ten rented spaces. It was a good location and he'd shared details of the unit with Taylor including the monthly fees—$550, plus utilities, and a minimum year lease.

"Hi, I'm Helen." A trim middle aged woman with long braided hair and no make-up waited on the side walk outside the strip mall. She wore an ankle length tie-dyed skirt made of wool and smelled like soap.

Steve grabbed the woman's hand and shook it vigorously, "Good to meet you, I'm Steve. This is my assistant, Taylor." Orange-colored taco sauce formed a thin outline at the corners of his mouth. "Now, let's have a look at this unit. Outstanding location and very modern."

Taylor said nothing as she watched Steve give Helen a tour. Across the street the drive through at Coffee By the Bay was packed on both sides. The weather was turning cool, making lattes enjoyable at all hours of the day. Taylor thought up drink names to share with Melissa that would promote autumn weather: Fuzzy Sweater (caramel and marshmallow) and The Hottie (cinnamon mocha).

"Time to go, Taylor Ann."

At the sound of her name, mom-style, Taylor snapped to attention. Helen had already left the building, her bright colored skirt visible in the parking lot where she was opening the door of a vintage Volvo.

"Uh, only my mother is allowed to call me that."

"I needed to get your attention. Again." Steve raised his eyebrows. "Now let's head back to the office so you can do some filing for me. Then we'll review a list of clients you can follow up with."

"So what did Helen think?"

"Too expensive. She wants to sell her organic goat milk soaps and lotions. This space is clearly out of her league." Steve shook his head in disgust, "Just what we need in Bellingham, another Earth Mother selling soap."

"Maybe it's her dream."

"Dreams are overrated; she needs to get her head out of the clouds. Or maybe its out of the earth." He laughed loudly, his belly wobbling close to the steering wheel.

"What about helping people get what they *need*? As you were saying awhile back."

Steve's eyes suddenly narrowed. "So you were listening. Good to know." He belched, filling the car with the smell of cheap Mexican food. "People hardly know what they need, that's the problem. I help them get what they *really* need. In her case, its a road side stand." He laughed again.

"What *I* really need now is a smoke." Taylor cracked the window and spoke into the blessedly fresh moist air outside as they pulled into Northcoast Realty.

Steve turned off the car and sat for an extra minute as if pondering the situation. He finally looked at his watch. "Five minutes." Without waiting for her response he lumbered into the building.

As Taylor sucked on the cigarette she pondered how to tell Steve she had a potential deal. Should she tell her mother first? Steve was the head broker at the office, not to mention her mentor. She'd have to rely on him to help her and make the deal work. He probably wouldn't take Melissa seriously. Like Helen she had a dream, but no money. Was it possible for a single, 21-year-old woman to get financing for $89,000?

☙

## Chapter 13

Taylor grabbed a six-pack of Corona out of the refrigerator. Pulling on a wool sweater she flopped into a lawn chair on the porch. Across the street the gathering dusk muted the shapes of the gravestones. The shadows of the enormous evergreens that surrounded the cemetery seemed as if they were swallowing the space. Taylor shivered and popped the top off a bottle. She turned her attention to Rain's small field where she could still make out a silver shape that moved here and there, gleaning the last bits of hay Taylor had fed her not long before.

The air felt moist and icy on her skin, warning of the coming cold weather. No longer the warm blanket of fog that visited the earth in early fall, it had turned raw and penetrating, as bracing as the ocean in Puget Sound only a few miles away. It would be a cold night. A night perfect for snuggling deep under the flannel sheets and featherbed her mother had given her. If only she wasn't terrified to go to sleep.

Taylor took long pulls on the bottle in her hand. A couple beers should do it. She wished there was some way to sleep outside with Rain. Maybe the horse could ward off the spirits tormenting her. She'd love to stretch out on Rain's broad back and drift off to the smell of horse and the sound of a steady heartbeat.

Since bringing the mare home Taylor was coming alive a little more every day. Rain invited her to engage in life again and she became a friend Taylor looked forward to seeing each morning. Her very presence invited peace. But then the dreams had started, a recurring dream that left Taylor sobbing in despair. Her heart would pound in her ears upon waking, breaths coming in frantic gasps, as she tried in vain to shut out the images in her mind. Panic attacks. That's how the website diagnosed her suffering. Perfect. Forget a head shrinker; she now needed drugs, too.

A sliver of light illuminated Rowan's deck next door. Taylor popped another beer and watched the woman approach in the near dark, her dreadlocks a ropy silhouette. *Like Medusa*, thought Taylor through the warm haze of a buzz. She laid her head against the stretchy back of the chair and imagined it disconnecting from her body and floating like a balloon into the darkness.

"Hello there." Rowan climbed the two cement steps and leaned against the railing surrounding Taylor's tiny porch. "I brought you some dried Echinacea. Good in case any germies befriend you this winter."

"Oh, thanks." Taylor reached for the brown paper bag of herbs. Rowan's crop of flowers were mostly dried and mixed into natural herbal potions to sell at a tea shop in town. She also cultivated a smaller plot of medicinal plants: Calendula, Bee Balm, and various mints. "How do I use it?"

"Steep in hot water and strain to remove the leaves. And don't drink with sugar." Rowan wagged her finger at Taylor. "Sugar breaks down your immunity. I call it The White Death."

"You sound like my mother."

"I think you could use some mothering, my dear." Rowan jerked her head toward the six-pack that had quickly become a three-pack.

"Do I need to worry about you?"

"Nah. I only drink at night. Alone." Taylor giggled, enjoying the detachment she felt between her physical body and her brain. "Thank you again for letting me keep Rain here. I just love her so much."

"She is good for you, I think." Rowan looked closely at Taylor, her green eyes wise. "Horses are good teachers."

"I hope I'm a good owner is all ..."

The cozy, alcohol-induced feelings suddenly evaporated. Taylor felt tears prickling. She wondered if her brain would explode from all the feelings that wanted to leak out.

"Why wouldn't you be a good owner? You love her; you care for her."

"I'm having bad dreams since she came ..."

Taylor knew tears were coming. She placed her empty bottle down and reached for another. Rowan grasped her arm before she could remove the Corona from its cardboard cubby.

"Tell me about the dreams."

Taylor allowed her arm to go limp. She leaned back against the chair and looked up at the square of porch roof over her head. A family of spiders had made homes in all four corners. She shivered again.

"I started to have this dream about a week after Rain came." Taylor squeezed her eyes shut for a moment. "In my dream I see Rain waiting to be fed, morning and night like she always does. But instead of feeding her, I get busy doing other things. She keeps appearing at the fence, waiting for me, looking at me with her big, kind eye. But I don't feed her." Taylor stifled a sob. "One day, I go out and she's dead, withered away from hunger right in front of me. I didn't care for her. I killed her."

Sobs choked the end of the sentence. Taylor dropped her chin to her chest. She felt Rowan's warm, rough hands grasp her own and squeeze gently. She said nothing for a few minutes.

"Dreams are important windows into the soul. Do not discount this dream." Rowan looked serious when Taylor finally lifted her head to meet her eyes. "You do not trust. That is what this dream reveals. You have been given a life to nurture but you do not trust yourself to do it."

Taylor nearly gasped out loud at the truth of the statement. Rowan didn't wait for her to respond. "You must learn to trust yourself. Go deep into your true self and you will find that self is worthy of trust, worthy of esteem. See, Rain shows up at the same time day after day. She believes you will arrive, she believes you are trustworthy. She will help lead you to your true self."

Rowan massaged Taylor's forearm as she spoke, sure of her advice. It was a shallow comfort. Taylor wished she could be sure of such a thing, that she was trustworthy. Going deeply into herself, as she had done in the last year, had not produced peace. She felt at times only inches away from a stint at the Funny Farm, that's what excessive self-analysis had gotten her. Rowan did not know what she had done. The woman nurtured *flowers,* nurtured *dirt.* She would probably never kill a living thing.

"Thanks, Rowan. I should probably go to bed now." Taylor took her arm away.

"Anytime you can share your dreams with me, I will interpret them for you." Rowan smiled. "Don't forget to drink the tea; build up your immune system. And don't neglect your true self."

"Will do." Taylor tried to smile as she shut the door.

One more beer, that's what her true self needed right now. To drown out the last bits of the dream she had not shared with Rowan, the part where she was back on that metal table shivering uncontrollably as blood drooled between her thighs. The nurse had patted her arm, "It will be over soon, just relax." How could she relax with the whir of the vacuum? In her dream her mind screamed to get off the table, to run away before that machine sucked out every piece of her soul. The doctor had not looked at her. He finished his business in silence, only sharing one word with a watching colleague as he disposed of something wet into a waste bin. The word stabbed her through the fog of horror and medication. "Female."

And Taylor knew he was not referring to her.

# CHAPTER 14

Taylor left Rain tied to Liz's trailer and walked to the covered gazebo to sign in. Horses and people of every color, size, and shape milled around waiting for the start of the poker ride. Taylor silently took a copy of the waiver and glanced at the terms before signing her name.

*Rider is aware that horses, by their very nature, are unpredictable and horseback riding is an inherently dangerous activity. By signing, Rider accepts all risk and will not hold The Back Country Horsemen of Washington liable in the case of injury or death.*

Blah, blah, blah.

She signed her name. Few things in life were not "inherently dangerous" and when compared to, say, falling in love, horseback riding was a cakewalk.

"How many hands would you like to buy today?" A chubby, sixty-something woman wearing a plaid vest took Taylor's waiver form and gestured toward a bag of poker chips.

"Uh, just one." Taylor dug in her pockets for a five. "I'm really here for the ride."

"And we hope it's a dry one." The woman smiled and looked toward the heavens. "Ridin' on faith today."

Taylor stuck her poker hand in her back pocket and made her way to the trailer. She breathed in the moist, fall air. It felt good to be outside being active and getting dirty. All that time in California had made her soft, citified. She remembered suddenly that as a child she'd loved the outdoors: collecting bugs, building forts, playing with animals, and being in the action. She'd pulled back over the last two years, stayed inside and avoided engaging too deeply with anyone or anything, her skin turning pale and sensitive as she cocooned in her own thoughts.

Protect, that's what Taylor had tried to do for her body. It seemed the least she could do. But instead of getting stronger, she'd felt more and more vulnerable. Like the callous that builds up on the soles of tender feet exposed to sun and different textures, a person needed to risk to become strong and healthy. Since Rain had come into her life she had felt the pull to engage in life again.

*Rain…. Why was a strange man touching her?* Taylor's steps quickened as she approached the trailer. A man stood by Rain's side, stroking her shoulder. He seemed to be talking to the horse but Taylor couldn't hear any words. She cleared her throat.

"What do you call her?" The man glanced up briefly but kept his attention on the horse.

"Rain."

"Rain?"

The man made an effort to enunciate the word clearly, considering the choice. He furrowed his brow and ran long fingers through a thick mop of wavy brown hair. Taylor looked him up and down. With his longish hair he could be a hippy, but the high tech riding gear suggested something different. An athlete. She noted his riding tights, half- chaps over hikers meant for the stirrup, and Patagonia vest. *Note to self: Buy a vest of some sort.* A multi-tool snuggled at his hip, clipped to the belt. This guy knew horses and liked to be active. He watched her with probing hazel eyes.

"I *like* Rain." Taylor crossed her arms. "Why else would I live in this part of the country."

"Good point," the man chuckled and stuck out his hand. "Jacob Wilson."

"Taylor."

She ignored his hand and pretended to adjust Rain's headstall, pulling the mare close. Jacob looked disappointed. He ran his hand once more down the crest of Rain's neck and over her shoulder.

"Well, Taylor," Jacob seemed to be committing her name to memory, "I'll always have my own name for this horse—Belissima." He smiled, "Enjoy your ride."

Taylor did not answer. *Move away from the horse, you weird cute guy.*

~ ~ ~

"My ass is killing me." Taylor maneuvered Rain next to Toby, Liz's rangy bay gelding. The horses made their way, unguided, to the horse trailer.

"What do you want, a medal for completing the ride or something?"

"How about at least a winning poker hand? I needed to win that Carhartt vest. Would help me fit in with the natives." Taylor glanced back at a large circle of riders eating an after-ride lunch of chili and hot dogs. At least half wore a vest of some kind.

"That was barely ten miles. Get yourself in shape and I'll take you on a real ride." Liz pulled Toby up by the trailer and dismounted. She swayed for a moment and grasped the horn to steady herself.

"You knew most of the riders today."

It was a statement more than a question. Though Liz kept to herself and avoided company on the trail, it seemed every person at the poker rider acknowledged her in some way. Though she hated herself for thinking it, Taylor wondered if it was because of Liz's handicap, like the way one felt compelled to say hello to the guy in the wheelchair at

Wal-Mart who greeted incoming shoppers.

"*I like horses because they do not feel sorry for me.*"

Taylor suddenly understood why Liz was always alone, why she shunned company or needless conversation.

"I know some of them." Liz pulled the latigo free. She lined her weak side up to Toby's shoulder and shimmied the saddle off his back, guiding it to the ground to avoid having to heft the full weight herself.

"Do you know Jacob Wilson?"

Liz looked sharply at Taylor. "Everyone knows *Doctor* Wilson."

"Doctor?"

"Doctor of Veterinary Medicine. Wasn't for Wilson, your horse there would have been put down. He patched her up free of charge, took care of her for a month, and then asked us to find her a good home."

Taylor dropped Rain's sweaty saddle pad to the ground as her brain clicked into rewind, sifting through images like a slide show—the photo of the hand holding the bullet; the intimacy of his exchange with Rain; the mare's obvious affection for him. "*I'll always have my own name for her.*"

"You didn't hit on him did you? Or insult him?" Liz's odd features twitched repeatedly as she studied Taylor's reaction.

"Not exactly. But I wasn't nice, either. Why didn't you tell me he was here?"

"You didn't ask."

Taylor watched Liz push her saddle into a carrying bag, then drag the bag to the tack room. It was a resourceful way to take care of her equipment without having to ask for help.

"Do you know what Bellissima means?"

"You gonna load up or what? I don't have all day." Liz jerked her head to Taylor's saddle lying where she had let it drop. Dirt scuffed the cantle. Liz frowned.

"I'm going, I'm going … "

After loading the rest of the tack, Taylor put Rain into the trailer where Toby already waited. Liz immediately turned the key and the

F250 rumbled to life. Taylor hurried to the passenger side. How was it possible she consistently couldn't keep up with a handicapped woman?

"Why would he patch up a stray horse for free? Especially one like Rain?"

"Obviously handicapped for the rest of her life, you mean?" Liz glanced in her rear view mirror. "Why waste resources on that sort of individual?"

"Yeah."

In the silence that followed Taylor forced her mind from Jacob Wilson and considered her verbal blunder. With Liz it was hard to know when to keep talking and when to shut up.

"I didn't mean it like that."

"Like what, exactly?" Liz looked quickly at Taylor. She ignored her own question. "Guess he saw something worth saving. *Bellissima*, by the way, means 'beautiful'."

Taylor did not reply. In the space of a few hours she'd insulted both people responsible for saving her mare's life. Best to keep one's mouth shut. She focused instead on the sun bleached stubble on the fields outside and the poetry of one word: Bellissima.

## Chapter 15

Taylor watched her windshield wipers smear the first drops of rain into undulating channels across the glass in front of her. The long Indian summer had ended suddenly in early October, the day dawning with a brisk wetness that contrasted sharply with the sunburned shoulders Taylor had received on a trail ride the previous day. As much as the rain was refreshing, she fought the melancholy bubbling inside. The regular weekly trail rides with Liz would soon cease and she'd be forced back inside to fight memories of the past and contemplate her bleak future in real estate.

The wet weather and impending soggy winter were foremost on her mind when Taylor finally pulled up to her mother's stylish condo in Edmonds for dinner. It wasn't *just* dinner, Taylor reminded herself, shaking smoke from her jacket. It was an inquiry, a test, and marching orders. She'd earned her Washington State real estate license and a broker's license was next on her mother's agenda. Taylor had no interest in becoming a broker, no interest in being made into a mini Ann Archer. The two things she currently enjoyed most were a one-eyed horse and making mochas. Taylor punched the bell outside the building and scrambled for a way to explain *that* to her mother.

While waiting, Taylor fought the anxiety of an evening with her mother by returning to a recent victory: Rain's moment of trust. It was a small, inconspicuous moment, yet carried the deepest of messages.

She'd almost missed it, lost in thought about Melissa and the real estate deal she hoped to pull through. Then it dawned on her: she was standing at Rain's blind side and the horse had not moved. Taylor looked down at the white head, muzzle lipping up stalks of hay, the sightless socket bobbing as Rain chewed quietly.

"Thanks for trusting me," Taylor stroked the mare's neck in their usual ritual, feeling the euphoria of passing a difficult test with flying colors. Rain lifted her head a few inches above the hay and paused as if she were listening. Without turning, a whiskery nicker answered, so faint it was hardly more than a fluttering of the nostrils.

The moment was real and true in a way few things were. Not that her mother would understand.

At first she'd been ecstatic to hide Rain's existence and her secret riding life. Now she felt compelled to get the information off her chest, confess and get on with it. Secrets were like that.

*"You keep the secret, then the secret keeps you."*

Taylor only needed to think of that particular motherism to relive a wave of seven-year-old shame: the night her mother discovered the package of Bubblicious she'd stolen from the grocery store.

She hadn't meant to. Really. She'd only wanted to hold the sparkly purple package of grape gum that her mother would never buy for her. When it was time to take the cartfull of groceries out of the store she'd stuck it into her coat pocket without thinking. Shame washed over her in waves as she sat in the back seat of the car, fingering the secret package hidden in her pocket. She wanted to take it back, but there was no way now. And there was no doubt in her small mind that telling her mother was out of the question. No, she would throw the gum in the trash when they got home and forget she had done something so dishonest.

By the time they pulled into the drive, Taylor was certain the horror of what she'd done was written all over her face. Inside, she removed her shoes, eager to get to the bathroom, and hide that pack of Bubblicious at the bottom of the white wicker wastebasket.

"Wait. Your jacket is soaking wet." Her mother had grabbed her arm. "Let's take that off so you don't drip water everywhere ... I swear this rain makes me feel like a slug."

Her mother grinned and began to slide the jacket off Taylor's shoulders. It slipped to the floor. As if in slow motion Taylor watched her mother pick up the jacket, feel the unbalanced weight in one pocket and stick her hand inside to investigate. She withdrew the gum.

"What? I didn't pay for this."

And so began a nightmare that lasted several months. The disappointment was the worst. Taylor had cried and cried; had said she was sorry. She hadn't meant to; truly, it was a mistake.

"But, you did it anyway, Taylor Ann. You broke a bond of trust between us and it doesn't come back just like that." She'd snapped her fingers, dark eyes serious.

Even after returning the gum and going to confession her mother insisted on checking her hands and pockets after each shopping excursion. She seemed to enjoy having the attention of fellow shoppers and the checkout clerk. The shame of a public audience would surely serve as insurance that Taylor's dishonesty would never be repeated.

"You may be forgiven, Taylor Ann, but nobody really forgets. They think of stealing every time they see you."

The incident was the first of many that produced the opposite of the honesty her mother had been trying to teach. The truth Taylor learned is that living with the shame of revelation is worse than the secret itself. Cover up your sins as best you can because God may forgive, but He remembers forever.

If her mother had ever been ashamed of anything only the priest at the Catholic Church knew about it. Ann Archer's mistakes were not fodder for discussion; they were attended to in stoic solitude.

As tempting as it was, revealing Rain might open Pandora's Box. Things about herself her mother didn't know and didn't want to know would spill out unbidden. Like the fact that they had nothing in common and probably never would.

"Come on up, Taylor Ann."

A moment later Taylor walked through the door and was immediately greeted by the smell of ginger and garlic and the excited yapping of a furry tornado.

"Hi, Twit." She bent down and scooped up Minnie, planting a kiss on the dog's tiny head.

Her mother beamed in approval. She leaned toward Taylor's cheek, her lips lightly brushing hair. "Welcome. I've got stir-fry cooking. Make yourself at home."

Taylor removed her shoes and wandered into the living room, her feet sinking into plush white carpeting. White. Who besides her mother would purposely install white carpet? Black and white Ansel Adams photos were arranged on one wall and issues of *Seattle Magazine* fanned neatly across a glass-topped coffee table centered between black leather couches. The only other furniture was a piano. It dominated one corner of the room, facing a large window that looked out over Puget Sound. Quiet and dignified, the piano matched the calm waters outside.

Taylor caressed the glossy, near-black surface of her mother's piano, an antique Story and Clark upright concert grand worth a small fortune. A genuine heirloom, the piano had been owned by her grandparents and great-grandparents before them. Her mother had paid several thousand dollars to restore it to complete magnificence. It was now worth in the neighborhood of twenty grand.

Taylor pulled out the bench and sat before the ornately carved behemoth of an instrument. It stuck out in the stark environment, an anomaly in her mother's otherwise stylish, modern home. She had missed the piano like a dear absent friend. It oozed history and memories—hers and those of countless people before—and had lulled her to sleep on many nights when she lay listening to her mother play Chopin.

She touched the keys, cool ivory on her fingertips. They had the power to transform a person, a curious white magic.

At the piano's suggestion her mother, the woman she had never seen cry, exhibited a full range of emotion from little shakes of her head to the definite careful way she stroked each key, gently brushing some, firmly pressing others, to encourage subtle nuances of harmony. She would often look at the ceiling as her fingers danced over the keys of their own accord, lost in some timeless place. With the piano as partner, her cool and practical exterior evaporated and she became a woman of passion, emotion swirling like a hidden current moving beneath the placid surface of Puget Sound.

A picture of a wavy-haired maiden playing a flute in a stand of trees had been carved at the front of the piano, deeply etched into the grain of the wood. As a child Taylor needed only to look at the carving to be transported into a fairy tale, a fairy tale of music that beckoned the listener with a nocturne or prelude called *Raindrop* to enter another reality.

"You've redecorated since I was here last." Taylor brushed her fingers once more across the piano and looked toward the kitchen where her mother measured rice into the rice cooker.

"I've had that piano forever."

"I know. But the condo wasn't set up like this when I lived here."

"Real estate's been good to me the last couple of years—it will be good to you, too. Then you'll have the money to redecorate that country mansion of yours."

Taylor felt instantly annoyed. She wanted comfortable, dependable things, not new, stylish ones. She missed her mother's old mismatched furniture, like the worn beanbag that had once faced the picture window. A favorite reading place, the spot provided hours of reflection within view of the majestic Olympic Mountains. No doubt her mother had worked hard to afford more, but Taylor couldn't shake the feeling Ann Archer had been waiting to move into her true inheritance— stylish, successful, modern woman—until the ball-and-chain daughter vacated the premises. The piano alone remained, a relic from childhood when her mother was the wavy-haired maiden sharing the gift of music with a lonely child.

"Music is an example of something that doesn't add up from an evolutionary standpoint," Taylor remembered her father say while talking theology with Tom once. "Music doesn't serve a basic need for survival of the species or follow animal instinct. It's beauty for no practical reason. Perhaps music is the only thing that suggests to me there is a god."

The few times her father mentioned Ann, he always talked about the music: how beautiful her mother's playing was, how much he enjoyed listening to it. It struck Taylor as astonishing that her mother was the one to show him a bit of heaven.

Taylor watched the rain increase, pelting the surface of the Sound until the line between water and grey sky melted into a single smoky palette.

"I'd forgotten how much rain this part of the country gets. I sort of missed it in California, but I'm already depressed about an entire winter of this crap."

*Because then I won't be able to ride.* The words longed to come out and shock her mother.

"Watch your mouth, Taylor." Her mother hated coarse language, no matter how mild. "We live in a rain shadow here, what do you expect?"

"Rain shadow?"

"A rain shadow is a weather pattern dictated by topography, the lay of the land. Didn't you learn this in school? The Cascades ensure we will *always* be wet; just as the east side will *always* be dry. Nothing anyone can do about it."

*In the shadow of rain with nothing anyone can do about it. Great.*

"Shall we eat?"

Taylor moved to the dining area and a mahogany table with high backed chairs. Her mother ladled out servings of rice and stir-fry and they began eating in silence. The wall behind the table was painted a deep chocolate. A huge, frameless painting of a Japanese Maple in full fall foliage accented the wall. If she had seen the painting on its own, in a shop somewhere, Taylor would never have imagined it would compliment her mother's dining space so well. The oranges of the feathery leaves fairly glowed against the otherwise dark solemn colors in the room. Funny how unexpected things could complete a scene. The picture on the wall proved the power of a special accent. Like a one-eyed horse.

Taylor thought of the mare and an overwhelming urge to tell her mother swelled inside. Pushing away the fear and ignoring her pounding heart, Taylor took a sip of water and opened her mouth.

"This is great stir fry."

"It's all about the lean protein." Her mother smiled and took a tiny bite of food.

*Just say it.*

"I have a horse."

"Pardon?" Her mother's thin eyebrows furrowed.

"I adopted a horse from the shelter where I work on Sunday's. Remember I told you?"

"You said nothing about a horse. Ever. *That* is something I'd remember." Ann placed her fork beside her plate and dabbed at her mouth with a fabric napkin.

"It's a mare—her name is Rain—I don't know if you remember but I always loved horses." Taylor kept talking as if more information would help with absorbing the fact she'd been hiding a thousand pound animal from the person responsible for paying the bills on her life. "Rain got shot in the head, but she lived. It's a miracle."

Her mother didn't appear to hear additional information, unimpressed with Rain's spectacular life story. "How, on earth, can this go along with your current plans for real estate and getting your life on track? That's all I want to know."

"Well it doesn't, exactly." Taylor looked around the room for help. She saw Minnie watching them hungrily in the kitchen. "You have a pet. It's like that. Rain is company for me; I don't have any friends."

"A five pound Miniature Pinscher is nothing like a stinky, filthy farm animal that eats into the double digits *every day*. How are you affording this, by the way?"

"The shelter donated hay this year, and other stuff. I'll be able to afford her when I'm on my feet."

"This is ridiculous Taylor Ann. Having a horse—much less a one-eyed one—is senseless. You're no cowboy."

Anger swelled and gave strength to the vulnerable feelings vacillating inside.

"How would you know that? You know nothing about me."

"I must say, since you've lived with Neal I don't recognize much." Her mother kept her voice deliberately even and low, as she did with colleagues in the office when they were upset. It gave her a professional edge—avoid drama, stay in control. Taylor wished, for the hundredth time, to see her out of control just once.

"I've always loved horses. I loved the piano, too, but you never got me lessons because you said I didn't have any natural ability. You never accepted me, just like you never accepted Dad."

Her mother pressed her lips together, a sign the conversation was going somewhere she didn't like. She pushed her plate away and started to get up. Then she sat back down.

"You assume *I* was the one who rejected your father. It never occurred to you that perhaps *he* was the one that never wanted me. I loved him once, very much, but my love wasn't reciprocated."

Abruptly Ann rose from the table and began clearing dishes while Taylor sat in stunned silence. She'd never considered that her mother had actually experienced the vulnerability of being in love. It was impossible to imagine. In the kitchen her mother's brisk efficient movements were punctuated by the patter of Minnie's following paws. Taylor heard her coo to the dog and give her a bit of chicken from the stir-fry.

Taylor knew the conversation was over. There would be no talking real estate or her sort of first job as agent for Melissa, no more talk about Rain. In the silence she thought of her assumptions about her parents and about the secrets that kept her mother. Perhaps they had something in common, after all. The knowledge felt strangely comforting.

## CHAPTER 16

The twisting ribbon of road, glossy with moisture, appeared and disappeared around corners cutting through the thick fog that blanketed Whidbey Island. Taylor took her foot off the gas pedal and turned down Paul Brandt's *Leavin'* that blasted over the Toyota's wasted speakers. No sense getting a ticket. Or missing a foggy turn and ending up in the drink.

She glanced at the ghostly form of a lone man floating in a small boat on the serene surface of a roadside lake. She had plenty of time to make the 10:30 Keystone ferry. Her mother was to take the Edmonds ferry and meet her in Port Townsend for an agent seminar on marketing. Forget marketing, Taylor had a few questions about how to help a client secure a business loan. The information might be the only thing worthwhile about the day. Like the song, Taylor felt like leavin'—her new career, for starters.

The road twisted up and over Deception Pass on its way to

Coupeville. Heavy fog cloaked the space between the bridge and the ocean below. Stunningly beautiful on a clear day, the bay remained dangerous for water lovers. Various pockets of undertow churned beneath its surface like ingrown tornados.

Taylor wondered about the name: *Deception Pass*. Who had been deceived and over what? She imagined an explorer perhaps, on a warm day in summer, removing his clothes for a dip in the bay; the natural beauty of the place deceiving him about the nature of the current that eventually sucked him under. Just another example of why outer appearances couldn't be trusted.

Once on the ferry, Taylor joined the stream of people leaving their cars and making their way up the metal staircase to the cabin. She sat down and leaned her head back, listening to the soothing drone of the massive engine below. It vibrated up through the seats and into the bones of her spine like a giant electric massage chair. Outside Puget Sound glowed with an otherworldly pallor. The sky and sea appeared a single boundary-less mass. Though no sun was in sight, the milky opaque light hurt her eyes.

After leaving the solid dock at Whidbey Island, the ferry disappeared into a pale haze missing a horizon. The fog obliterated everything but a few feet of water that sloshed ahead of the vessel. Nothing in the world outside appeared solid save the dripping metal rails of the deck and an occasional ropy sea weed floating like a green skeleton on the surface of the water. Every few minutes an unseen captain blew the fog horn, its blast echoing brave and wet.

Unnerved by her voyage on a vessel straight out of *Pirates of the Caribbean*, Taylor lay back against the faux leather seats at the edge of the cabin and closed her eyes, drifting into a shallow sleep. When she awoke, she sat up and glanced at her watch, expecting to find it was nearly time for the dark outline of Port Townsend to emerge out of the mist. Instead, the clock showed barely ten minutes had passed.

Flashes of color suddenly caught Taylor's attention outside the ferry windows. Clutching the rails and peering into the fog stood three girls of around thirteen years. They wore orange and purple and red, fingertips flashing matching snatches of color as they brushed tendrils of damp hair from laughing rosy cheeks.

From behind Taylor could see the subtle signs of emerging womanhood blossoming in rounding hips and thighs broadcasted proudly under figure-hugging denim. They turned in unison to greet a passenger holding the leash of an enormous Newfoundland. Taylor watched one of the girls, a blond whose wide smile glinted silver with orthodontia, kneel and passionately hug the neck of the dog as if she were a small child. It was an unselfconscious, vulnerable gesture that made Taylor smile even as her heart tightened.

*Don't grow up.*

The thought popped into her brain unbidden. For the first time it occurred to her that perhaps Ian's affection, though she still grieved it, was not the thing she missed most. What she missed was the girl that had been lost, the innocent girl who stood at the railing of life and looked to the future expecting to discover something beautiful, the girl who opened her arms wide and loved without holding back. That girl did not hide inside a bottle of Corona.

The fog horn split the air, startling the threesome outside. They jumped and giggled, then high-fived as Port Townsend's coast line slid into view.

After parking in a strip mall lot, Taylor made her way to a small office. She looked in vain for the silver Lexus and tried to remember the last time her mother had been late. For anything.

"Taylor Ann."

A male voice boomed across the parking lot. She turned to see the hulking shape of Steve shut the door of a black El Camino and make his way toward her. As he approached an unmistakable scent filtered into her nostrils: *Obsession for Men.*

It was an aptly named fragrance for Ian's favorite cologne. Forget that it now drifted from the body of a man she despised. Taylor couldn't stop herself from inhaling deeply as memories popped to the surface like reincarnated ghosts ready to possess her physical body. She pushed them away, but not before she remembered falling asleep on

Ian's chest, the spicy cologne a shadow of scent on his skin, warm and sleepy under the covers. She missed him suddenly in a feral, visceral way that denied rational thought.

Smell was one of the more powerful senses, she'd read somewhere. It had to be for her to crave the smell of the bulging man beside her who walked like a giraffe. Taylor looked at the sweat circles already spreading under Steve's arm. The sight brought her abruptly back to reality, a cold splash of water when one has taken leave of their senses.

"Why are you here?"

"I don't get a 'hello' from my favorite assistant?" Steve dropped his keys in a pant's pocket and winked at her.

Taylor ignored him. Between the winking and using her mother's way of address, she was done being polite for the day.

"I'm supposed to meet my mother here."

"Not coming."

Steve put his hand on her elbow and attempted to steer her in the direction of a sandwich board advertising *Agent Marketing Seminar*. Taylor shrugged him off.

"Do you mind? I'm not a five-year-old."

"Aren't we bitc ... I mean *touchy* today." Steve scowled and raised his arms, showing her the palms of his hands.

His attempts at friendliness never fooled Taylor. A subtle disrespect for women simmered beneath a façade of chivalry, like the undertow at Deception Pass. It swirled openly anytime his precious pride was threatened.

"Your mother had something come up. She called and asked me to escort you through this seminar. I'm here *for you*."

"Right." Taylor stared hard at him. "Well, I don't need babysitting. We clear?"

"Crystal." Steve narrowed his eyes and enunciated the word slowly.

Without further conversation they entered the building and took seats on opposite sides. Taylor rummaged through her purse and found a stray piece of gum. She popped it in her mouth and thought of the little talk she would have with her mother about Steve. Soon.

At break time Taylor slipped outside and lit a cigarette. She felt Steve approach just as she took the first eager drag.

"So, what do you think?"

His tone again friendly, Taylor slowly exhaled and counted to ten. No sense being rude.

"It's okay. I guess I just don't like the thought of treating everyone like," she thought for a minute, "like a resource. You know? Always working an angle to get a sale. Just not me."

"Everyone *is* a potential resource. Don't be naïve, Taylor. You're not a five-year-old, remember? Or do you think all your 'friends' on Facebook are actually friends?"

He laughed, hard and jeering.

"Obviously to *you* people are resources. Not everyone thinks that way."

Taylor took another drag off the cigarette and blew it toward Steve's face. He fanned the air but stood his ground.

"Listen, if you want to succeed as an agent you better change your attitude. And I'm saying that for your own good." He looked serious for a moment, then a slow grin turned up the corners of his lips. "Besides, nothing wrong with being a resource or *using* a resource. Long as everyone gets what they want."

Taylor wondered what kind of dates the man had ever had. *Date*, come to think of it, was probably too decent of a description.

As Steve walked back to the room Taylor considered what he said. There was truth in it, unfortunately. And that was no doubt the key to the reason behind Steve's position of head broker at Northcoast. Her mother was obtuse, but she wasn't stupid. She knew how to use a resource.

࿔

# Chapter 17

"So, don't talk too much today, okay?"

Taylor shut the door of the coffee stand and walked toward her car with Melissa following.

"You've told me not to talk twice now. Why are you being so bossy and weird?" Melissa stood at the passenger side door of the Toyota and stared hard at Taylor.

"I'm not trying to be bossy. Steve is just … you'll see. I want him to be on our side. I'm a new agent so any deal we can make for you to buy this place will be a 'team' effort with Steve as the leader."

Taylor started the car and looked at her friend before easing out of the parking lot toward a late afternoon meeting at Northcoast Realty. Melissa had dressed special for the appointment: knee high lace-up army boots hugged shapely legs encased in skin tight purple plaid pants. An equally snug black v-neck sweater was accented by a chain choker that dangled with charms—hearts and pistols. Highlighted with a flush of purple eye shadow and extra thick liner, Melissa's eyes seemed darker than usual. Steve was gonna love her, maybe more than the hippy lady.

"You think I'm too young, uneducated, *tacky*, to buy a business?"

Melissa's voice was even but her tone leaked a confrontational edge, defensive and hard. When Taylor heard the old, pre-friend voice return she thought, as she had many times, that Melissa was a girl used to fighting for any scrap of good fortune that came her way.

"Of course not. I'm your friend, remember? This guy is a putz, that's all. I've been working on my deal-making pitch for days now. I just want the chance to practice it."

She smiled at Melissa and, after a solemn moment, her friend smiled back.

"Hell, I *am* too young and uneducated." Melissa picked at fuzzy pills on her sweater then rested metallic green fingertips on a three-ring binder that said "Business Plan" in neatly printed block letters.

"You have a business plan? That's pretty impressive." Sisterly, protective feelings swelled inside. Taylor felt like a butcher leading a lamb to slaughter.

"Peter helped me with it. And he's got a contact who's a mortgage broker."

"So you and Peter are going to finance the coffee stand together?"

"Nah. Peter's not interested. After graduation he'll be going to South America for a couple months. Some environmental study. He's supportive but … " Her voice trailed away.

Taylor filled in the blanks in her head. *But we aren't at the point of planning a future together.*

After parking the car, the girls walked to the office. Even from outside Taylor could feel Steve watching them approach. She took a deep breath and pulled open the door.

"Hey Steve, this is my client Melissa that I told you about. She wants to discuss putting in an offer to buy Holy Grounds."

Instead of rising from his leather computer chair, Steve remained seated, his eyes roaming up and down Melissa's body. He took a swig of an extra large can of Red Bull and finally rose to his feet and extended a hand.

"Steve."

"Melissa. Nice to meet you."

"Are you prequalified?" Steve ran a large hand through his thinning hair then checked his Blackberry as if waiting for an important call.

"Um, not exactly. But I'm heading to my mortgage broker after this. I thought that, maybe, we could discuss offers. Then I'll know how much to try to qualify for."

Steve did a poor job of hiding a smirk. "No sense talking about offers when you don't have any money, Sweetheart."

"Melissa knows the coffee business, Steve. She's perfect for this place. I thought it would be helpful to go over some of the steps of putting in an offer, what to expect from the seller, etc. I'm sure she'll get financing."

There were few things Taylor was less sure of, but she stared hard at Steve. "I've already talked to my mother about this deal. She said you'd be willing to go over details, even without prequalification. For practice."

Small lies were only venial sins, easily forgiven. Taylor watched Steve's eyes narrow slightly before roaming over to Melissa again.

"Have a seat." He pulled over two chairs and got out a pad and paper. "I have an appointment, but here are some things to expect. Bank is gonna want to see some history on this place, profit and loss." Steve scribbled illegible notes on the paper.

"I've put together a business plan." Melissa offered the binder to Steve. He ignored it.

"As for offers … $89,000 is the asking price," Steve paused, "which is absolutely ridiculous. Definitely shouldn't pay more than 80, even with the equipment included as a total package." He seemed to be talking to himself, "$89 thou and its not even a real business … for crying out loud. You have money to put down, right?"

He allowed Melissa only a second to respond before continuing, "Cause you're gonna need at least ten percent. Don't waste anyone's time if you can't get money—as in cash—to put down."

Melissa swallowed. "Okay. I'm going to work on all that today. Then you—and Taylor—will put an offer in for me?"

"Sure thing. Taylor will get right on that, Sweetheart. You let us know how you make out at the bank." Steve grabbed his Blackberry. "Now I've got some calls to attend to, thanks for coming in."

He allowed his eyes to rest somewhere below Melissa's neckline before punching at the numbers on his phone. Taylor squeezed Melissa's arm and they made their way out the door.

"Wow, that was stressful," Melissa fanned her face with the binder.

Fighting the urge to curse, Taylor considered her friend. It was strange to see Melissa vulnerable. They rested in silence beside the Toyota for a moment before getting inside. Melissa buckled her seat belt then looked at Taylor.

"What an asshole."

Taylor laughed out loud, relieved to see the scrappy barista she knew reappear.

"Was he totally checking me out *and* treating me like an idiot?"

"Yeah. You should work with him all day. I'm a candidate for the freaking sainthood after the last couple months. Swear."

"Let's get the hell out of here. I'm going to go to the bank, get that loan, and stuff it right in his balding *head.*"

"Don't you mean *face?*"

"Whatever."

Taylor glanced at Melissa reapplying purple lipstick. "You don't have to use me as an agent, you know. Seeing as I come with such unattractive baggage."

"I want you to get a commission. I'll get that loan somehow, wait and see."

Taylor drummed the steering wheel as she drove Melissa back to the coffee stand. She wanted desperately to hear that a young, cranky barista without support had the chance to make a future.

~ ~ ~

The cell phone trilled an alarm as Taylor swallowed the first crisp mouthful of Corona, relishing the tang of a lime wedge on her tongue. It had been an exhausting day with Steve; she didn't want to speak to anyone. Glancing at the number on the display Taylor sighed, laid her head against the futon and punched *Talk*.

"Taylor."

"Hi, Dad." Without giving him a chance to respond Taylor began a guilt-driven ramble. "I'm really sorry I didn't return your call a few days ago. Just been real busy. But I've been thinking of you—how are you? How's Tom? I hope Anthony's feeling better."

It had been over a week since she'd heard the latest from her Dad. Anthony had been hospitalized. Again. Maybe it sounded heartless, but the boy basically rented a bed at the hospital. A visit didn't exactly qualify as newsworthy anymore. She felt bad but, honestly, it was hard to talk to her father sometimes when she knew the conversation would center on the only readily available topic—Dad's passion and purpose: Saving Anthony.

"Are you there? Sometimes reception sucks out here in the boonies."

The phone remained silent.

"Dad?"

"Anthony," Taylor heard her father clear his throat, "he ... he passed away last night, Taylor."

Taylor heard her father's voice catch and the phone seemed to go dead. Something heavy settled in the pit of her stomach, curdling the taste of the beer she'd so desperately wanted only a few moments before.

"My God," she stared into the cemetery across the road. Hulking head stones rose into the deepening twilight like demons coming to life in the dank November air. "The doctors said at least 15 ... he can't die yet."

Tears swelled and spilled down Taylor's cheeks. "I'm sorry, Dad. I knew he was in the hospital, but I thought, I thought it was just like usual."

*Usual.* Even horrible realities can become normal. That's what the short time she'd spent with her adopted brother had taught her. She'd shed tears in private for him, yes, but mostly his life—its horrid reality—had become usual and expected.

Had she loved Anthony? That now seemed terribly important. Not that it changed anything. Mostly she'd kept herself distant from the terrifying reality of a terminally-ill child, a child who stole the time and affection from the father she needed.

She had loved the boy. And resented him deeply.

~ ~ ~

"Where the hell's Acorn Drive? I thought I knew every street in Bellingham ... "

Taylor deliberately avoided helping Steve locate the address of a future listing. Besides being preoccupied with her trip to San Diego for Anthony's funeral, she was still angry at his treatment of Melissa. The guy was lost, in more ways than one, and as far as she was concerned he could stay that way. She checked her watch.

"Listen, I gotta work in an hour and I've got a ton of stuff to do. Can you just drop me off at the office so I can get my car?"

Steve blew out an exasperated breath. "Fine. I'll have to do the background on this property on my own time. But I *do* need to stop at my apartment first. I forgot something."

"What?"

"Just something, okay?" Steve's voice was conspicuously absent of its assertive, macho edge. Instead, he sounded worried. "My apartment's only a few minutes away."

Just what she'd always wanted, a personal tour of Steve's apartment. Plus, she was dying to go pee and needed the clean office bathroom, pronto. Taylor forced herself to breathe deeply. A tour of the apartment was bad enough, having to use Steve's toilet would be much worse.

"Wanna come in?" Steve leaned his head in the car before shutting the door. "I'll be a few minutes."

Taylor hesitated. There was no way she'd make it to the office. "I guess. I need to use your bathroom."

"Sure, no problem." Steve didn't wait for her, but hurried to a ground floor apartment door across the street and disappeared inside.

Taylor followed more slowly, cautiously picking her way along a crushed rock walkway studded with dormant weeds. Once inside she made a beeline toward the hallway and the first doorway on the left. Making a conscious effort not to focus on the filthy sink, overflowing trashcan, and the boxer shorts crumpled in one corner, Taylor took care of business and washed her hands with a large bar of soap. She glanced at a hand towel smeared with trails of dried toothpaste and wiped her hands on her jeans instead.

Steve paid her no attention when she reentered the living room. Taylor glanced around the small "man space." *The guy's a pig, what a surprise.* A battered tan couch and glass topped coffee table were the only pieces of furniture. Two pairs of jeans, one with belt still hanging from the waist loops, were thrown over the back of the couch. On the coffee table sat an open pizza box, one lone piece of petrified pepperoni announcing its prior contents. Two open cans of Red Bull guarded an empty box of powdered donuts. Beside the couch a magazine rack bulged with periodicals and several newspapers. At the base of the rack several novels teetered in an unstable stack, the one on top a Dean Koontz.

"Go ahead and have a seat. I'll be as quick as I can."

"I'll just stand," Taylor wrinkled her nose at the couch," thanks anyway. What are you doing?"

Turning her attention from the disarray of the bachelor pad, Taylor took a few steps toward the small kitchen. Steve was hunched over the counter top, rummaging inside a box of what looked like medical supplies. Ignoring her question, he called into the empty space of the apartment.

"Princess, come here sweet girl." Steve's tone oozed affection.

Taylor fought the urge to laugh. Who on earth could he be talking to?

At that moment a cat padded silently past the couch and toward its master in the kitchen. The creature was petite and feminine and had the most beautiful coat Taylor had ever seen. A sleek, tri-colored collage of orange, black, and grey, the cat's pelt was strikingly leopard-like. Even from a distance Taylor could hear a rumble coming from its chest. It sounded like a swarm of bumblebees.

"There you are, Beautiful."

Steve waited for the cat to approach. It jumped gracefully onto a chair and then onto the counter itself. Purring even louder, it sauntered past the box of supplies and into Steve's waiting arms. Taylor watched him cradle the animal and kiss its furry head. He removed a needle from the packaging.

"What *are* you doing?"

"Princess is diabetic. I need to monitor her glucose levels closely right now. We had a scary bought of hypoglycemia a few days ago. She lost her coordination and got really weak. She could have gone into a coma … "

"You have a *diabetic* cat?"

Taylor shook her head. *This* was not something she'd have predicted.

"Yeah." Steve seemed oblivious to her surprise. "Cats get diabetes just like people do. I have to closely watch the type and amount of food Princess eats and monitor her water intake and urination. It can be fatal." He rubbed the cat as he spook. Relaxed in his arms, Princess's gold-flecked eyes looked into his face with what could only be described as complete adoration.

"You don't look like the pet type."

*Male Chauvinist/cat lover. Who knew?*

"Yeah? Guess you don't know me very well."

His tone matter-of-fact, Steve remained focused on taking Princess's blood sugar. Taylor perched on the edge of the couch and watched for a few moments, fascinated with the scene in front of her, before turning to examine the apartment more closely. A few framed pictures hung at odd angles on one wall: an elderly woman with tan wrinkled skin and a baseball cap, a smiling blond-haired woman, and a man and young Steve posed in front of an open field with dark clouds in the background. Above a shelving unit filled with dusty football trophies hung a larger photo. Half the image was missing. Taylor rose from her seat to inspect it.

The young Steve *had* been handsome, she thought, looking into the photo. Outfitted in his football uniform, Steve smiled into the camera, a shock of once thick blond hair swept to the side. His smile was genuine and full of joy. It had a youthful vulnerability that had since aged to defensive posturing. One broad shoulder was behind a mystery person who had been torn from the photo. A girl. Taylor could make out her fingers, nails painted bright pink, at Steve's opposite side. As she pondered the photo—or lack-there-of—she felt certain that a picture told a story worth a thousand words. Or more.

Taylor glanced back at Steve, Princess's furry tail curled around his forearm, and felt something unexpected. Empathy. It contrasted sharply with the disgust she had become accustomed to nursing while in his presence. Suddenly awkward, she scrambled at small talk.

"Looks like rain again. Don't you love living in a rain shadow?"

Steve didn't answer immediately. He measured some food into a bowl, spoke softly to the cat, and grabbed his car keys. On the way to the door he paused and made eye contact.

"We actually don't live in a rain shadow. The *shadow* is the dry part, eastern Washington." He jerked his thumb in what Taylor guessed was an easterly direction. "But you are correct in that the weather pattern is collectively called The Rain Shadow Effect."

"I figured the shadow was the dark, rainy part."

"Nope. It's the sunny part." Steve smiled at her, without winking. "How topography influences weather is pretty fascinating. You have rain shadow effect—uniquely evident in Washington State—and stuff like lake effect snow in places like New York. Weather is wild, but surprisingly predictable if you know the science related to it."

"Are you a science guy, too?"

"Surprised? People aren't as predictable as weather, Taylor." An edge of defensiveness crept back into Steve's voice. "I always wanted to be a weather man; I think it's amazing. My dad and I used to follow tornados and build weather stations in Oklahoma where I grew up. Crazy weather out there."

Taylor followed Steve out of the apartment and waited while he locked the door. "You're from Oklahoma?"

"Yeah. Dad left when I was in middle school. Mom got cancer and he couldn't handle watching her die. After her funeral I moved to Bellingham to live with my grandmother. When she passed away I handled the estate and learned a fair bit about real estate. I needed a career and it wasn't happening in football … or as a weatherman. Not my dream job, but I've done pretty well."

"It's not my dream job, either. In case you hadn't noticed." Taylor laughed and Steve joined in. For the first time she felt at ease with an equal.

On the way to the office Steve shared more about himself: how he'd loved a grandmother who made the best biscuits, the knee injury that ended his football career, and his fascination with the elements required to make a "sweet" tornado. While he talked, Taylor considered the rain coming down outside and the fact that light could be found in a shadow.

༄

# Chapter 18

Why did airlines continue to build planes constructed for six-inch-wide human beings? Taylor stuffed her boarding pass into her purse and glanced above the seat to check the number: 15B. Middle seat. Next to the window sat a pimply teen with iPod ear buds stuck in his ears. The boy slouched in his seat and stared blankly out the window at a soggy Seattle sky line as rap music pounded an angry, audible beat. On the aisle sat an extra large Italian grandpa, his broad middle pressed between the narrow sides of the seat. A gold chain winked against a dark chest visible between the wide lapels of a half open Hawaiian shirt. He looked up, a smile crinkling the corners of his eyes.

"You next to me?"

"Yeah."

Did she have the worst luck or what? She felt like part of a sandwich, stuffed like a piece of lettuce between salami and, Taylor glanced at the teen's greasy face, cheese. Yuck. Fortunately the plane ride was only a couple of hours.

After take-off Taylor laid her head back and closed her eyes. She wasn't tired. The too-close proximity of strange males gave her the heebie-jeebies. Closing her eyes simply provided an illusion of personal boundaries.

Instead of peaceful calm, Taylor's mind raced under closed eyelids. Jumbling thoughts jockeyed for position. Besides seeing her dad again and dealing with the sadness of Anthony's funeral commencing the following day, there was the past that lurked in shadowy corners of the city known for sunshine. Just knowing she'd once again be in the same locale as Ian was somehow distressing. He'd married and moved on. Probably had a kid by now. After a few moments, Taylor opened her eyes, eager to focus on something else. Twinkly brown eyes gazed back at her.

"No sleep?"

She shook her head at grandpa.

The man had an open wallet on his lap, its leather surface as worn and creased as his olive skin.

"I am Salvadore. I do not like this flying."

He gestured toward the front of the plane, the thick gold links of a man's bracelet collapsing onto his forearm, then fingered the wallet.

"I look at my familia; it helps."

Salvadore began flipping through photos encased in plastic sleeves stuck deep within the interior of the wallet. He stopped at one and handed it to Taylor for her inspection.

A black-haired, olive-skinned girl of about eight smiled back at her. She had warm brown eyes and gaps in her teeth.

"Bella."

Just saying the child's name made him emotional. Taylor looked up and saw tears glistening in the old man's eyes as he put his hand to his heart.

"She is my sweetness. Just like her grandmother, God rest her soul."

Taylor watched Salvadore make the Catholic sign of the cross.

They spent the next hour talking about family—mostly Salvadore's.

Taylor told him only the most basic details of her own life. She left out the upcoming funeral and most everything else about her parents. Instead she listened with genuine interest to his stories of the wife he'd cherished for fifty-seven years—recently deceased, large holiday feasts, baby baptisms, and the weddings of children, grandchildren, and cousins.

Taylor felt as if she were peering inside a Norman Rockwell painting of the type of life for which she had no frame of reference. The stories were vividly told with great emotion. Salvadore alternated between belly jiggling mirth and wiping at tears that came without effort as he relived precious memories. Taylor wished she could crawl inside the pictures he painted.

All too soon Salvadore's tales of family life ended. He seemed to grow tired and closed his eyes in the last few minutes before landing. Taylor, too, fell silent and watched the aircraft gradually decrease altitude and land before taxing toward San Diego Airport. Even from behind the plane's thick window panes she could see the change in air quality—clear and dry—and, Taylor remembered, free of annoying wet weather insects. Palm tree fronds swayed slowly in what she knew was a warm fall breeze. It was a stark contrast to her view just a few hours before: The snow-covered Twin Sisters, their imposing granite sides a vision of icy stoicism that softened only at dusk when they melted briefly into pastels before disappearing altogether into blackness.

Grabbing a duffle bag stuffed with two changes of clothing, Taylor said farewell to Salvadore and made her way out of the plane and into the terminal. She immediately spied her father leaning against the wall. A desperate feeling surfaced as she watched him walk over to greet her, a thin smile on his tired face.

Their interaction remained what it had always been, a stiff sort of dance where he moved carefully and waited politely for her response. Measured. Today was no different.

"Hello, Daughter." He slipped an arm around her shoulder and squeezed.

It seemed to Taylor the squeeze was tighter and lasted longer, but she respected the distance she always felt in his presence and only rested her cheek on his shoulder for a moment.

"Hello, Father."

"I'm so glad you came."

"I'm glad to be here. I'm sorry I didn't ... "

"No, no. No sorrys," her father shook his head. "How could you have known? Anthony *was* in the hospital a lot. None of us expected him to ... " His voice trailed off as if he could not bear to say the words.

"Let's get out of here, huh? Bet you could use an In-N-Out Burger."

Taylor followed him to the car in silence. They made small talk—mostly about Seattle geography and real estate—and ate In-N-Out Burgers and strawberry milkshakes. Her father soon fell silent, retreating to some internal sanctuary where, Taylor imagined, children did not die and relationships were simple. The food a soothing weight in her stomach, she felt content to watch traffic snake by them in the lazy waning daylight. Apathetic fog rolled in from the coast, shrouding and softening the edges of the city.

By the time they pulled up to the neat two-story stucco home with the Pepper Tree out front and a sea of Mister Lincoln rose bushes in back, Taylor was yawning. Though only five o'clock, the November light felt as fragile as the atmosphere in the car. It made her tired.

"Good to have you, Taylor." Her father's partner, Tom, pulled her into a hug as soon as she walked through the door.

"Glad to be here." Surprised, Taylor patted his back as if he were a child. Tom did not *hug* her.

Her father had met Tom when he worked as a nurse. The director of hospital house keeping, Tom was the polar opposite of the quiet reserve and dignity that characterized her father. Gregarious and outgoing, Tom had probably never "come out of the closet." For anything. Taylor couldn't imagine him hiding in a closet literally *or* figuratively.

Still, for all his boldness Tom had given Taylor a wide berth from the beginning. Perhaps it was because he had never fathered children. Whatever it was, she seemed to represent something sacred and untouchable. At first Taylor had been hurt and confused by Tom's apparent lack of interest in her. This mellowed to acceptance, even relief, when she realized he would never attempt to parent her. They were polite with each other, not warm.

"I'm going to bed." Her father barely acknowledged Tom. Instead he gave Taylor the whisper of a kiss to the cheek and ducked into the hallway. "I'm exhausted. Talk more later, Honey?"

"Sure, Dad."

His "later" equaled her intention to call back "soon." Good intentions seemed the extent of what they were able to offer each other.

Before she could make her way to a bedroom, Tom made eye contact and gestured toward the kitchen. "Can we talk for a minute?"

Taylor nodded. She set her duffel bag down and sat at the small breakfast table. Across from her a crude painting of a single red rose made on computer paper adorned the front of the stainless steel refrigerator. The letter "A", drawn in sweeping lines, served as an artist signature. Affixed by four stout magnets at the corners, the picture was the only decoration in the kitchen save a purple African violet above the sink.

"Neal's pretty bad off, Taylor." Tom ran trim fingers through a salt and pepper Caesar cut. "He's lost to some desperate place where nobody can reach him. Not even me. I loved Anthony, too, but we have to go on somehow. We always knew it would end like this … "

Tom looked down at the table, rubbed his eyes, then rose and walked to the sink. He poured a glass of water and offered it to her. When she shook her head, he poured it down the drain and replaced the glass in the cupboard.

"I'm sorry; you're probably tired from the trip. Get some sleep. But look for an opportunity to speak to your Dad after the funeral tomorrow. I'm afraid for him, Taylor. He needs you."

She didn't know what to say and simply nodded and squeezed Tom's arm.

~ ~ ~

There was nothing so tragic to behold as a small coffin. Taylor walked slowly toward it, willing herself to be strong and say a proper goodbye. An organ whined a tired tune in the stuffy air as if it was trying too hard. Taylor wished her father had chosen the piano to escort the spirit of her adopted brother into heaven. Pianos would be in heaven, no doubt about that. Along with plenty of macaroni and cheese. As she looked into the casket, Taylor remembered something Anthony had said shortly before she left for Washington.

"God will make macaroni and cheese for me."

He'd been blissfully partaking of his favorite meal, a special treat during a spell of "doing better." The thought blossomed out of nowhere during a contemplative moment between cheesy fork-fulls.

"Oh yeah?" She'd only been partially listening, lost in her own world and the dramas that existed there. Anthony had the worst sort of drama, yet appeared immune to its daily horrors. Instead he pictured God in a chef's apron and imagined the perks of heaven from a place no ten-year-old should be allowed to visit—the waiting room of the dying.

"Yeah, God's like that. He knows all our favorite things."

Taylor had feared the moment of seeing him dead, but it didn't scare her in the ways she had imagined. The frail shell that lay in the coffin dressed for a baseball game—complete with oak bat beside him—looked like something made of wax. It only vaguely resembled the boy that had told her on the occasion of their first meeting, "You're pretty for a girl." That boy smiled back from a framed photo that sat near a church podium and a large carved glass vase stuffed with red roses.

Roses—red ones no less—might have struck some as an unusual floral choice for a funeral. They didn't know her father. "Gladiolas are hideous," he always said. It was one of a handful of strong opinions he readily shared. The red roses weren't Mister Lincoln's, but they'd have to do. Like his precious son, the presidential blossoms in the backyard had withered and died.

# Chapter 19

After the funeral, the three-some returned home to a dinner of carnitas, her father's favorite.

Taylor sat in the kitchen watching Tom work while her father retired to a spot on the back deck. As she sipped Corona, Taylor watched Tom's neat fingers prepare pork, chop a pile of cilantro, onion, and tomato for fresh pico de gallo, and assemble shredded cabbage for a bowl of coleslaw.

"I don't remember you cooking this when I was here."

"That's because I didn't. Carnitas are your Dad's specialty," a tired smile lifted the corners of Tom's mouth. "I've been doing more since Anthony passed. Your dad needs support."

*"He needs you."* Taylor thought of Tom's words from the previous evening. She rose from her chair. "Think I'll go outside and keep Dad company while you finish."

The French doors leading to the deck stood ajar. Twilight shadows bathed the backyard in shades of purple and deep cobalt. Her father sat with his back to her, elbows on his knees and head bowed. At the funeral he had spoken for a few minutes about the four short years of life celebrated with a special needs boy. Afterward he wept discreetly and avoided talking to the few friends who had come for the ceremony.

Taylor padded outside on bare feet. She pulled a chair close to her father and sat down. For a long time nobody spoke.

"What will I do without him?"

It felt weird to hear such a vulnerable question from a parent. Taylor cleared her throat. "You still have me, Dad. You still have a daughter."

She didn't expect the swell of emotion that bubbled up. Her voice wavered on the words and she looked away, pretending to search for a suitable spot for her beer. When she sat back she felt her father's eyes on her. He clasped his hands together, lacing the fingers into a fist.

"I have failed you. I know that." He lay his head back on the chaise lounge, sighed, and looked into the inky heavens. Stars winked like crystals scattered across heavy velvet.

"She was destroyed, utterly humiliated, when I asked for the divorce. You were only a baby ... "

Taylor made no sound or movement. She wanted nothing to derail the train of thought gaining momentum in the space beside her.

"The only thing she ever wanted was a family. I stole that. Since I couldn't love her it seemed that the kindest thing I could do was leave her alone. I wrecked her life, but at least she had you. You were always *hers*, you see."

It was strange how some things that sound like love don't feel like love. And visa versa.

Her father continued speaking in a distant voice, the voice of one seeing something afar off that had never been clear until just that moment when his soul was raw and exposed.

"I guess I succeeded in not loving you, either." He touched her knee and Taylor heard the tears in his voice. "Only I do. Can you forgive me? Can you love me, too?"

Without a word she shimmied the deck chair closer and wrapped her arms around her father, leaning into his neck. "I've always loved you, Dad," she whispered.

A great sob caught in his throat, releasing the pain of the day—and so many before—as he squeezed her tight. "We are broken people, Taylor, broken people."

They hugged each other for a long time, enjoying the peculiar companionship of brokenness. Through the French doors the scent of cooking pork and corn tortillas warming in olive oil mixed with the clean pungent smell of onion and garlic. It snuck over the deck and hovered over the space of sorrow, inviting fellowship and the making of memories. Life birthed a second chance while God welcomed a little saint home with a plate of macaroni and cheese.

She thought of Anthony and the sweetness of Salvadore's family memories—happy *and* sad—as she gazed up at the awesome majesty of the dark universe overhead.

"Anthony said I was pretty for a girl, you remember that? When we first met?" She giggled at the memory and swiped her leaking nose.

Her father chuckled. "You *are* pretty for a girl." He nudged her shoulder with his, teasing, then stood. "Shall we eat?"

~ ~ ~

On the way to the airport Taylor told her father about Melissa, Liz, and Rain. She thanked him for the summer horseback riding camps that made horse ownership doable, if not easy. She invited him to visit.

"You just have to meet my horse, Dad, she is amazing."

Her father looked thoughtful, "That's something you got from me—did you know that?"

"Love of horses?"

"Yep," her father nodded his head, "purely my genes."

"I didn't know that."

"I grew up with a pony. Rode him all through the woods growing up. His name was Trigger."

"That's original."

Her father laughed, "Isn't it? I think my happiest days were in a saddle. It may sound weird, but I always felt understood by my pony. I miss that feeling. Never followed after it, but I see you've picked up the genetic thread."

He sounded proud, relieved to discover Taylor had never been solely *Hers*.

"I know exactly what you mean, Dad. It's not weird. You simply must meet Rain—you'll come visit?"

"I will."

And she felt deep inside that the days of shallow good intentions had come to an end for both of them.

# Chapter 20

Taylor could not say exactly what woke her. Only that she was drawn from sleep as if hearing a voice from far off, or the repetitive strains of familiar music. She drifted to the window, as she always did on sleepless nights, and looked for the pale shape of the horse.

Late at night Rain could always be found lounging in the corner of the field nearest Taylor's bedroom, her leg cocked and head hung in a horse's fitful sleep. Taylor knew the choice of location was probably because the ground there was especially spongy, or the views more encompassing or simply some odd animal instinct. Whatever it was, knowing the mare chose a spot close by brought overwhelming comfort. Taylor couldn't shake the feeling that Rain sensed the battle that took place when the sun went down and the nightmares haunted her.

"Did you know horses only sleep a couple hours a day?" Liz had shared once.

"Sounds like me."

"They really only doze and it adds up to like three hours of actual sleep next to our need for eight."

Ever after Taylor thought of Rain as her pale sleepless guardian, an angel of the night.

Feeling dreamy and disoriented, Taylor's heart skipped a beat as she gazed into the deserted pasture. A full moon illuminated a crispy December landscape, the stiff grass glittering as if crusted with tiny diamonds. Rain was nowhere in sight. Suddenly awake, Taylor shivered and pulled on a pair of jeans and wool socks. She shrugged into a jacket and hurried out the door.

Outside silence covered the hibernating earth like a heavy cloak. Taylor's ears tingled with an increased sense of hearing. She thought she could hear the rustle of a bear turning over in its den somewhere in the surrounding hills, sense the curled up shape and tiny breaths of a mouse cocooned at the base of a tree. Her boots became cymbals crashing in an orchestra of woodland whispers as they crunched over diamond-studded vegetation.

Entering the lean-to, Taylor sighed in relief. Rain stood huddled in a corner. Instead of nickering, the mare bobbed her head twice and bit at her flank, her ebony eye troubled.

"What's wrong, Sweetie?"

At moments like this, Taylor became painfully aware of her lack of experience. She walked around the horse looking for obvious injury. Nothing appeared to be wrong, but she noted Rain had not finished her dinner. Left over hay littered the earth around the mare's feet. Taylor retrieved some grain and offered it to Rain. The mare ignored the treat and shifted her position.

"Liz says not eating is serious business. What's up?" As Taylor talked she watched in horror as the mare's knees buckled and she dropped to the ground. Rain rolled to her side, first one way, then the next, the way she might do after Taylor removed the saddle. It was not a natural thing to do late at night, on rock hard ground, when she would normally be snoozing.

"Okay, okay … think, think." Taylor fought panic as she watched the mare rise to her feet, only to drop again and roll. What was it Liz had said about veterinary care? *If anything happens, call Dr. Wilson.* He would want to treat Rain in case of emergency. *His number's in the packet.*

Heart pounding, Taylor sprinted to the house. She glanced at the clock inside: 10:30. The vet hospital wouldn't be open. What then? She fumbled through her real estate paperwork and finally found the packet Liz had given her detailing Rain's injury and recovery. At the bottom of one sheet she saw what she was looking for: South Valley Large Animal Clinic. A phone number followed and Taylor punched it into her cell.

"Dr. Kelso and Wilson's answering service," a dry, tired female voice picked up on the fifth ring.

"Hi. My horse is sick or something. I need Dr. Wilson to come look at her."

"Dr. Kelso is on call tonight. I'll have him give you a ring right away."

"No. I need Dr. Wilson."

"Miss, *Dr. Kelso* is on call. He will speak to you shortly and you can tell him what the problem is."

"Please, just call Dr. Wilson. He saved this horse. He knows her and will want to be the one to see her." Taylor felt breathless, gulping for air like a fish out of water.

"I seriously doubt that."

There was silence for a moment then Taylor heard a sigh on the other end of the phone. "What is the name of this animal?"

"Her name is Rain," Taylor hesitated, "but tell him Bellissima is sick."

"Ooookay." The woman hung up without saying goodbye.

Taylor had paced three circles around the living room when her cell phone trilled. When she picked up a deep voice answered.

"Dr. Wilson here."

"I'm so sorry to call late, Dr. Wilson. You may not remember me ... Taylor. I met you at the trail ride in October ... "

"I remember."

"Something's wrong with Rain. I woke up and went outside and she wasn't sleeping where she usually does ... " Taylor hesitated.

"Horses normally move around. They don't sleep the way we do."

"I know, Liz told me." Taylor's thoughts felt as scattered as seeds blown by the wind. "Do you know Liz?"

*Of course he knows Liz.*

"I know Liz. Taylor, if you don't mind, it's nearly 11 o'clock. Is something else the matter with Rain?"

"She looks uncomfortable. And she isn't eating the rest of her hay. She rolled three times when I went out to see her just now."

"Rolled?" The veterinarian's voice sharpened. "Anything else?"

"She was biting at her flanks and refused the handful of grain I tried to feed her."

"I'll be right out. Where do you live?"

When the truck pulled in the driveway its headlights illuminated twin shapes in the paddock. As instructed, Taylor had haltered the horse and Rain walked in circles at the end of a lead rope.

It took only a minute for Dr. Wilson to confirm his phone diagnosis.

"What's colic?"

"Basically a bad stomachache." The vet pulled out a tube of paste and inserted it into Rain's mouth, depressing the plunger. "I'm giving her something to relax her intestines, if it's a simple colic."

Taylor's heart beat faster. "What if it isn't a simple colic?"

"If it's a twisted gut colic she'll need surgery." Dr. Wilson was matter of fact. He did not make eye contact with Taylor but focused on Rain, running his hand up and down the length of her spine and stroking her neck.

"Can horses die from colic?"

"Yes."

"Oh God, really?" Taylor began pacing the length of the lean-to. She stuffed shaking hands into her jacket pockets and felt for a cigarette.

The veterinarian turned his attention from the horse. "Don't worry, yet. This could be a simple, mild stomachache. If it is, the medicine will relax Rain's gut muscles and she'll begin eating again. That's how we'll know. In the meantime, why don't you show me her hay? I'd like to see if I can determine why she's uncomfortable."

After a tour of her sparsely filled feed and tack area, Wilson gestured toward the paddock. "Do you have water out there for her?"

"Of course."

Taylor felt herself relax as they walked to the water trough. An inch-thick layer of ice covered the surface of the metal tub.

The veterinarian frowned, "How long has it been like this?"

Horror mixed with panic as Taylor examined the miniature ice skating rink in front of them. "I don't know."

"Well, that is certainly your problem." The vet put his hands on his hips. "Horses need just as much, if not more, water during cold weather. Hard telling how long Rain's been without. That's why she didn't finish her food and why she's so uncomfortable now."

"I didn't know … I checked the water and filled it a couple days ago. I didn't think … "

The guilt that waited to pounce on Taylor every minute of every day took its opportunity. It pummeled her, stealing away the joy of Rain's companionship. She did not deserve to have the horse. She had hurt her and would certainly fulfill the dream. Tears filled Taylor's eyes and made trails down her frozen cheeks. She looked away from the vet. "Maybe I'm just not a good home for her. I'll go break the ice now."

Dr. Wilson looked from Rain to Taylor and back again. He glanced at his watch. "How about I break the ice and keep an eye on your horse. Seems to me she might be perking up. Would you be willing to make me a cup of coffee in the meantime? It's a good forty minutes back home."

Taylor wiped her eyes. *Coffee, that's something I can do without screwing up.* "Sure."

By the time the coffee was done, Rain had consumed half a bucketful of warm water and a couple mouthfuls of hay.

The vet looked happy. "She'll be fine, but I'll drink a cup of coffee and give her a few more minutes to show otherwise." He followed Taylor to the house, stamped his feet on the door mat, and sat on the futon after receiving a steaming mug of coffee.

"Thank you."

Taylor didn't know what to say. She sat across the small living room and slid a cigarette out of the pouch, sucking hungrily at the end after lighting the pale cylinder. In the uncomfortable silence Dr. Wilson sipped his coffee and watched her smoke, a thoughtful look in his hazel eyes. She avoided his gaze for what felt like an eternity then blurted out the only thing that came to mind.

"You think smoking is disgusting."

It was more a statement than a question. Taylor immediately wondered why she cared what a veterinarian thought of her personal habits.

"Disgusting? That isn't what I was thinking. The way you lit the cigarette reminded me of my mother." Dr. Wilson took another sip of coffee. "She died of lung cancer a few years ago."

"Oh." Taylor took a few more drags then snuffed the cigarette out in an ash tray.

"Don't stop on account of me. I should go anyway." He drained his coffee and set the cup down. "I *am* curious what you plan to do with Rain. Are you riding her?"

"Yeah," Taylor relaxed. "I love it. She's maybe the best thing that's happened to me. Ever."

"She's a remarkable horse."

"Why didn't you keep her after all the work you did to save her life?"

The vet looked thoughtful again. "I've seen many gunshot animals at the clinic, Taylor, but none like Rain. It's a flat miracle she lived. So, it seemed to me she had a special purpose to fulfill. " His eyes were probing.

Taylor looked away and grasped for another subject. "Do *you* ride?"

"Oh yes. My passion is Ride and Tie events. But my horse is getting old. I retired him last fall."

"What's Ride and Tie?"

"It's a team event. Two riders and one horse in a relay cross country. One rides ahead while the other runs. The horse gets tied up mid-way and the first runner gets on and rides while the rider runs the next portion of trail."

"Sounds hard." Taylor thought of her first ten mile ride with Liz and frowned.

"Nah. It's fun and exciting. Not to mention great exercise in beautiful country. You should try it. There's a club in the area and yearly rides in spectacular settings."

Even under a veterinarian's union suit and a jacket, Taylor could see Dr. Wilson's masculine shape. He had an athlete's body that paired naturally with the challenge of outdoor adventure. She tried to imagine herself jogging through mountainous country, flabby thighs stuffed into a pair of running shorts, alternating between gasping for air like a beached fish and puffing on a cigarette. Not a pretty sight.

"I don't have a partner. Plus, my horse only has one eye. We're not exactly obvious athletes."

"Rain would do just fine; she's intelligent and level-headed. Plus, she's an Arabian. They excel in distance sports. If you change your mind give me a call. I'll be your partner, show you the ropes." The vet smiled and walked toward the door. Taylor followed.

"What do I owe you for the farm visit?" She cringed inside, imagining the $23.51 that made up her checking account until pay day.

"Nothing. First visit's on me. Just remember that water."

"Dr. Wilson … "

"And call me Jacob, please."

"Are you sure? I feel bad."

Jacob paused before pulling the truck door open. He looked at her. "It was an honest mistake."

Taylor bit her bottom lip, feeling as if she might cry again.

"You'll do fine, Taylor. Give a call if you're worried and remember what I said about Ride and Tie." He smiled and disappeared inside the dark interior of the pick-up truck.

# Chapter 21

"You're late."

Taylor handed change and a triple shot mocha through the window to a woman in a yellow Volkswagen and heard the door click shut behind her. She turned and watched Melissa push her small backpack into the cubby beneath the cash register. Instead of the usual headband her hair hung long and heavy, a dark fringe that obscured her face. When she rose and made eye contact Taylor stared into eyes naked of makeup. They were rimmed in red.

"You look like crap."

Taylor waited for a comeback. Melissa said nothing. Instead she began scribbling on a sheet of paper by the register.

"What are you doing?"

A car had pulled up outside. Taylor hurried to take an order for a skinny latte then crossed her arms and waited for Melissa to respond.

"We need syrup. Crème de menthe I think."

"No we don't." Taylor jerked her head toward the double shelf of syrup behind them. The tall glass bottles were arranged alphabetically, labels perfectly aligned like soldiers ready for action. "You just went through the syrup order last week, did you forget? Nobody uses crème de menthe anyway. It's gross." Taylor wrinkled her nose. "But, if you want to be useful you can empty the used grounds. While you've been filling in for Sleeping Beauty I've sold a ton of mochas." Again Taylor waited for a response.

In the four months she'd been working morning shift, Melissa had never been late, or forgotten anything that had to do with the coffee stand. Some days it seemed as if she was already the owner, ready to take Holy Grounds to the pinnacle of small business success.

Taylor watched her remove the plastic tub under the machine. The pressure of expressing made the coffee grounds into compact brown discs. They looked like miniature hockey pucks. As Melissa tapped out the container Taylor noticed her hands shaking.

"Are you okay?"

Melissa straightened and replaced the tub. "Yeah, just had a hard night."

Taylor furrowed her brows. "And … "

Melissa dropped her arms to her sides. Her shoulders sagged and she seemed ready to burst into tears. "Can I ask your advice on something personal?"

Taylor glanced into the parking lot outside the kiosk and, seeing there were no approaching customers, grabbed the 'closed' sign and stuck it to the drive-up window. She pulled the shade down to obscure their presence.

"Of course."

"My sister called me last night. She's pregnant and considering an abortion. Her boyfriend doesn't want the baby … I don't know what to tell her."

Taylor saw tears shining in Melissa's eyes. Her own stomach churned into a knot. "Good thing she has you to talk to."

Melissa did not look her in the eye. Instead, she leaned her back against the wall and slid to the floor keeping her knees pulled tight to her chest.

"Hmmm ... there's one problem," Taylor slid down beside her. "You don't have a sister, Melissa. You must have forgotten telling me about being an only child. Remember— *'The one thing we have in common?'*" Taylor imitated her husky voice.

A sob caught in Melissa's throat. Taylor felt her own cocktail of emotions rising inside. She said a silent prayer, the only prayer she was capable of saying anymore: *God, please help me.*

"So, you're pregnant."

Melissa gave an almost imperceptible nod. Her shoulders trembled. "Really dumb, I know. I should have used protection every time. I knew better. I have a future to protect." Melissa gestured around the kiosk, "*Had* a future." She put her head in her hands and sobbed.

"What does your boyfriend think?" Taylor tried to think of one thing she knew for sure about Peter besides his affinity for protecting the environment and all things sold at REI.

"Peter says now is not the time to have a child. He wants me to have an abortion; he gave me the money already."

"Do *you* want to have an abortion?" There were so many words, so many feelings inside that wanted to come out. Taylor wished she were older and wiser and that the perfect words would magically come out and make the situation better. Instead she waited. And listened.

"I don't know. The counselor told me every child deserves to be wanted. I think that's true, don't you?" Melissa wiped at her eyes and searched Taylor's face. Her chin trembled. "I'm not ready to be a mother; you know my plans for this place. Plus, Peter doesn't want it. What does that mean for *us*?"

Taylor wondered if the truth was written all over her face as she heard Melissa repeat the familiar words: *Every child deserves to be wanted; He doesn't want it; What does this mean for us?* She squeezed her eyes shut.

She hadn't thought seriously of the future of "us" when she'd started sleeping with Ian. Somehow she didn't want to have to think about details when he'd wanted her and just being in his presence felt like enough. When she started loving him it seemed like that, too, would be enough, enough to figure out the details of life with another person—a home, jobs, personal habits. An unplanned baby.

Didn't everyone say love was enough? How did you know the love you experienced with someone was big enough for something as life changing as a child? There were levels and limitations to love, a *Note to Self* for future relationships. She'd suddenly, painfully, understood the limitations to love when she saw the look on Ian's face after she told him. She could still see him pull out his wallet and count the hundred dollar bills, hear him say to himself as she left without drama, "It was worth it."

Love shouldn't hurt that much.

# Chapter 22

Minnie glanced hopefully at the door. When Taylor ignored her she whined and jumped up on it, resting there with her front paws. Turning her tiny head she stared at Taylor.

"You can't possibly be ready to play again. Plus, it's cold out there. Give it up, Min."

Taylor returned to the computer and typed "business loans" into the search engine. There simply had to be a way to find money for Melissa's dream. It had become an obsession.

Minnie waited a few moments more at the door then began trotting around the small house. Alert and purposeful, she made rounds of the kitchen before disappearing into Taylor's bedroom.

"It's not in there, Min," Taylor called in exasperation after the little dog, "I hid your ball. And for obvious reasons."

At the sound of the word *ball*, Minnie raced back into the living room and looked expectantly at Taylor.

"Oh, all right. I'll throw it a few more times. Mom should be here any minute to pick you up." *And won't she be surprised*, Taylor thought.

She glanced at a paper bag of Minnie's things that sat by the door, awaiting her mother's return from a post holiday Mexico cruise. She'd used none of its contents: a doggie purse to carry Minnie around in, several outfits, and doggie shoes in case it was overly cold when she took Minnie for a walk. Ridiculous.

Her mother would be shocked to discover that her pampered "child" loved the farm life and, especially, playing fetch. She had even gone after small rocks Taylor had thrown into the icy waters of the Nooksack River. Plunging her head under water, she'd retrieved the rocks over and over again like a tiny Labrador. Taylor had laughed until her sides ached, a new respect for the dog blossoming inside.

Later, she snuggled Minnie in a warm towel beside her on the drive home, amazed that dog sitting the "useless" Miniature Pincher had turned out to be so much fun. She couldn't wait to tell her mom about the athletic ability that lurked inside five pounds of pampered pooch. She'd make sure to neglect certain parts of the dog's stay on the farm. The river outing, for instance, and the fact that Minnie had certainly consumed her weight in horse manure in the last ten days.

"Ready?" Taylor held up the toy dog sized tennis ball she'd bought and Minnie gave a sharp bark.

The ball sliced through the chilly fog and flew across the driveway and into the cemetery. Minnie resembled a black torpedo as she raced after it, disappearing into the fog for a moment before reappearing with the ball in her mouth.

"Be careful near the road, Twit. You gotta watch where you're going."

Taylor wrestled the ball out of Minnie's mouth and the dog panted happily, a doggie grin plastered across her face. At that moment Taylor heard tires crunch as her mother's car pulled into the drive.

Barking hysterically, Minnie ran to the car.

"My sweetie!"

Taylor watched in silence as her mother scooped up the little dog.

"Dear me ... look how wet you are, Min Min. You must be freezing

"… and you stink." Ann wrinkled her nose.

"Hi Mom, welcome back."

"Thank you, Taylor Ann." Her mother smiled for an instant, then turned serious. "You should have put a sweater on Minnie, she's shaking like a leaf. This kind of weather isn't suited for a fragile, short-coated dog like Min. Let's get her inside."

Taylor watched her mother fuss over the dog as if she were a newborn. Finally she spoke up.

"I think you'll be amazed to know your *fragile* Minnie is a hoot. We've had lots of fun outside together playing fetch. She's like a Labrador Retriever, Mom. It's a crack-up."

Her mother looked skeptical. "Retrieve?"

"Yeah, you've gotta watch her before you leave. Seriously, she's hilarious."

"It's too cold for her."

"No, she loves it. Wait and see."

Her mother's brows remained furrowed so Taylor continued.

"It could be good blogging material. Let's see … unexpected potential in a client? Untapped opportunities in a property? You could talk about Minnie's new skill and tie it into real estate in your next posting."

Taylor wasn't sure why it felt imperative to show off Minnie's new talent except perhaps to prove she had done something right, as if getting close to the Pride and Joy would somehow help her get closer to its owner.

At the mention of the blog her mother softened. "I suppose just once would be okay."

"Hey Min, wanna get your ball?"

Catapulting out of her mother's arms, Minnie pranced around Taylor's feet, tongue hanging happily out of her mouth.

"Ready?"

Her mother stood, arms crossed, and watched Minnie give a sharp bark. Taylor suddenly paused, "You should do it, Mom. Come on."

Taking the wet ball with manicured finger tips, her mother drew back an arm and flung it in a wide arc in the direction of the street.

Before it had even left her hand Minnie bolted in the direction of the throw.

Taylor didn't hear the car approach. It appeared silently out of the mist, cresting a swell in the asphalt just as Minnie plucked the ball from the roadway. Like a film in slow motion, Taylor watched in horror as the tiny black dog disappeared under a front tire.

"Minnie!"

A shriek split the thick moist air and several things seemed to happen at once. Taylor saw her mother sprint for the asphalt and a cacophony of noises—her mother's frantic breathing, the car's tires crunching on the gravel as it pulled over, her own heart beat pounding, and the agonized cries of a wounded animal—jumbled together. Taylor raced after her mom.

"It just came out of nowhere!" A man wearing a cowboy hat called to them as he exited the car and made his way over.

Taylor ignored him. Instead she focused on the black form writhing on the pavement. Minnie reminded Taylor of a Daddy Longlegs spider she tried to kill once. Instead of ending the spider's life, she'd simply mangled one of its legs with a swat of the rolled up newspaper. The spider had continued to flee, big body bobbing, its thin graceful leg twisted the wrong direction. Like the spider, one of Minnie's twig-like legs was bent at an unnatural angle. Blood seeped into a puddle from a hole in the skin where pale broken bone was visible.

"Oh God, oh God … I can't look." Her mother alternated between reaching for Minnie and looking away as she wrung her hands. Her face had turned white, the blue veins in her neck bulging.

"I swear I didn't see your dog. I'm so sorry."

"It's not your fault. Just go, okay?"

The motorist looked from Taylor to her mother to the broken dog at their feet. "That doesn't look good."

"Oh, God … "

"Just *go*. I mean it." Taylor gestured toward the car then ignored the motorist completely as she knelt beside Minnie. "Shhh," she cooed to the dog, "you'll be okay."

The high pitched wailing continued as Minnie repeatedly tried to rise on the shattered limb.

"Let me." Voice trembling, her mother reached a shaky hand toward the dog. "She's my baby."

Abruptly the wailing ended and Minnie laid her head back on the pavement. Her eyes glazed over and an ominous sound rolled from the depths of her small chest. "Grrrrrr." Buzzing at first like a swarm of bees, the sound turned to a growl that parted Minnie's black lips showing her pearly white teeth.

Her mother snatched her arm back as if bitten by a snake. "My god, what's happened to you Minnie?" Wringing her hands again, tears began to spill from her eyes. "She's *never* growled at me before."

"Mom, she's in pain." Taylor put her arm around her mother's shoulders, suddenly sure of what to do next. "Go back to the house. I'm going to call a friend. He's a vet; he'll know what to do."

Her mother appeared dazed and confused as she walked toward the cottage. As Taylor watched she thought of the many times she'd wished to see the woman emotional or out of control even once. Now that the moment had come it cut her to the heart. Quickly she punched some numbers on her cell phone.

"Hi, I need to speak with Dr. Wilson. It's an emergency."

# Chapter 23

Jacob Wilson carefully unbuckled the muzzle from the back of Minnie's sleeping head. With what seemed like affection, he gently slid the nylon apparatus from the dog's slender nose. "I don't think she'll be biting anyone now."

As Taylor watched it occurred to her that, once again, the veterinarian was patching up a creature that was vitally important in her life.

"She won't try to bite my mother while she's recovering, will she?"

"Highly unlikely. When an animal goes into shock they can do all sorts of things that are contrary to their normal personality."

"My mom was just devastated."

The vet said nothing. He was busy connecting an IV and assembling what he needed to repair the broken limb.

"So she'll be alright?" Taylor paced the small room, considering the tools of a veterinarian's trade as she chewed her nails down to the nubs. She felt certain Dr. Wilson had violated the rules of the clinic by allowing her to follow him back to surgery and observe procedure. Her fear of letting Minnie out of sight, not to mention tenuous grasp on self-control, had no doubt made him more flexible than usual.

"My mom would just die without this dog; she's seriously like the most important thing in her life. If only I hadn't taught her to fetch ... "

Again Taylor had hurt something dear to her. This time it included *someone*. Her mother would probably never trust her again. Taylor glanced at Minnie lying motionless on the table. The little dog wouldn't be playing with balls anymore. A tear oozed from the corner of her eye and she wiped it away.

"The break is pretty bad," the vet spoke with his back to her, "but I should be able to patch her up enough so she can walk again. She may always have a limp. Perhaps a reminder she's not a Labrador?"

Dr. Wilson looked at Taylor then, a warm smile playing at the corners of his mouth. When he saw her face he frowned. "I'm sorry. I didn't mean to make a bad joke. Just trying to get you to smile. I'll take good care of this dog, okay?"

Taylor watched him brush his fingers over Minnie's side, the masculine hand a study in contrast next to the petite creature on the table.

"It's just like with Rain and the frozen water ... I wasn't paying attention." Taylor looked away.

"Bad things happen, Taylor. Sometimes it's nobody's fault. Now, you must let me work. I'll call you when I'm done. Why don't you let me deliver Miss Minnie after she's recovered from surgery tomorrow? Then I can see my favorite girl."

Though she knew he was talking about Rain, Taylor felt her face flush. Fortunately the veterinarian was leaning over Minnie, already utterly consumed with the task at hand.

"Okay. I'll tell my Mom she can see Minnie tomorrow?"

"Yes."

Taylor looked once more at the back of the veterinarian and let herself out of the surgical room.

After calling her mother, Taylor switched on the computer. She punched in a web address and nursed a third beer while waiting for the images to load. A moment later, Minnie's alert laughing face appeared on the screen. She sat upright on her mother's lap outside the real estate office. The blog title read: *Minnie Musings: Thoughts on the Market and Man's Best Friend.*

Taylor had never bothered logging on and reading her mother's silly attempt at social networking. It didn't seem so ridiculous when she looked at the number of followers—85—and the many comments that appeared under posts. She scrolled to the last entry, posted from Mexico four days before her mother had returned from the cruise. The title was *Anniversaries.*

*Aloha friends. Oops, wrong vacation! Buenos Noches. A beautiful evening here in Mexico and though I'm without Minnie and supposed to be taking a break from real estate, I thought I'd say a few words about anniversaries. Anniversaries are important to celebrate whether it's a wedding or the purchase of your first home or condo. Make a special meal or, better, commemorate the purchase of your first dwelling by doing a renovation or improvement. Doesn't have to be big. As my sweet Minnie would tell you, special things come in small packages. Install a new fixture on the sink or invest in a needed appliance. Of course, if you have the funds, the renovation of a bathroom or kitchen really builds your home's value. On a personal note, today is the anniversary of my father's death. I'm lonely without Minnie's company, but enjoyed a margarita and remembered Dad tonight—may he rest in peace. I'll be back in the Pacific Northwest soon, land of beautiful real estate and a certain perky Miniature Pincher. Call, comment, or come by. I'd love to talk shop, or "dog" with you.*

Grandpa's death. She's forgotten it of course. The passing of an angry alcoholic she barely remembered wasn't something to highlight in the day planner. Her mother's post reminded her that regardless of the messy, tequila-colored details, Grandpa had been a father to a little girl once. A little girl that grew up to be a woman who still thought of him. The conversational tone and subtle vulnerability of the post took Taylor by surprise. Her mother had a warm heart beating under the perpetually cool exterior. Ironic that it seemed most comfortable appearing to acquaintances and complete strangers.

# Chapter 24

Taylor paced the length of her small living room and waited. She watched the daylight begin to fade outside. In the cemetery, a headstone extended its shadow—the looming shape of a cross—nearly to the road. Even though weathermen said it was the warmest February on record the days were short and the night would still be bone chilling. Prematurely warm days with temps in the 60s had lured lilacs to begin budding and behind her Rowan's tulip beds were a sea of thick green stalks.

Taylor alternated between watching the road and watching her landlady—in bright red boots and yellow woolen cap—erect a "nightgown" of plastic sheeting over raised beds. She huddled over the plants like a hen with a brood of chicks. Taylor watched her lips move and knew she was talking to the plants and fussing about temperatures plunging again and killing off the new growth. Outside of Dr. Wilson, the woman was perhaps the most nurturing person Taylor had ever met. She seemed to have missed that gene altogether.

At the sound of tires crunching gravel, Taylor bolted to the door. She greeted the veterinarian at his truck and chewed at a thumb nail.

"How is she?"

Jacob didn't answer. Instead he opened the narrow door of the extended cab and withdrew a small pet crate. Inside Taylor saw Minnie lying on her side, a splint on her broken limb.

"My mother is completely freaking out. She's called me twice today and is, in fact, on her way up from Edmonds now."

"Let's take Minnie inside. She's been sleeping a lot today, but she's about ready to wake up I think."

Jacob's long legs took the two porch steps in one stride. He pushed open the door and walked in the house with Taylor following. He placed the crate on the futon and sat down beside it. Taylor knelt on the floor and peeked inside. Minnie's glossy brown eyes looked out at her as a short stump of a tail wagged back and forth ever so slightly.

"Ooooh." Tears sprang to Taylor's eyes as she considered both the splint on the dog's leg and the lively expression creeping back to her face. Animals did not feel sorry for themselves. It was one of the great mysteries of life that no matter what happened they were always ready to move on, forget and forgive whatever caused them pain.

"I'm afraid to touch her."

Taylor looked at Jacob. Without a word he opened the crate and with impossible gentleness lifted the dog out and set her on the futon. Minnie tried to move but immediately collapsed on her side again. Taylor stroked the gleaming black coat as the dog licked her fingers.

"When she recovers a bit more she'll figure out how to sit up and then hobble around."

"Really?" Taylor brushed the broken limb with a finger.

"Really. You'll be amazed. I'm leaving instructions with you for her care and also medication. I'll need to see Minnie again of course and remove the pins, but your mother can take her home. Now it's a matter of the body healing itself."

Taylor watched Jacob remove a pen from his coverall pocket and begin writing on a pad of paper. Above the pocket was stitched, *Jacob Wilson, DVM*.

"Did you always want to be a veterinarian?"

"Hmmm." Jacob continued writing.

"Why?"

Jacob scratched a few more words, then the digits of a phone number. Replacing the pen in his pocket he finally gave her his attention.

"I love animals." He ran calloused fingers through his hair and sighed as if there were more to the story. "That's the short answer."

"Did your parents want you to be a vet?" Taylor wanted him to stay, wanted to hear the long answer, so she kept shooting questions like a four-year-old stuck on *why*.

"Not exactly. *Veterinarian* was about as bad as *librarian* in my dad's opinion. Not manly." Jacob flexed his right arm at the word 'manly.' Taylor watched the bicep bulge under his shirt.

"Fixing up toy dogs for ladies didn't match his idea of the masculine life."

Jacob chuckled and stroked Minnie's side while he talked. There was no bitterness in the words, only a hint of old—and very manly—emotion that had been shrink-wrapped and packed safely away.

"You became a vet anyway." Taylor wasn't sure what else to say. Jacob acted like he was ready to leave, the sooner the better. "And me, Rain, and Minnie are glad you did."

Instead of rising from the futon, Jacob leaned back and looked at the ceiling. He took a deep breath. "I knew I wanted to be a vet when I was ten. About the time Dad killed our German Shepherd, Duchess."

Taylor watched Jacob pull at his chin, scratching the stubble of an emerging goatee as he rifled through old memories.

"Duchess was a dog we got from the pound. A real beauty. But she was food aggressive. Dad got tired of it after awhile and tied her to a tree in the back yard, said she wouldn't get any food until she learned to be polite at meal times."

"Did it work?"

"Duchess had a history of starvation and neglect so withholding food only made her more anxious and aggressive. She was my dog—never growled at me—but Dad was determined she should respect him as the man of the house. When he finally offered her food and took it away she bit him pretty good. I watched him kick her repeatedly in the throat. She died a day later."

Jacob's jaw clenched slightly at the memory. "Dad said, 'A dog should know better than to bite the hand that feeds her. You're better off without her son; quit the cryin.' Guess I never got over the fact that I stood there and watched him kill an innocent creature."

Atonement. Maybe Melissa was right. Maybe people lived a lot of life trying to atone for the things they did. Or didn't do.

"Your dad wouldn't have appreciated Minnie, huh?"

Jacob laughed loudly as he shook off the memory. "Not even a little. Now, I've gotta get on the road. I'll just say hello to my girl on the way out. That is, if you don't mind."

"Of course not."

Taylor followed Jacob out of the house and waited on the porch. She watched him walk to the fence line where Rain was waiting, as if she knew he would come to her. He stroked the horse's neck and face, his deep voice rising and falling with words Taylor couldn't make out. After a moment he returned to the truck and opened the door.

"Oh," Taylor raised her voice to catch his attention, "I've been thinking about doing that Ride and Tie thing you mentioned a couple months ago … "

Jacob paused. "Yeah?"

"Yeah. Would you show Rain and me what to do? Maybe be practice partners?"

"Sure would," Jacob grinned. "I'll call you with a trail date—soon."

At that he got in the truck, closed the door, and raised a hand in farewell. Taylor returned to Minnie and pondered her sudden, intense interest in physical exercise.

☙

# Chapter 25

"Ride and Tie is called 'the thinking athletes sport.'"

Taylor watched Jacob clip a cantle bag on the back of his saddle and mount a tall black gelding he called Titan. Though its face was freckled with the white hairs of advancing age, the horse fidgeted with anticipation.

"So I have to think *and* be athletic?"

Jacob chuckled. "Yeah. You ready to go?"

Taylor nodded. She'd discreetly smoked half a cigarette under the guise of needing to find the "facilities" while Jacob saddled up. The nicotine should hold for the duration of the ride. She didn't want to smoke in front of him again.

"We'll only ride a few miles today so you can get an idea of terrain and how to condition and prepare for an actual Ride and Tie race. There's a training ride in a couple of months that we can do together if you feel up to it—only fifteen miles."

*Only fifteen miles.* Taylor shook her head, remembering how she hurt after the last "only ten miles" logged with Liz. Out of the corner of her eye she gaped at Jacob's muscular thighs flexing under form fitting riding tights. She had *a lot* of conditioning to do.

"So you sort of need to be a marathon runner AND distance rider?"

Jacob positioned Titan beside Rain. "I wouldn't say *marathon* runner but, yes, you need to be able to run. Ride and Tie is like a relay race with the horse as a baton. In the Old West it was a way to cover ground when there were two riders but only one horse. One rides ahead, ties the horse to a tree, and continues ahead on foot. The first runner gets to the horse, rides ahead of the second runner, ties the horse again and runs on. You get to rest—sort of—when it's your turn to ride, but you'll need to get in condition."

"And why would people willingly sign up for this sort of torture?"

Relieved she'd worn baggy clothing that hid her flab, Taylor squeezed Rain into a trot without waiting for his answer. As ridiculous as it was, she felt an urge to prove her ability to at least *ride* at some sort of speed.

Jacob's horse easily paced Rain. He grinned at Taylor as they trotted, side by side, down an old logging road.

"For the competition, the mental and physical challenge, and, especially, the team aspect of it. Horses are herd animals. They naturally gravitate toward joining up. You, Rain, and I would become a herd working together for a common goal."

Taylor felt her face warm in the chilly March air. She briefly considered the fact that Jacob simply mentioning her in close familiarity made her self-conscious.

"And you think Rain can do this?"

Jacob slowed his horse to a walk and ran his hand down the crest of the gelding's neck. "Titan has arthritis; I need to get him thoroughly warmed up at the walk before doing too much trotting. Do I think Rain's up for this? Absolutely. Arabians are built for distance racing and she's intelligent and personable. I think she'd love the team aspect. Every member of the team has weaknesses to consider, like Rain's limited vision, but it can be worked with."

"Is my smoking a weakness?" Taylor brushed a damp lock of hair from her face and looked at Jacob, waiting for the lecture to commence. Everyone knew smokers were lower class citizens who knowingly, and stupidly, ruined their health. Worse than a diet of Twinkies or snacking on pure lard. Why did he want to do this with her anyway? It made no sense. He needed some super healthy and cute tri-athlete girl, preferably blonde with shapely legs.

"That's for you to decide." Jacob reached behind the saddle and withdrew a water bottle. He tilted his head back, took a long swig, and smiled at her. "Ready for a bit of trotting now?"

They jogged slowly at first, keeping the horses side-by-side. After a few minutes Jacob seemed to think Titan was sufficiently warmed up. He gestured to a single-track dirt trail on Taylor's side of the road. She turned Rain onto it and pushed the mare into a long trot that was intended to keep them well ahead of Jacob.

The air was thick and chilly; weak sunlight struggled to penetrate the foggy layer. The appearance of sun was cheery, if not exactly warming. It beamed thin golden shafts through the air resembling the filmy illumination of light through deep water.

Rain soon found a pace she liked and Taylor alternated between posting the fast trot and simply standing in her stirrups, the mare's hooves thudding a rhythm in the dirt. Like slalom skiers they wove, faster and faster, around slender trees hung with moss, pushing aside huge branches and maple leaves dripping with water at face level. When a downed tree appeared ahead Taylor did not slow the horse. Instead she kissed to her. Without missing a beat, Rain gathered her energy and neatly jumped the obstacle. She tossed her head and snorted, pleased with the opportunity to express herself in such a way.

As they cleared the jump and trotted on, an almost forgotten joy swelled within Taylor, the wonder at losing the limitations of an earthly body and being carried along with the majesty and power of something much grander than herself. She felt the heavy fog condense on her face and trickle like tears down her cheeks as they pressed through it. Without thinking she laughed out loud. Riding this way reminded her of surfing off Mission Beach: the incredible rush of standing atop a ridiculously small piece of fiberglass as the awesome power of the ocean heaved beneath her.

"Whoa, hold up there cowgirl!"

At a bend in the trail Taylor pulled Rain up. Titan approached and stopped beside them. The horses were breathing hard, small clouds of warm air rising above their heads like a smoky fire. Still exhilarated, Taylor began talking before her brain could catch up.

"That felt so good! Reminds me of surfing, just that power under you."

Jacob studied her curiously. "Aren't you full of surprises? Here I thought you weren't athletic and needed to take it easy. Yet you leave me in the dust, Miss Surfer Girl with the awesome balance."

At Jacob's observation Taylor's enthusiasm evaporated. *Surfer girl with the awesome balance.* In a moment she was transported back to a certain day that felt a lifetime away from a misty trail in the Pacific Northwest.

She'd been unaware Ian was watching her ride the waves at her favorite spot. He stopped her as she carried the board up the beach after an especially sweet ride, hair whipped into soggy ropes, the sun kissing her bikini-clad body. *You have amazing balance.* Hotter than the sunburn blooming on her skin, his hand had brushed at the sand clinging to her shoulders, bicep flexing under a barbwire tattoo that encircled it.

All her friends had discovered the opposite sex naturally, effortlessly. Taylor remained a late bloomer, afraid of venturing into a domain that her mother seemed both wary of and resistant to. But she felt pleasure at being watched and admired that day, her 18-year-old body suddenly alive in a disconcerting way. And so it had begun. Even after two years the memory was painful, sharp and immediate like a punch to the gut.

"It was a long time ago. I'm not athletic anymore." Taylor looked away, her fingers finding Rain's mane and twining around a segment of coarse grey hair.

Jacob furrowed his brow. "Well, you could have fooled me. How about we start looping back? I've gotta work today."

Taylor simply nodded. She waited for Titan to take the lead and maneuvered Rain behind him. As they rode she pushed her own memories aside and considered the man riding ahead of her. He was handsome, no doubt about that. And kind. Also a bit mysterious. Taylor noticed he wore no wedding band yet he seemed somehow attached. Gay? No. That didn't seem possible. And what was up with his interest in her? It didn't seem physical, yet Taylor caught him studying her more than once.

Liz also seemed confused by the friendship. Before Taylor could retrieve any useful information about Jacob Wilson and his attachments she'd insulted the woman, yet again, while working at the shelter one Sunday.

"So, you're going riding with Dr. Wilson?"

"Yeah. We might do a Ride and Tie race together after Rain and I get in shape."

"Lucky you." Liz handed her a broom as they cleaned outside the dog kennels.

"I guess."

"You guess?" Liz's mouth began to twitch. "Wilson's only one of the most eligible bachelors in the horse community. He's a hottie, that's for sure." She whistled then.

Taylor stared back in surprise. *Hottie* didn't seem like it should be a word in Liz's vocabulary.

Instantly reading her mind, Liz scowled. "I'm handicapped, Taylor, not blind. Just because men don't look at me doesn't mean I don't look at them." Liz's voice was sharp and sad. She shoved the broom in the corner and hobbled back to her desk leaving Taylor alone to ponder unasked questions and an extra dirty kennel.

৵

# Chapter 26

It was Rain who made her quit. No special nicotine gum, hypnotist, or twelve step program needed. Taylor had to laugh as she considered the television commercial that could be made of the event: Young woman and horse arrive home after an especially fun and exhausting training ride. Cameras are in wide angle, taking in the glory and abundant life of a sunny spring day in Washington State.

Woman dismounts, reaches in her pocket and retrieves a slender cigarette. Music builds. As she prepares to light the pale cylinder, the camera zeros in on her lips, then pans to a solemn grey horse face. Rain fixes her with both the dead eye and her amazingly wise, alive eye. Cameras further close in on the cigarette and the hollow deadness of an empty socket. Text flashes on the screen: *Don't be blind, smoking kills.*

Sure, she'd cheated a few times since Rain gave her "the look," but knowing the mare was working hard to get in shape and overcome her blindness—her weakness—stirred something deep in Taylor. Maybe it sounded weird, but the horse made her want to be a better person. Or at least a healthier person. And so she'd slowly, surely, cut out the cigarettes. First she quit smoking while riding, then during any and all activities related to horses—including mucking out, then to smoking while on the phone or in the car. Finally Taylor cut out the hardest time of all—smoking while drinking. Her confidence grew along with the muscle in her thighs.

~ ~ ~

"Let's put up our tents there, by the tree line."

Jacob gestured toward the edge of the meadow and maneuvered the truck and horse trailer into one of the few remaining spots. Taylor rested her arm in the open window on the passenger's side and watched the activity outside. Horses stood tied to trailers or grazed in temporary circles of electric fence, children played, and men and women sat in lawn chairs in front of campers. An excited energy filled the air, anticipation for the Ride and Tie competition that began at six the next morning. Taylor felt her own excitement rise and fall: first swell in anticipation of finally competing after three months of training, then drop to anxious worry that she'd disappoint Jacob or do something harmful to Rain.

"You're not nervous are you?"

"Whatever gave you that idea?" Taylor grimaced.

"Oh, I don't know," Jacob shrugged his shoulders, a teasing look on his face. "Your hands are only balled into fists right now and you have a certain 'deer in the headlight' stare."

Taylor looked down at the fists she didn't know she was making.

"Let's just hope I can run like a deer tomorrow."

"I have faith in you. So does your horse."

With a spring in his step Jacob walked to the back of the trailer and unloaded Rain. While he set up a temporary fence for the horse Taylor got out the two small tents they'd be sleeping in for the night and began setting up camp. Tonight they'd have Rain vetted to ensure she was sound for the 15 mile ride ahead and she and Jacob would talk strategy. They were one of ten teams eager to test their abilities in the vast, mountainous land surrounding pristine Black Lake. Though within easy driving distance of civilization, the area still felt like wilderness.

At least one of them was eager, thought Taylor as she watched Jacob make his rounds of the campsites that were scattered around the small meadow. Even from a distance she could tell he was excited, his arms gesturing as he made conversation with what appeared to be a village of old friends. The man was in his element. Once in awhile she'd watch him motion to their camp and she felt self conscious sitting alone in her collapsible chair. As minutes turned to hours anxiety built and began to roll and crest in her stomach like never-ending waves on the beach.

She felt worse the next morning.

"I might get sick, Jacob, are you sure you want to do this with me?"

They both were stretching in the chilly early morning air, listening to the hum of camp activity. Horse's whinnied and pawed in anticipation of race day. Rain's head was high, ears perked, as she kept tabs on the situation. Jacob remained quiet as he held a toe stretch.

"Have you not trained, ridden miles, even quit smoking to do this?"

"Yeah, but … "

"*But* nothing. You'll be fine once we get going. Everyone has jittery nerves at the start."

Taylor didn't respond. Instead she went to the horse and did a meaningless check of tack. Even though Rain was light and easily recognizable Jacob painted their team number on her rump— #21.

"Your age! This is a good sign." Jacob was cheerful about everything; it was almost annoying. He fairly glowed with competitive energy.

She'd been assured, by several nice folks at the pre-ride meeting, that 15 miles was a cinch. Right.

Excited, prancing horses jockeyed for position at the start line as Taylor followed Rain and Jacob to the trail head. They'd discussed strategy the night before as they ate hot dogs around the camp fire.

"The second third of the race will be hardest, Taylor. I recommend you jog first, over the flats. I'll get us through the mad dash of the opener, tie up Rain and do the Stony Mountain Loop. You tie Rain after you make it over and run the last bit, which is mostly over flats, too."

She said nothing.

"Unless you want the mountainous part. I don't want to steal anything from you." Jacob took a huge bite of his hot dog and chewed.

"No, you're right. You ride first."

Pride never partnered well with jittery nerves, something she was reminded of the following morning as she surveyed the group of horses jigging and snorting, their bodies tense with suppressed energy. Hill or no hill, she wasn't ready to handle the stress of the starting line just yet.

Taylor milled around within the group of runners who kept to the side of the dirt logging road, well out of the way of the riders. She watched Rain fidget and chomp the bit. The mare had clearly plugged into the highly charged energy and her dark eye had adopted a faraway look, the gaze of a race horse focused on a far off finish line. Taylor also recognized something happy beneath the veneer of nervous energy. She thought suddenly of Liz then and the pleasure the woman received from competition. It was an honor to pursue feats of glory.

As she thought of it, Taylor bent at the waist and stretched her hamstrings and the backs of her legs. Time to run toward glory. When she straightened and looked again to the horses, she frowned. Brenda, a trim blond, stood at Rain's shoulder and looked up at Jacob, a laughing smile on her face. She was too far away to eavesdrop, but Taylor clearly made out the woman's annoying cackle. No doubt she was rolling her big goldfish eyes, too. Not unlike Steve's winking, Brenda appeared unable to resist an obsessive urge to roll her eyes during conversation. She'd done it plenty during the socializing that occurred after the pre-ride meeting.

At first Taylor had felt special to walk at Jacob's side, the chosen partner of an obvious athlete. The vet was popular and his appeal rubbed off. Then Barbie Doll Brenda appeared and everything shifted. Jacob introduced her as "an enthusiastic newbie with a great horse." Suddenly Taylor got it. It was about Rain; it had always been about the mare.

Even though the every other day runs had trimmed Taylor's figure to a size eight, she felt about as appealing as baggage when considering the other runners. She pulled at her t-shirt and watched Brenda's metallic gold hair bob as she flipped it around. The woman was perfectly toned and looked like she belonged. Well, except for the tan. Nobody in the Pacific Northwest was that brown in early May. It looked all the more artificial in the pale light of the grey sky over head.

Maybe it was the eye rolling, the too-tan skin, the perfect body; whatever the details, she instantly disliked Brenda. And the feeling was mutual. The two women completely ignored each other.

Taylor fought the urge to walk over and interrupt the cozy scene across the road, jar Jacob to his senses, to the steady, authentic person Taylor had come to know. Around Brenda's preening and effervescent questions the vet seemed to grow a couple inches and was encouraged to engage in intellectual monologues on equine alternative therapies and their usefulness, among other things. Taylor wished she had a dollar for every time he said the word *modality*.

Did he really want to impress a woman like Brenda? Taylor felt unsure as she stared at the woman's lean backside and watched her put a hand on Jacob's forearm. Taylor was certain he was enjoying a rider's view of Brenda's big boobs squished tight inside a hot pink sports bra. Men.

Why did she care, anyway? Taylor wished Melissa were around. She'd make some crack about Brenda's frizzy gold hair and rolling eyes and help Taylor see how silly it was to be jealous of such a person. Was she jealous? Jacob was in his 30s, too old for her anyway. She had no right acting possessive. Maybe it indicated a need for male approval or something—another item for the Headshrinker's List.

Still, even her horse craved Jacob's attention. Though the vet was totally engrossed in conversation he laid his hand on Rain's wither every few minutes, his touch settling her amidst an anxious crowd of jostling horses. Taylor felt insecure about their intimate exchanges. He'd saved the mare's life, after all. Rain probably loved him more. Maybe she wished to be his horse and do away with the newbie owner she'd gotten stuck with.

Glancing quickly at her watch Taylor pushed the thoughts away. Only two minutes to start. She kept her eyes on the light grey horse and waited as her muscles tensed.

*Bang.*

The sharp crack of a pistol echoed in the meadow. What looked like chaos followed. A swell of bodies crested onto the trail ahead like a hairy calico wave: bays, chestnuts, blacks, a palomino, and a couple of ghostly greys all broke at a dead gallop.

Pure adrenalin propelled Taylor into a sprint. She ran for several yards, carried by the horses' energy and the momentum of the runners around her. One by one, the horses melted into the forest ahead. She watched Jacob's back disappear around a bend in the dirt road and dropped to a jog as she patted the back pocket of her stretch pants. The map was still there, crinkly under her fingertips.

# Chapter 27

The trail master had explained the 15 mile loop in detail the night before: a winding, rolling first five miles followed by the much more challenging middle five of Stony Mountain. Not technically a *mountain* yet more than enough for someone who'd only been training for about three months. Fortunately Jacob was a serious runner. He'd finished the Seattle Marathon three times. After descending the hill on horseback she'd tie Rain to an available tree and jog two and a half miles. Jacob would sprint the last two and a half.

The first mile was predictable. Taylor had come to expect the heaviness in her feet, the way her body felt utterly earth bound when she began to run. But, inexplicably, the weight would lift and it felt easier. For awhile. Then the battle to keep running would commence after about mile three. This was followed by exhaustion and later the notorious "runner's high." It wasn't like nicotine, but Taylor had come to crave it. The whole running thing—the burning in the muscles, the tingling in her skin, the way her face felt warm—insisted she fully inhabit her physical body. Jacob said it would become an addiction.

The crowd began to thin after a couple of miles. No horses were in sight at first and the faster runners—Brenda included—went on ahead. But soon Taylor came upon mounts tied to trees, some whinnying and pawing the ground in anticipation. Since it was a shorter training ride, strategy was completely unique to each team. Some teams switched every mile or so. That way, Jacob said, the runners could go faster with more frequent rests on horseback. In an actual race there were rules governing the number of times runners had to switch and more rigorous vet checks. The flexibility of the training ride ensured Taylor could avoid Stony Mountain by running a longer distance at first.

The technicality of the sport was intimidating. Taylor watched in awe when she observed the first "flying exchange," a coordinated passing of the horse with the rider dismounting on the off side and the runner swinging into the saddle without anyone stopping. She tried to imagine such a feat as she ran along the bumpy red earth trail, its edges punctuated by lacey groupings of ferns and imposing fir trees.

Overhead a featureless grey sky was visible in between hunter green tree tops spiking heavenward. It hinted at rain. To keep her mind off straining muscles, Taylor tried to name the plants and trees in the forest around her. Though she'd grown up in the northwest, she'd never been interested in flora and fauna. Not like Jacob who knew that Foxgloves were poisonous, Salmon Berries edible, and that the stalks of Fireweed could be used to make rope, if necessary.

There weren't many flowers on display in the lush undergrowth, but Taylor identified several kinds of trees. From time to time she noted a rotting stump offering its services as the "pot" in which a leggy young fir rooted itself. The base nurtured in the decomposing crumbles of the tree that came before, the seedlings gained strength. "Nurse Stumps" Jacob called them. Ever after Taylor felt a tender affection for the stumps.

Soon they would run through a clear cut and, after, an old gravel pit that carved out the trail just before Stony Mountain. There Taylor would find her horse waiting. The air felt humid, the warming before a shower, and insects fluttered at face level. Sweat began to bead at her temples and Taylor swiped at a swarm of gnats.

The longest Taylor had ever run at one stretch was eight miles. Never mind she'd about died doing it. The vet check midway would ensure the horses were not pushed beyond what they could endure, but she worried about her own endurance. She wanted to make Jacob proud.

She heard Rain's husky nicker before actually seeing the pale rump materialize through the branchy undergrowth. Taylor ran faster, relieved and comforted by the mare's greeting.

"How'd you know it was me?" Taylor patted Rain's neck as the horse bobbed her head in anticipation. She untied the lead quickly, looped it around the saddle horn and swung onto the horse's back. Rain immediately started jogging, as if she knew there was no time to waste. Taylor began posting the trot. Refusing to acknowledge her screaming thighs she instead pondered the uncanny way that the horse sensed things, like the way she recognized her owner's approach without the use of vision.

"Horses are highly aware, Taylor," Jacob shared once, "prey animals have to be. They sense everything about the environment to an extreme. We're the ones who become dull, block our feelings and sensations. Horses never do that."

"But how does she always seem to know where I am?"

"Seeing is over-rated. People who are blind will have highly developed senses of hearing and touch. I bet something similar has happened with the loss of Rain's eye. She probably follows your breathing patterns."

Taylor considered that now. Yes, it was probably the breathing. Rain often lifted her nose to Taylor's face and paused. The mare would breathe slowly in and out, her whiskery muzzle hairs tickling bare skin.

"Horses can't see very well up close," Liz shared once after observing one of Rain's regular facial inspections. "And this horse *really* has to compensate for lack of vision. She's making sure of you; checking to see that you're still breathing."

Liz had smiled, the knowing smile of one who has shared a similar experience. Taylor wondered then if what hurt the most in human relationships was a dismissal of details, the way one could quit breathing and nobody ever noticed.

It took longer than Taylor expected to lap Jacob. She saw his navy running tights with silver reflective panels first and watched his arms pump rhythmically side to side. As they trotted up to him, Rain nickered softly and Jacob cocked his head without turning.

"Hi, girls. How's it going?"

"Better than you, I think." Taylor noted the damp hair at Jacob's temples. She slowed Rain to a walk and considered the gradual incline before them. The hill would peak and then begin to descend into the valley again and the last leg of the race.

"I'm doing okay. Rain passed the vet check with flying colors, just so you know. We have a champion developing."

Jacob grinned proudly and Taylor pushed down the warm feelings of being included in "we." It was Rain he was interested in … and probably Brenda.

"Good to know."

"See you on the flip side," Jacob raised his arm in farewell. He never broke an exaggerated, methodical stride that resembled running in slow motion.

"Okay."

Stoney Mountain had been part of a clear cut and gravel pit area at one time, which meant almost no mature trees remained and vision was unobstructed. Taylor pushed Rain into a faster walk and focused on the push for the top. Once there, she nearly gasped at the beauty of the valley that lay verdant below them. Overhead the grey cloud cover had broken into neat columns of puffs that gave the illusion of ripples in a vast pond, as if God had thrown a stone into the atmosphere and broken it up on purpose.

As they cleared the top and began the descent on single track, Rain picked her way carefully around large rocks, tree roots, and slowly decomposing slash piles. Taylor removed the map from a back pocket and looked for the color coding of the trails. An orange ribbon would be her sign to tie Rain and continue on foot.

The fluttering ribbon appeared before the descent was completed. Taylor saw the flash of color between tree branches; it marked a fork in the path and continued down the mountain. She located a slender branch from which to secure the horse and dismounted stiffly.

"Ouch! How am I going to run anymore, Rain?"

The mare bobbed her head and swung her body this way and that. Clearly she didn't want to be left alone.

"Just watch for Jacob. He'll be here in no time, okay?"

Taylor rubbed the horse's broad forehead, took a moment to stretch, and made her way down the path at a slow jog. Rain nickered at her back.

## Chapter 28

Going downhill shouldn't be so difficult. Taylor forced her feet ahead, knees protesting at every step. She'd passed and been passed by more than one team, but no Rain and Jacob. Too early. Jacob would be tired and moving slower.

Overhead the sky had changed once again. No end to the shades of grey and forms of precipitation in Washington State. The clouds, some tinged with charcoal, were moving restlessly, influenced by the atmospheric energy on a far hillside.

Taylor watched in awe as a beam of light opened the heavens and shone golden through the curtain of mist that covered the lone hillside with rain. It would move their way in time, Taylor could already feel the moist air cooling her cheeks. But above the curtain, through heaven's porthole, a cerulean blue sky peeked, complete with wisps of cotton candy clouds that flitted across it. The scene was a sharp contrast to the grumbling grey masses to the west.

Looking as she was to the heavens, Taylor momentarily forgot to keep an eye on the undulating earth below her. In an instant the poetry of Mother Nature was replaced with its harsher realities as Taylor caught her toe on a root and tumbled forward. Her arms broke the fall, but offered no protection for a knee that squarely made contact with a jagged boulder at the trail's edge.

Rolling to one side, Taylor instinctively clutched the knee to her chest. The blow had hit just the right nerves and her entire limb throbbed with a bright, tingling pain. She gritted her teeth and writhed this way and that as the knee pulsed. When she removed her hands from the leg to examine the joint they were streaked with blood.

"Great, just great," she moaned.

"Everything okay?"

At that moment, a white-haired man on a chestnut gelding appeared seemingly out of nowhere. He pulled his horse to a stop and looked at Taylor in concern, crow's feet wrinkling into folds at the corners of his eyes. The man's skin was as weathered as a football, a lifetime etched in deep lines that endlessly merged and converged with each other. Despite the obvious years the man was somehow ageless, sitting the horse with the grace of someone much younger.

"Yeah, fine. Really." Taylor dragged herself farther away from the trail's edge. "I'm just going to stick something on this scratch and be on my way." She tried to smile.

"I'd be happy to turn around and find your team—Dr. Wilson, right?"

"Please, don't worry about me. I'll be fine."

*I need NO help from Dr. Wilson.*

Reluctantly the man trotted on. As she watched his posting backside disappear from view Taylor pondered the fact that a grandpa was smoking her.

The sound of hoof beats in the distance, rhythmic and driving as an African drum, announced another rider approaching. Taylor picked up a scalloped edged leaf and wiped at the blood on her knee. Hopefully she could be on her way before Jacob saw her predicament.

"Taylor? Are you okay?"

Jacob appeared at her side. He gently touched her knee cap and immediately began digging in his pockets.

"Right on the joint, that must have hurt. Good thing the cut's superficial. I've got a bandage here."

*Of course you do.*

Taylor watched Jacob in silence. She felt Rain's lips above her head, nuzzling her hair, and breathed in the salty smell of the horse.

"Did you trip on that boulder there?" Jacob gestured toward the offending chunk of rock by the trail.

Taylor pointed at a spot above the rock, "Root." A sinuous loop broke the surface of the dirt like the hump of an under water sea serpent. "I *fell* on the rock. Too busy staring at the sky."

"Head in the clouds, huh?" A teasing smile perked the corners of Jacob's mouth.

"Something like that." Taylor watched him brush the broken skin with a wet wipe. A moment later he had removed the adhesive backing on a bandage and placed it gently over the wound.

"Is that the best *modality* of treatment for this injury, Dr. Wilson?"

Jacob chuckled, his dusty face crinkling into a smile that revealed both dimples. "I'm afraid it's the best I can provide on the side of a mountain, *Ms.* Reed." He stood and offered his hand. Taylor allowed him to pull her upright. She winced immediately and bent the injured knee.

"Why do scratches hurt so bad?"

"Lots of nerves close to the surface of the skin, but I think you'll live."

Taylor moved to the trail and examined the cracked boulder. It glistened a deep green that perfectly reflected the shade of the surrounding fir trees growing in scattered groupings at the trail's edge.

"Olivine."

"What?"

"The stone is called olivine." Jacob moved to her side and bent to examine the boulder. He picked at the crack and a small piece crumbled off. "Olivine is a common mineral used for lots of things. The Twin Sisters have the largest reserves of olivine in the United States." He gestured toward the mountains in the distance, their majestic granite faces devoid of vegetation, a solemn testimony to eternal forces.

Jacob had a far-away look on his face as he gazed at The Sisters. "'I will lift my eyes to the hills, where does my help come from?' My mother liked that scripture." He considered the rock again. "Did you know that the gem form of olivine is peridot? Birthstone of August."

"That I know." Taylor smiled at him, "My birthday's in August."

"Mine, too."

"Really?"

"Really." Jacob scratched the stubble on his chin. "32 this year … Geez I'm getting old!" He laughed. "Let's see if I can remember the properties of peridot: Love, peace, truth and good luck, for starters. Can't remember what else."

"Is mineral healing one of your specialities? Do I get a read of my horoscope, too?"

Jacob laughed again. "No. My Italian Catholic mother passed on all her superstitions. She read the Bible, but if a rock or rabbit's foot could influence the supernatural she was all for it: 'Good to cover all the bases,' she used to tell me. She's the reason I know so much nature trivia."

"Well, I'll take all the good luck I can get. Not that I'm having much of it today … "

Jacob seemed unconcerned. "I swear Rain wanted to find you. She was in a big hurry before we got here, like she knew something was up."

Taylor walked to the mare and considered his words. The horse bumped her elbow then picked a mouthful of scraggly grass. Taylor laid a hand on her wither, "She always finds me."

Jacob watched the mare graze for a few minutes, a thoughtful look on his face. "How about you ride the rest of the way and I'll run? We don't have far to go and it'll save your knee."

"But, you're tired. We're going to get beaten by geriatrics today, Jacob!" Taylor frowned.

"This is a training ride, remember? It's okay to be a beginner. There'll be another time. As for the geriatrics, a few of them regularly finish 50 mile endurance rides. Not your average grannies out here."

# Chapter 29

Taylor followed Jacob toward a cedar-sided house. A grill smoked at one corner of an expansive covered deck where most of the Ride and Tie participants milled and chatted in groups of two or three. The home was a picture of domestic bliss. Pots of petunias in red, white, and blue sat at the corners of the deck and spilled over the side. A yellow lab lay snoozing in the sun and wind chimes tinkled in the whisper of a breeze. The smell of charcoal and meat mixed with the essence of spring air recently moistened by a shower.

They'd finished last at the race, but Jacob didn't seem to care and all the riders congratulated Taylor on a job well done—she'd made it through and next time would be easier. Or so they insisted. Mishaps and battle scars made for good stories later on. She glanced down at the rainbow colored bruise already blossoming like a sloppy tattoo over her knee cap.

Jacob had insisted she accompany him to the after ride get together the day after the race. It was fun to be included, but now all she could do was fidget after getting through shallow "hellos" and "good jobs." It was different for Jacob. People were drawn to the vet like a magnet and they peppered him with questions on all things equine: tack, feed choices, past injury care. She went into the house and approached the hostess, Tina.

"Can I help with anything? Carry some food out?"

"Thanks, but I've got everything covered. Unless you want to keep an eye on Mariposa for a couple minutes while I grab some more chairs?" Tina gestured toward a toddler in the corner. "She just got in a little trouble, didn't you Pumpkin?" Tina's voice turned warm and nurturing.

"Sure."

Taylor flicked her eyes from the child to the retreating back of Tina. She sat on the floor with her back to the couch, as far from Mariposa as she could get, and watched. The little girl had a thatch of naturally curly red hair, and matching dimples. A blue clip-on ribbon nested in the curls. She was utterly engrossed in the contents of a large rubber bucket filled with toys, completely unaware that a stranger was charged momentarily with her care. Taylor watched her pull out a chunky book, open a page, and push it into her mouth. She chewed on the edge of the cardboard for a moment or two then threw it to the side. Chubby fingers clutched the side of the bucket, helping balance unsteady legs that were still bowed like an infant.

"Peetie." Mariposa reached into the clutch of toys and pulled out a doll by its fake frizzled blond hair. She held it up, examined the find for a moment, and proclaimed again, "Peetie."

"Yes, *pretty*. She is a *pretty* baby."

Tina reentered the room and patted the child's head on her way to the kitchen. Taylor watched her open the refrigerator door covered with photos of Mariposa: an ultrasound print, at birth, nestled in her exhausted mother's arms, various family pictures, and a smiling baby in the bathtub. She cleared her throat.

"She's such a cutie, will you have more?"

Tina sighed deeply. She bent over to pull a bowl of salad from the depths of the refrigerator and shut the door before responding.

"I'd like to, but I just don't know … "

As she watched Tina's face bunch with conflicting emotions Taylor immediately regretted the inquiry. Her heart began to beat faster. She needed to escape, perhaps excuse herself by begging exhaustion from the ride. She would simply ask Jacob to take her home. Tina appeared oblivious to her discomfort.

"We had a hard time conceiving. I lost two babies before Mariposa, the second after in vitro, which is such an ordeal. I couldn't cope with life after that. It's just so emotional…. " Tina looked out the window into a distant time and place. Then she smiled at Taylor, "You'll see someday."

As she listened the pounding inside increased. It seemed to beat up into Taylor's brain until she was certain it was visible, her eyeballs pulsing freakishly like a Halloween mask. She thought of the girls in the recovery room, the haunted expressions as they clutched their empty wombs. The same expression she knew was etched upon her own face. *Emotional*, yes. Receiving, losing, birthing, and taking life were all emotional experiences. It seemed ridiculous to describe it with such a matter-of-fact word.

"But then I got pregnant again," Tina's voice turned warm and full. "I was so scared to lose another child." Her eyes brimmed with the memory and she blinked the tears away as she watched her daughter innocently make a mess, unaware of the affect she had on her mother even before birth. How could a ball of cells have such power over a grown human being?

"When she was born it was like happiness fluttered inside my heart for the first time in a long time. I knew I had to name her Mariposa—*butterfly*." Tina smiled at the memory and walked to the door, the salad in hand.

Taylor suddenly recognized the significance of a stained glass ornament that hung in the kitchen window. Beveled pieces of vibrant glass—periwinkle, deep violent, and pale pink—formed a delicate butterfly.

Sunlight shone through the glass, forming a collage of soft pastel hues that danced across the opposite wall. A child was like that, changing the look of life in subtle and stunning ways, softening and sharpening the edges. She'd once read in a magazine that choosing to have a child was deciding forever to have your heart walk around outside your body. Her heart didn't exist inside or outside her body. Instead, it hung in an excruciating sort of purgatory.

Mariposa dropped the doll into a pile of toys cast off for various reasons known only to herself. She seemed to notice Taylor's presence for the first time and tottered into the center of the room, turning her full attention on the stranger within her house. Unshed tears from whatever infraction she had been guilty of earlier still shone in her eyes, turning them an otherworldly shade of blue. Drool wet her chin. She stared at Taylor, solemn and unashamed.

"Peetie," Mariposa proclaimed. She lurched forward and sat down hard before crawling purposefully toward the couch. Taylor felt her heart race as the child crawled to her side. A smile crinkled Mariposa's chubby cheeks and she reached forward. Instinctively Taylor offered her hand and Mariposa took it as she struggled to her feet. Trapped, Taylor gazed into the little girl's face and waited for whatever judgment might come next. She felt weightless, as if she might float away at any moment. Mariposa suddenly leaned forward and laid her head on Taylor's chest. Small hands patted reassuringly, "Peetie."

Wisps of curly hair tickled Taylor's cheek as she breathed in the smell of baby powder and milk. The voices outside sounded far away and Taylor felt like she was falling into a bottomless well. Just when she thought she might pass out a voice pulled her back to the present.

"You never told me you had such a way with kids." Jacob leaned into the doorway.

Taylor slowly raised her head and met his gaze, unable to hide her tears. The smile evaporated from Jacob's face. He studied her for a long moment then straightened and entered the room.

"We've gotta go, Tina. I promised Taylor I'd get her back home for … an appointment."

"Oh?" Tina looked surprised. "We haven't eaten yet."

Taylor carefully deposited Mariposa on the couch. She kissed the child on the top of the head and mumbled to Tina, "I'm really not hungry. But thanks for your hospitality." She focused on the door and avoided making eye contact.

They didn't talk for several minutes. Taylor knew she owed Jacob some sort of explanation. She mentally groped at options before deciding on something, far-fetched as it was.

"Sorry to cut dinner short, but thanks for rescuing me. Mariposa is really cute. It's just she reminded me of my niece … who died."

"How did she die?"

Taylor hadn't expected any further questions. She thought fast.

"SIDS. You know, Silent Infant Death Syndrome." At least that was somewhere closer to the truth.

"Hmm. Sounds tough." Jacob steered the car with one hand. He kept his eyes on the road. "Well, I'm still hungry. You want to come to my house? I'll fix you dinner and then take you home. We can talk about your next trail riding adventure."

"Okay."

She would have agreed to just about anything to take the conversation in a different direction. *Was this a date?* No, they were just friends, united by the love of a special horse. Nothing weird about that. As they drove Taylor watched the sun complete its descent into Bellingham Bay. Within minutes they arrived at Jacob's house.

"Make yourself at home. I'll see about whipping us up some pasta, good for replenishing energy. You like vegetables?"

"Sure." *On somebody else's plate.* She wasn't about to be the least bit of trouble for Jacob, even if it meant choking down a few veggies.

As he disappeared into the kitchen she wandered into the living room and took her time examining the furnishings and décor. The place was masculine and spare—no sign of a woman's touch. A single black couch took up one wall in what would be a proper dining room. There was a stereo system opposite. For dining there was only a small, two person table set in the kitchen. Simple, elegant frames were scattered in collages everywhere she looked. One large black and white print of a wild horse, its abundant mane and forelock blowing in the wind, was positioned above the couch.

Taylor walked to the stereo and examined a basket of CDs for his musical taste. You could tell a lot about a person by the type of music they listened to. Outside of a few anomalies—Billy Idol, the Red Hot Chili Peppers, and Michael Jackson—Jacob seemed partial to classical and piano music. Interesting. She picked up a CD.

"You like George Winston." It wasn't a question. Jacob had five Winston CD's. She examined the one called *December* and read down the list of songs.

"Oh yeah." He glanced her way between washing green peppers and chopping up mushrooms and onions. "I've seen him in concert twice."

"I don't think I've heard his music. My mother plays though. I grew up listening to Chopin, and lots of other dead guys."

Taylor wandered across the hall into a darkened living room and noticed the piano for the first time. A Baby Grand, no less. Its surface shone, glossy as patent leather.

"I love piano, especially Chopin's preludes. *No. 15, Raindrop*, is probably my favorite. Makes me sort of melancholy, in a good way. If that makes sense."

"It does." The sound of chopping paused, then resumed. "I can play lots of 'dead guy' selections."

"*Canon in D*? That's another one of my favorites."

The chopping stopped. "I played that at my own wedding. You could say I'm well practiced on that one."

Taylor cringed. "I didn't know you were married."

There was silence for moment and she heard a cabinet door open and close. She turned her attention to the photo collages and pretended to be vitally interested in them.

"My wife left me for another man. Last year."

*So that's his mystery.*

"Oh. I'm sorry to bring it up." Taylor allowed herself to make eye contact for a moment.

"No worries." A tired smile appeared on Jacob's face, his game face. "We're still officially married, but I expect she'll file for divorce soon."

He offered nothing more and Taylor didn't ask. Instead she went back to examining photos. One was of a younger Jacob in church, a rosary clutched in one hand.

"You're a practicing Catholic?"

Jacob laughed, "Get out while you still can."

Taylor giggled and the stiff atmosphere of painful facts that swirled around instantly broke into something softer and more comfortable.

"I didn't mean to say it that way. I'm Catholic, too."

"Where do you go to church?" Jacob asked as he drained fettuccine noodles into the sink.

"I don't, can't do confession anymore. I'm too guilty."

Jacob nodded but said nothing so Taylor continued talking. "I just can't confess to a guy that probably gets speeding tickets, drinks too much, and looks at short skirts. Why should I think I need forgiveness from him?"

"You've got a point. I suspect my priest has an eye for the pretty ladies." Jacob seemed unconcerned as he tossed vegetables with white sauce and poured it over the noodles. The kitchen air was moist and smelled of garlic and onion. He pulled out a chair and motioned Taylor to sit.

"Then why do you bother with all the confession crap?"

Jacob sat down and arranged silverware at both of their plates.

"The Bible says to 'Come boldly to the throne of grace to find mercy in time of need.' Doesn't bother me one bit what my priest does or doesn't do, thinks or doesn't think. I need grace and mercy, that's all I know." Jacob chewed for a moment or two then continued. "Plus, it's good to air your secrets to another human being, helps to share the burden."

For several minutes they ate in silence. Jacob poured her a glass of white wine and removed garlic bread from the oven. Taylor watched him and tried to imagine who his wife had left him for. When they were finished eating Jacob rinsed the plates and gestured toward the piano.

"Can I play you some after dinner music? Helps the food digest."

"Sure. I may fall asleep though, all this good pasta after a hard ride. I'm high on serotonin right now." Taylor patted her stomach.

Jacob chuckled and Taylor followed him to the Baby Grand. She sat, cross legged on the floor for a moment and then stretched out on her back, flexing her ankles and working out the kinks from the recent hours spent in a saddle. She watched Jacob's bare feet. They hovered for a moment, poised over the pedals, then depressed as his fingers moved over the keys. A melody rolled from the depths of the piano.

Taylor lay on the carpet and let the music sink in. She could no more stop it than she could stop rain wetting her bare skin. The notes reached somewhere deep inside, the place where love lived—or should live, the place she longed to lose sight of after a few beers. They danced over her heart, whispering insistently to the sadness lodged inside, inviting it to come out into the light.

Time passed, but Taylor was unaware. She watched the tendons on the tops of Jacob's feet flex as he worked the pedals, watched his calloused fingers work a melody on black and white. Suddenly the music paused.

"Do you want me to stop?" Jacob looked down at her, his hands hovering over the keys.

"What?" Taylor felt as if she had woken after a dream, slightly delirious and unsure of her location or if she was drooling.

"You're crying."

"I am." *I am.* Taylor raised an arm and put her hand to her face. Her temples were wet, a stream of tears coursing on either side. For some reason she was not embarrassed. *I am what I am.* "Can you just keep playing?"

Jacob's fingers returned to the keys and the music rippled in waves. It felt good to be carried along and not fight anymore. Tears dribbled to the carpet and when the playing stopped twin damp spots marked her place.

For a long moment Jacob sat quietly. He looked to the ceiling then pulled the piano key cover down.

"That song is called *Thanksgiving*. I thought you might like it."

Taylor said nothing.

"They say music is processed by the emotional part of the brain, the amygdala. Stored forever like a giant iPod. Even for people with progressive diseases like Alzheimer's the music is there. It can be a way to reach them." Jacob hesitated before rising, as if waiting for her, then continued. "When I first got your mare she was practically unresponsive. Some of it related to her injury, but she was traumatized emotionally, too. I sang to her. She liked *Amazing Grace*."

Taylor pictured Rain, unable to communicate in words, the refrain of a song reaching into her horsey amygdala:

*Amazing grace how sweet the sound,*
*that saved a wretch like me,*
*I once was lost but now am found*
*was blind but now I see.*

Blinded, but found; how sweet the sound.

"Ready to go home?"

"Yeah, I'm tired. Thanks for the food and entertainment."

"I consider it a success if I can make a lady cry."

Taylor giggled. "I know I'm probably freaking you out. Sorry. I just, I can't … " She let the thought trail away.

Jacob simply smiled, "You can make me cry next time, okay?"

"If I cook for you that'll be guaranteed."

# Chapter 30

A gentle breeze lifted the hair from the back of Taylor's neck, chilling the sweat that trickled down her back. She shivered and watched a cloud momentarily block the brilliant May sun. She felt the tingle and itch of overworked leg muscles and though she knew it meant pain later on, it felt good to be alive.

"Will you go to a wedding with me?"

The question startled Taylor, jerking her away from thoughts of burning calf muscles and the remaining mile left to run.

"Kinda early in our relationship for a proposal, isn't it?"

The broad grin that stretched across Jacob's face revealed nearly every one of his teeth and a lone dimple high on his cheek. She watched the fine lines at the edges of his eyes wrinkle into the smile and felt her own face warm beyond simple physical exertion. She looked away and, without thinking, rummaged in her pockets for a cigarette.

Jacob raised an eyebrow. "Rain's watching."

Taylor glanced sideways, straight into Rain's one-eyed stare. Somehow the mare had managed to maneuver herself less than six feet from where Taylor rested. She had stopped grazing and a mouthful of grass poked out either side of her whiskery muzzle. Taylor sensed disappointment.

"Damn. I just need something … in the worst way."

"Here," Jacob rocked to the side and pulled a disc from the back pocket of his shorts. "Protein Bar."

The package was compressed thin from 200 pounds of muscular backside pressing it into a saddle for half a day. Taylor took it, immediately recognizing that the only thing remotely appealing about the snack was its recent intimacy with Jacob's body. She unwrapped the bar and took a small bite, jawing it like a geriatric chewing on a piece of steak.

"Mmmm, this satisfies *exactly* like a shot of nicotine." Taylor looked at Rain. The mare bobbed her head once and resumed grazing, moving away toward more promising forage.

Jacob laughed loudly. "I swear, I've never seen such intelligence in a horse!"

Taylor frowned. "Right now I find animal intelligence overrated. Now, about that wedding … "

She discreetly stuck the rest of the bar in a hole at the base of a nearby tree and brushed her hands together to remove the crumbs and dirt.

"Yeah, here's the deal: an old friend from vet school is getting married next week. If I don't bring a date he'll set me up with every single girl at the reception."

Taylor raised her eyebrows. "I'd have to wear a dress. That's, like, a serious favor, bested only by helping you move or something. I don't know … " She broke a twig in two and picked at the tread of her hiking boot.

"I did say I'd collect fees for that farm call one day … " Jacob winked.

Taylor dropped the twig. "God, I forgot about that! Guess a dress is the least I can offer you."

She felt her face flush at the suggestive connotation. "I mean, well, you know what I mean."

Jacob chuckled. "It's going to be worth the sacrifice. I guarantee you've never seen a ceremony like this one."

"Why?"

"The pastor is a ventriloquist. She's giving the entire ceremony with the help of a dummy."

"You're serious?"

"Oh yeah. Pat is odd enough on his own, but he married a ventriloquist comedian. Her idea."

"Sounds awesome."

*Ventriloquist/pastor.* That was one her father hadn't heard before.

"Okay then. Pick you—and your dress—up next Saturday at one."

~ ~ ~

The search for something suitable to wear to a wedding began several days before the event. Finances being what they were, a brand new dress was out of the question. Instead of mall shopping, Taylor found herself in front of her own closet, staring at the dismal contents. There were really only a couple possibilities.

She withdrew a trim black suit and considered it in despair. Her mother had purchased the suit on sale at The Loft and mailed it to her in California hoping, no doubt, that her daughter would put it on and morph into her namesake: Ann Taylor. So *not* happening. Even with controlled-top panty hose there was no way her thighs were fitting into a size six skirt.

Taylor brushed dust from the jacket's shoulders. It was a spare, classy suit. She could see it on her mother, a matching pair of heels and colorful scarf knotted at the neck for accent. She held the suit away from herself. Why had she kept it? It had only been worn once, to a job interview. Now the suit, in all its classiness, regarded her with contempt. It seemed disappointed in the woman she had become.

"I don't like you, either," Taylor said to the suit. "Off to Goodwill with you."

Taylor threw the clothing on the floor and removed the other feminine object in her closet, a colorful broomstick skirt. Just looking at the skirt made her feel sick to her stomach. Definitely an article of clothing that deserved disposal. She fingered the creases in the fabric and remembered how they brushed crinkly against her legs: Solana Beach with Ian on one of their first dates. She had aged a lifetime since driving down Pacific Coast Highway, radio blasting, the sun toasting her arm as it rested on the window of his truck.

After walking the beach and jumping waves, Ian had made a fire to dry the bottoms of his jeans and the skirt that was wet half way up her legs. They sat on beach rocks, tired from the sun, and watched the fire flicker as a fog rolled in. The air between them hung heavy, an intoxicating mix of salty ocean, waning sunshine, and smoke. Ian had an intense look in his eyes, hungry. At that moment Taylor sensed a power she had never imagined wielding over a man.

"You're so beautiful," he had said. And for the first time in her eighteen years, Taylor felt that it could be true.

Looking back she could see clearly that the signs were there from the beginning of the relationship. Ian desired her, but from a measured distance that kept his true, vulnerable self protected. He loved her in the way he loved looking at a painting in a museum, one that would never hang on the wall in his own home. As their relationship progressed the nagging feeling of distance increased along with her need for him. She would think of his fiancé, Leah, at those times and worry it all would abruptly come to an end. And so it had.

"Join Miss Priss for a journey to the Goodwill." Taylor pulled the skirt from its hanger and threw it on top of the suit. She had no desire to keep clothing that reminded her of women she would never be, of things she could never have.

Walking to her chest of drawers, Taylor pulled open the bottom one and rifled through looking for something to inspire an outfit. Stuffed under a too small pair of jeans she spied a long rayon skirt and pulled it out. It was fitted and nearly ankle length with a pattern of large flowers in shades of blue scattered on a creamy background. Her father had given it to her shortly before she moved back to Washington.

"I found something that just looked like you," he'd said, and passed her a shopping bag.

"You don't buy clothes for me."

"I know. But this had your name on it. I thought ten was about your size." He smiled and Taylor recognized regret in his eyes along with many unspoken words. She removed the skirt for inspection, amazed at the choice of gift from a man she feared didn't know her and never would. It was perfect. Even now, as Taylor smoothed the fabric of the skirt, she felt the warmth of being known.

## Chapter 31

"You look different." Jacob leaned against the hood of his truck and watched Taylor lock the front door. He wore khaki pants and a button-down shirt with narrow green stripes.

"*Different* can be good or bad."

Taylor walked to the car and waited for Jacob to open the door. "Be careful with that word."

"You look beautiful; how about that kind of different?"

Taylor felt her face flush from the compliment and immediately tried to joke. "So, I've never looked beautiful before?" She raised her eyebrows.

"Actually, you looked the most beautiful after stumbling into that mud puddle a couple of weeks ago." Jacob laughed, his hazel eyes teasing.

Taylor punched him in the arm. "I did that on purpose, making noise, you see, to ward off bears. I had you and Rain in mind the whole time."

"Right."

Taylor considered Jacob's profile as he turned out of the driveway and sped toward town, shaking his head. Easy, that's what their relationship had become. A friendship *"like an old pair of shoes"* her dad would say. Yet Taylor wasn't sure Jacob should be compared to old shoes. Not when she had to admit she felt something more, something she felt certain was not reciprocated.

Jacob felt sorry for her and needed a Ride and Tie partner. He liked her for her horse and that was that. She was too young, too damaged; he was too Catholic and too married, at least technically. Taylor watched Jacob's long fingers shift the truck into third gear. She suddenly wanted to tell him all her secrets—even The One—and discover she still had his friendship. But that could never happen.

Taylor turned her attention to the broad countryside that quickly evolved from a scattering of farms to the outskirts of Bellingham. She wriggled on the seat, feeling the fabric of the skirt that draped gracefully around her newly toned legs. Jacob made her feel beautiful, inside and out. She clutched at the feeling even if it could never mean anything more.

The church was small and wooden and very white. It had a graceful age and character that was missing from the more popular and anonymous warehouse churches around town. With no saint listed in the title, Taylor felt sure it wasn't Catholic but "Good Shepherd Community" didn't offer too many clues as to denomination. What sort of denomination would allow a ventriloquist wedding? It was absurd and hilarious and enviably creative.

Jacob led her to a pew adorned with tulle and pink roses and they sat down. A pianist coaxed a gentle melody from the depths of a large piano and Taylor relaxed against the seat. Jacob draped his arm behind her. It brushed the edges of her shoulders and made her skin tingle. The pews filled as the brilliant May sun cut through stained glass windows that flanked the front of the church. Multi-colored collages danced on the white walls. The scene was traditional and classy until a woman dressed in a black suit marched to the front carrying a toddler-sized doll, its wooden mouth carved into a huge smile.

Taylor stifled a giggle, leaned into Jacob's shoulder, and whispered in his ear, "I sort of thought you were joking. This is hilarious." He grinned and squeezed her shoulder.

The woman pastor spoke first. "Welcome friends and family to the joyous occasion of the wedding of Pat and Carla. Today the service will be performed by Carla's closest friend, Eleanor." She looked at the dummy and swiveled its head toward the audience.

"Hello friends," said Eleanor the dummy, "welcome to this most happy day. I always told Carla that men were animals. She finally finds one I approve of and come to find out he spends all his time *with* animals." The dummy shook her head and the audience snickered.

Throughout the ceremony—complete with a deliberately fumbled ring exchange that drove Eleanor crazy—Taylor and Jacob laughed and elbowed each other. The act was outrageously funny positioned next to the solemn formality of lifetime vows. Taylor's sides ached from suppressed laughter by the time, "Oh go ahead and kiss the bride, you animal," was commanded by Eleanor. Jacob sat, elbows on knees, his shoulders shaking. Taylor avoided looking at him for fear she would lose control completely. She wiped at her eyes, cheeks strained from a continual smile.

Finally the pastor left with Eleanor and the pianist began the recessional march. It took only a few notes to wipe the smile from Jacob's face. Taylor watched his shoulders stiffen. He dropped his head and laced his fingers together as *Pachelbel's Canon in D* swelled and filled the church.

Without thinking, Taylor reached her hand under Jacob's arm. She rested it briefly on his thigh and squeezed gently. Jacob did not look at her. Instead, he stared at her hand as if he did not recognize it. Then he took it, clasping it tightly between his own warm palms.

Taylor's heart pounded and she was certain Jacob felt the throbbing deep within her fingers. But he did not look at her or seem to notice, lost in another time and place, the music breaking his heart with every note. She decided she did not care that he thought of his own wedding or imagined holding his wife's hand and promising Till Death Do We Part. She only waited and focused on a cross that hung on the wall at the end of the pew.

Jesus hung there, as He hung in thousands of churches, face frozen in suffering as He looked heavenward. A cheap paint job positioned His pierced side higher up, almost to his shoulder. *Probably made in Mexico by six-year-olds*, thought Taylor. The sort of thing tourists bought as they waited at the border crossing in Tijuana, where garish ceramic statues were sold and packs of Chiclets were hawked by dirty Mexican children.

The last time she'd visited Mexico it was purely as company for her father. He made a trip to buy medicine at the much cheaper Mexican pharmacies. That and large bottles of whiskey for the hard nights when he couldn't sleep. Anthony had been up most the night, coughing so hard it sounded like his lungs would break into small jagged pieces, his frail body deflating like an old balloon unable to hold oxygen.

Taylor had put the pillow over her head as fear clutched at her. In the darkness, Anthony's death loomed inevitable and she felt guilty for her own life—the vitality of her physical body—and frustration that nothing could be done about the sadness of her brother's existence. When her father had asked for company on his trip the next day, she had jumped at the opportunity to be alone with him and have the chance to be normal.

Instead, her very private father had spent the trip distracted and sad, lost in a world she couldn't penetrate. Taylor finally gave up attempts at conversation and instead concentrated on the shabby Mexican venders that clustered beside the road. They remained persistent, ever hopeful that their worthless kitsch could extract a few precious American dollars from the plump wallet, they imagined, inside each air conditioned car.

Garishly painted ceramic statues tumbled together on Mexican blankets where dumpy women in tattered clothing flashed toothless grins and gestured toward giant Disney characters painted in otherworldly hues so bright they were probably visible at night. Ugly. Taylor closed her eyes and laid her head back against the seat as the car inched its way toward California.

"I've always wanted one of those."

Her father's deadpan voice came as a surprise, breaking a silence between them as solid as stone. Taylor opened her eyes and turned her attention outside. Her father pointed toward a huge ceramic hamburger, at least four feet tall, on display beside a vendor's shack. The bun was painted yellow, the hue of traffic lines on a roadway, with dark brown spots on top for sesame seeds. Stop-sign red and primary green paint had been smeared haphazardly in the middle, indicating, one might guess, tomato and lettuce. A section near the bottom painted black was no doubt intended to resemble a burger patty.

"I like my burgers well done."

Taylor began giggling. She imagined the ceramic burger towering next to her father's majestic Mister Lincoln roses that bloomed under the living room window. The roses were the only thing accenting the neat green lawn he took pains to keep weed-free and irrigated. Her giggle turned into a belly laugh that invited a chuckle from her father.

Soon they were both laughing so hard Taylor had a hard time catching her breath. Her dad wiped his eyes, his shoulders shaking. When they finally got control somewhere on I-5 north of Mexico, he squeezed her knee.

"Thanks for coming today, Love."

Laughter and tears were strange twins, opposite sides of a coin. Sharing either of them created an instant bond.

The Mexico trip, and ridiculous ceramic hamburger, remained one of a handful of memories Taylor cherished from her time in San Diego, rare snapshots of connection.

As she thought of her father and the origins of the cheap Jesus on the wall, light through the stained glass warmed the figure, highlighting the painted blood. Taylor stared at Jesus, considering his bloody shoulder, and thought of Rain—viciously wounded, but blessed by God.

Bellissima.

# Chapter 32

Taylor pushed open the coffee shop door and immediately found Melissa slumped at a corner table. She met Taylor's eyes but didn't move.

"Hi." Taylor slid into the chair across from Melissa, "I thought you weren't supposed to drink coffee when you're pregnant."

"Doc says a cup or two a day is fine. This is my "two." She took a tired sip from a styrofoam container.

"Yikes, styrofoam! That leaches toxins. Not good for baby." Taylor reached for the cup, but Melissa held it away.

"I know, I know. This place ran out of regular cups. I need this treat, even though it's swill. I swear, nobody knows how to make coffee."

"Except you." Taylor smiled, hoping to ease the anxiety on her friend's face. "And you're going to have the best coffee stand in Bellingham. So, how'd the appointment go?"

At three months pregnant, Melissa decided to make an adoption plan for her baby. She had called Taylor one night at 11 o'clock. They talked about babies and buying the coffee stand until the wee hours of the morning as Melissa wept and considered the options.

"I don't know why those dumb counselors talk about "choices" … they're all bad. I feel stuck."

"I know."

Breaking her vow to Rain, Taylor lit a cigarette and inhaled, grasping at the short lived euphoria of the nicotine as she held the phone to her ear.

"Only a bad woman, a selfish woman, would give up her own baby. Sometimes an abortion seems better for the baby, too. Then it won't grow up and know it wasn't wanted. It will come look for me one day, Taylor, and what will I say?" Her voice cracked and she hiccuped.

"What you will say is that you were young, and alone, and doing the best you can, Melissa." Strength from somewhere and nowhere uncurled inside Taylor like a kite picked up by a strong wind. It flapped high above the ground, carried with unstoppable conviction. "You will say you loved that baby enough to give it a life. It's going to rip your heart out, but you're protecting life—the baby's and your own."

"How do you know that?"

Taylor waited, the silence on the phone an exclamation mark. She took a deep breath. "I just know, Melissa. Trust me."

"It seems like now would be a good time to tell me how."

*Sometimes it's good to air your secrets to another human being.* Taylor thought of Jacob's words. They sounded right and yet giving words to her experience would give life to it again. Words had power. God supposedly brought all of creation into existence with just words. That's what talking about her abortion would do, give it life and breath and power. She couldn't allow it to move of its own free will.

"I can't talk about it, Melissa. Don't take it personally."

"I most certainly *do* take it personally," she bristled, then simply sighed, "You gotta do what you gotta do. Will you at least go through this pregnancy with me if I make an adoption plan? Would you do that for me?"

"Like go to birthing classes and all that?"

"Yeah. And help me pick out parents."

Something heavy settled in Taylor's throat. She tried to swallow. But who else did Melissa have? No mother, no father. A grandmother with dementia could hardly be a support and Peter was busy saving the planet.

"Yes, I will be there for you."

And so here she was, an hour before reporting to creepy Steve for another afternoon of Real Estate *From* Dummies. The man's brief transformation into an authentic human being hadn't lasted. Taylor assumed only Princess saw it on a regular basis.

"How was the adoption appointment?"

"They're so nice it's annoying." Melissa cracked the top of her coffee and stirred it with a spoon. "They gave me cookies like I'm a kindergartner and told me I'm beautiful. Please."

Taylor smiled. "Besides having good manners, what annoyed you so much?"

Melissa ignored her. "We looked at profiles of couples who are waiting for a child. I swear these people come from another planet: MBA this, engineer that. The women are perfect and motherly and just … annoying. I kinda liked this one couple, though," her tone changed abruptly. "The guy's a civil engineer and the wife is an interior decorator. They tried for ten years to have a child—in vitro, everything. Then the wife got ovarian cancer and it's like a freakin' miracle she lived and is now *totally* healthy. She can't ever have a baby though. You should have read the story about why she wants a child. It was so honest and vulnerable." Melissa's voice dropped and became almost a whisper. "She decorates houses for millionaires in Seattle and stuff, but she'll stay home for a baby. She talked about decorating a baby suite. A baby *suite*, Taylor."

"Sounds perfect. What kind of adoption do they want?"

"They'll do whatever I want the counselor said. They just want a child so bad. Isn't it weird how the one thing that is devastating to my life is a miracle for somebody else? It makes it almost beautiful.

Almost … "

"Like you." Taylor looked into Melissa's eyes and saw tears beginning to glisten there.

Melissa shook her head and dropped her chin. "I could never be that kind of woman, that kind of mother. Look at me!"

"But you make a *mean* cup of coffee." Taylor reached over and grasped Melissa's hands in her own. Tears swelled, blurring the room into softly moving shapes. "And you're the *bravest* person I know." She squeezed Melissa's hands, then dropped them and wiped at her eyes. "I've gotta go to the Shop of Horrors now. But call me if you want to talk about that family. Or whatever."

"Okay." Melissa remained lost in another world, but snapped suddenly at attention when Taylor rose to leave. "Don't forget the pregnancy and child birth class next Thursday night—you better be there." She pointed an index finger at Taylor.

"I'll be there."

~ ~ ~

"You're starting to do the duck walk."

Taylor walked slightly behind Melissa as they made their way down the long trail that skirted Bellingham Bay. The serene surface of the ocean seemed to stretch to infinity before them, melting into a pastel skyline. Melissa threw a rock into the water disturbing the glassy surface into ripples that multiplied into endless undulating waves that marched out to sea.

"Rearrange your center of gravity and see what it does to *your* walk, smart ass." Melissa flipped long locks of hair over her shoulder then adjusted her sagging jeans. "Bet I'll really be doing a duck walk when I have to push this baby out." She sighed deeply. Moving in wordless agreement they sat down on a bench beside the trail.

Melissa had drug her out for exercise with the excuse she already "looked like a small whale," but Taylor knew she wanted to talk about the baby.

"It's official, sort of."

"What is?"

"The adoption. It'll be open, but the parents don't want me to contact them. They have agreed to send me pictures and letters once a year."

"That sounds pretty good."

"*Nothing* sounds good." Melissa appeared to be scanning the horizon, a faraway look in her eye. "Some days all I can think about is keeping this baby, which is so hilarious. I never thought of myself as the maternal type. The books say it's hormones or something."

"You started knitting or anything yet?"

"Cross stitch."

Taylor laughed out loud. "Serious?"

"Don't laugh; it's your Christmas present this year."

"It's probably a skull and cross bones. On camouflage."

Melissa shot her a look of mock horror. "You've ruined your surprise."

They sat quietly for a few minutes, each lost in a private world, until Melissa spoke again. "I did ask for something special in the adoption agreement."

"Yeah?"

"The baby has to have 'Taylor' in the name somehow."

"No way." Taylor's eyes began to sting. "You can't *make* the parents legally give the child my name, can you?"

"No. But I told them you're the reason they're getting a baby and they should never forget that. Taylor's a cool, semi-trendy name, anyhow. Not like I suggested 'Mabel.'"

"Wow, I feel like a godmother or something … not that I'll actually get to be one."

The girls fell silent, each contemplating their losses. Taylor thought of the three birthing classes she'd attended so far with Melissa and the expectations every person had, that they'd end up with the miracle of life after nine months. A baby didn't affect just the one giving birth. There would be new grandparents, aunts, uncles, and cousins. Godmothers. Since the abortion she'd avoided children and any thoughts of them. If it were not for a lowly coffee shop job a birthing class would be the last place on earth she'd willingly go. Literally.

She hadn't expected to want to know Melissa's baby, to hold it in her arms and kiss its tiny head. A tear trickled down her cheek and she felt a hand squeeze her knee.

"Anyway," Melissa's voice falsely brightened, "I gave the parents ideas for names. You know, some famous people have 'Taylor' in the name. James Taylor, for instance, and Elizabeth Taylor. Cool, huh?"

"Definitely cool."

Taylor smiled at her friend. She wished bravery like Melissa's could be purchased in a bottle and sprinkled on at will. "Thanks."

# Chapter 33

"Freaking Sunday drivers!"

Taylor veered onto the shoulder of the road to avoid rear-ending the car in front of her. Lost in thought and oblivious to the red lights in front of her, she slammed on the brakes. Never mind that it *was* a Sunday and she'd been shamelessly tail gating.

An arm appeared out of the driver's side window of the car ahead, middle finger saluting her near miss. Drumming the steering wheel, Taylor scowled. Normally the weekly time at the shelter was a respite from life, but today she didn't want to spend a morning with Liz. She wanted to stay in bed and ponder Jacob's behavior. Ever since the wedding he'd been different, distant and unavailable. He canceled a scheduled ride with her on the way home and, shortly after, left an abbreviated message on voice mail. Even over the phone Taylor sensed his withdrawal from her life.

"I have to cancel our appointment," he said, the "appointment" being a casual meeting to fit Rain with a new saddle. "My schedule is too busy."

The new edge in his voice stung. It was the tone of a professional with firm boundaries on relationship, not the voice of a friend who teased her about being a klutz and told her she looked beautiful in a dress.

No matter what she told herself made sense, Taylor had not been able to stop her attraction to Jacob. His moment of vulnerability at the wedding only intensified her feelings, drawing her to him as surely as iron to a magnet. She wanted the other Jacob back, the one who fit like an "old shoe," an especially attractive old shoe.

*What would happen now?* Taylor turned onto the street that fronted the shelter. He obviously didn't feel the same way and no longer had time for her. As the days passed the sting of his rejection had begun to ache like a deep wound. Shallow cuts to the skin's surface hurt for a little while, but the pain was nothing like a deep piercing. The worst cuts didn't hurt until the body had a chance to realize the depth of its trauma.

In the end, Taylor knew it was her own fault. Jacob had just been trying to be nice and help her succeed with a horse he was invested in. It was mostly about Rain and always had been. He'd gone above and beyond the call of duty. As she pondered it Taylor remembered Evan—the hottest guy in junior high.

While most of their class stumbled into adolescence pimply and blushing, Evan remained cool and totally comfortable with the opposite sex. That he was also a nice guy only made every girl in the school want him more. Not that Taylor had given it serious thought. Evan was way out of her league; best to feign indifference and ignore him altogether. This worked well until freshman year of high school and the evening of the spring dance. Like every other girl in school, Taylor had dressed carefully and tried to play up her assets. She had traced her blue eyes with her mother's smoky grey liner and donned lip gloss, secretly hoping for an invitation to dance. Some girls had dates and Evan was top on everyone's list. Taylor had not considered asking him—or anyone—but had accepted her single status, convincing herself she preferred going alone.

After an hour of watching the rest of her class dance with no interest from the opposite sex, Taylor's self confidence began to wane. It was then that she noticed Evan watching her from across the room. He appeared to be alone and smiled, motioning to her. Eight years later it was pretty funny how the moment resembled a toothpaste commercial: the sparkly disco ball accentuating Evan's white teeth, the way the slow music seemed to start playing as if on cue. It was so obvious now that it wasn't authentic, hind sight being 20/20 and all that.

To her 14-year-old self there was nothing funny about hunky Evan taking note of her. There was only joy in being wanted. This was quickly followed by devastation in the girls' restroom.

"Why was Evan dancing with Taylor *Reed*; I thought *you* guys were a couple?"

From the safety of a closed stall Taylor listened to Stephanie Maple and Amy Bettencourt gossip as they primped in the mirror.

"We *are* together," Amy said. "Evan likes to make the dorks feel special. He calls it a charity dance. Did you see her face? She thinks he actually wanted to dance with her."

It suddenly felt unbearably hot in the restroom. Taylor tried to breathe quietly, praying nobody heard any movement within the stall. After the girls left she found a phone and called her mother, complaining of an upset stomach, and asked to come home.

It was hard to say what was worse, wanting someone who didn't want her or being completely clueless. Was it written all over her face that she wanted Jacob, too? Taylor felt sure of it. Why else would he have pulled out of her life? The "charity dance" had come to an end.

"Hi Liz." Taylor pushed her feelings away and walked into the shelter.

"Hey," Liz's lips kept twitching, even after she spoke. She hitched up her leg. "Got a new resident you might like."

"Really?"

"Take a look at the back of the kennel."

Taylor took a deep breath as she navigated the hallway leading to the dog kennels. It was a relief to concentrate on something else for a few hours. She didn't see any new dogs and the very last kennel appeared to be empty. She was about to return to the office when she noticed the tip of a long black snout poke out of the dog house at the back of the space.

"Hey pup," Taylor moved to the chain link and peered inside, "come out so I can see you."

She waited for a moment. When the snout disappeared and no dog came forth Taylor opened the kennel door and went inside. She moved slowly. The animals that came to the shelter all had a story to tell and it was usually an ugly one. She had learned to take her time making friends. They communicated when they were ready.

Crouching down she resisted the urge to put a hand inside the dog house and instead talked softly to the creature inside. "Hey, I'm your friend. Come out so we can meet."

From her vantage point Taylor could only make out a mass of black hair inside the dark structure. It pressed against the walls. She continued talking and after a few minutes heard a low whine and the movement of fur. She waited. The snout again appeared at the entrance to the dog house. Amber-colored eyes looked up at her.

"Come on, pup."

The dog didn't look angry so she extended a hand. The snout disappeared but quickly reappeared and a pink tongue licked her fingertips.

"That's the way. See, its friendly here."

Taylor sat down, cross-legged, and watched as two huge paws began crawling toward her. She gasped as an enormous German Shepherd puppy inched it's way over, lanky haunches trembling, and flopped into her lap.

"Whoa, you're a big fella!"

She stroked the dog's face, her mouth agape at the size of the paws that clawed into her jeans. The dog wasn't exactly a pup, more like a gawky teenager. It licked at her, desperate for acceptance, as if she were a long-lost friend.

"He's something, huh?"

Taylor looked up at the constantly shifting form of Liz. "He looks like a purebred."

"He is. The woman who dropped him off says he comes from European breeding stock, Romanian or something."

"How does that sort of dog end up in a place like this?" Taylor stroked the dog's dark, bushy ruff. He was almost completely black, his face sporting fringes of rust-colored hair that feathered into the black for contrast. He had clear amber eyes and an elegant head. When the dog grew into his body he would carry himself with the natural dignity unique to his breed.

"You still think only the handicapped and mismatched end up here?" Liz shook her head as if Taylor was dim-witted. "Two words: commitment and convenience. A dog like this isn't exactly convenient. He's big, dirty, has a double coat that needs brushing all the time, and probably knocks things over with his long tail. He looked cute at six weeks, but not so cute anymore, are you?" Liz's voice was rough, but her eyes were soft. As she talked her hand reached for the dog's muzzle and cupped it. "Commitment goes out the window when things get inconvenient."

Taylor pondered Liz's observations. She continued to pet the dog, her fingers finding a hard scabby place under the thick fur that ringed it's neck like a necklace.

"He must have gotten injured. Feels like an old scar or something here around his neck."

"That's from being tied to a tree with a collar that didn't fit. The woman who dropped him off rescued him from the Seattle area and intended to keep him. But she got a job in Bellingham and doesn't have room for this guy now. Abandoned twice and he's only ten months old."

"You think it will be hard to place him?" Taylor shifted her legs. They were going numb from the weight of the dog, but he didn't seem to want to move from her lap.

"Hard telling. The right person needs to come in, someone who likes German Shepherds and can handle the care and feeding for a dog this size."

As Liz talked one person immediately came to Taylor's mind—one who had once loved a German Shepherd and understood commitment. She thought about it the rest of the day while cleaning the facility and pondering each inconvenient creature in residence there. The dog seemed to speak to her, whining every time he heard her approach, further cementing the plan taking shape in her mind.

"Liz, my landlady has always wanted a dog for security purposes and to keep the deer out of her garden. Is there any way I could take Kreed home with me for a couple of days and let Rowan meet him?"

"*Creed?*"

"Yeah, with a 'K.'" Taylor smiled, "Like it?"

Liz shrugged, as if any name would do, and turned to the coffee pot behind the desk. After refilling her mug she sat down and nodded. "Two days. And it's only because I like you and know where you live. Take an extra large crate so you have something to keep him in at night."

~ ~ ~

As she drove to Jacob's house with Kreed snug inside a dog crate stuffed in the back seat, Taylor thought about Liz's compliment: *It's only because I like you.* Outside of her deceased mother, Taylor had never heard Liz positively declare affinity for another human being. She felt warm and grateful, committed to maintaining Liz's trust even in the midst of a lie.

What felt ingenious and inspired while at the shelter began to fade to foolishness the closer Taylor got to Jacob's house. By the time she pulled into his driveway she regretted her impulsiveness. Her heart raced while Kreed whined in the back seat.

Taking note of a new *For Sale* sign stuck in Jacob's front lawn, she shushed the dog and got out of the Toyota on unsteady legs. Jacob appeared almost immediately at the front door.

Taylor forced her feet to move in the direction of the house, grasping at what to say. She had no idea how to explain herself. It felt impossible to articulate the words inside, especially since most of them had little to do with an unwanted German Shepherd.

"Hi." Taylor hesitated, stopping short of the stone walkway leading to the front door.

"Hi." Jacob looked tired and confused. He had a weekend's worth of stubble on his chin and wore sweats and a frayed tee shirt advertising a college sports team.

"Hi." Taylor repeated the greeting while Jacob waited. "I was in the area and wondered how you were doing. Are you moving?"

Jacob sighed and ran his fingers through unkempt hair. "Yeah, I started packing this weekend. It's part of the divorce agreement. I'll still be in the area, just not in this house."

"Are you ever going to ride with me again?" she blurted, her thoughts coming out as they had appeared in her mind over several days, stark and rambling and raw.

"Taylor," Jacob sighed again, as if saying her name was exhausting. "I'm going through a lot of crap right now—the house selling, my divorce being finalized. My life is pretty messy."

"So. I thought we were friends. What about what you told me, 'sharing the burden' and all that?"

Jacob's expression softened and he smiled. "I did say that, didn't I? I should probably take my own advice. Just not with you, Taylor." His tone resolute, Jacob looked into her eyes as he spoke.

"Because you don't like me that way ... I get it." Taylor looked across his yard at the real estate sign and bit her lip hard to fight back the tears that were forming. She was inconvenient in the life of a good man who had enough to deal with. "I hope your house sells."

She turned to walk away and Jacob grabbed her hand. He squeezed it. "Thank you for being willing to share my burden. I just can't go there with you, okay? I hope you can understand."

At that moment a sharp bark punctuated the awkward exchange.

Jacob dropped her hand. "What do you have in there?"

"Something I wanted to show you, but it was a pretty dumb idea."

Taylor moved to the car and grabbed the door handle.

"You came here ... might as well show me." Jacob crossed his arms and raised his eyebrows, the teasing look on his face a shadow of their prior rapport.

"Okay." Taylor opened the back door of the car and released the dog. "Come, Kreed."

Kreed scrambled from the crate, nearly falling to the ground when his gangly hind limbs caught the edge of the seat as he exited the small space. When he saw Jacob he cowered and inched his way to Taylor's side keeping watchful eyes on the vet. She reached down and ruffled the hair at his neck.

"It's okay, buddy, he's friendly."

Jacob took a deep breath as he watched the dog. He crouched down, resting elbows on knees, and extended a hand. Kreed whined and, slinking into the submissive posture he regularly adopted, crawled over. When he reached the outstretched hand he licked the fingertips. Jacob laid one hand on Kreed's head and with the other stroked his neck. The dog wagged his tail and pressed into Jacob's knees, the sheer mass forcing the vet to sit on the ground. He then fell into the available lap as if he were Minnie's size.

Taylor watched Jacob stroke the dog, lost to another time and obviously enjoying the reprieve from reality. When Kreed was full grown he would be handsome in an intimidating sort of way. He'd possess great power and cunning, the sort of dog that chased down criminals. But for the moment he was only a clumsy instrument of grace, performing search and rescue for one man's heart.

"I thought of you when I met Kreed. He used to be tied to a tree, like Duchess. We're looking for a home for him. Not that you would want him, you're moving and busy. I just wanted you to meet him."

After several moments Jacob spoke. "Why did you name him creed?"

"A creed is a system of beliefs or principles, like a religion or something. You probably know that already."

Taylor fiddled with the strings on her hooded sweatshirt. Seeing Jacob with Kreed made her want to cry and she couldn't say who she felt most sorry for—Jacob, the dog, or herself.

"Liz told me most of the animals at the shelter are there because of lack of commitment or inconvenience. I think a good creed is committing for the long haul, even when something's inconvenient. I never really thought about that until I met this dog." Her eyes stung with tears.

Jacob rose from his cross-legged position on the ground and Kreed followed him to the car where Taylor leaned against the door. He wiped a tear trickling down her face and placed a hand behind her neck. Pulling her forward he pressed the side of her face into his, beard stubble burning her cheek, and buried a kiss near the curve of her jaw. He whispered into her hair, his breath sending shivers down her spine, "I like you *that way*, Taylor. That's the problem."

Taylor felt breathless when Jacob released her, uncertain what to say or do next. He didn't speak for a moment, but stared with sad eyes at the dog sitting beside him. Kreed looked up, his amber gaze pleading.

"I have a creed, too: Don't expect someone else to fix your woundedness. They can't and it isn't fair. Even though my wife left *me* there are things I have to figure out before involving someone else. I need time to do that."

On the drive home, Taylor thought about Jacob's creed. Even though his words hurt they felt strangely affirming. Perhaps relationships, more than anything else in life, needed an honoring creed to navigate by.

# Chapter 34

As surely as the sun rose in the sky each morning since the abortion, Taylor had known the moment would eventually come. Avoiding internet websites and anything baby related did not protect her. Rather, an unexpected friend unknowingly insisted she revisit the past. With heart racing, she watched Jennie smile and flip the large laminated pages at the front of the classroom.

"Fourteen weeks is an exciting time, guys. Your babies are all about the size of your clenched fist. Actually, they can clench their own fists now and even suck their thumbs."

"How cute is that?" Melissa whispered. She elbowed Taylor and put a hand on her stomach.

"Is it possible to know what sex they are?"

Amanda, pregnant with number four, was hoping for a girl. She smiled and added, "We'll be happy with another boy, of course."

Jennie grinned back. "Yes, your babies all have sex organs. They are growing hair on their heads and making faces. They can express themselves and make all sorts of movements, though you won't feel it yet. When I was pregnant with my third ... "

Taylor looked around the room, desperate for something else to focus on. She wanted to sprint out of the room, far away from the happy couples and smiley Jennie who used cloth diapers on her children and home-schooled so she could spend more time with them. They would all hate her if they knew the truth, that she had laid on a table at week fourteen and allowed a stranger to remove her thumb-sucking baby.

She hadn't intended to wait so long. The pregnancy counselor said the first trimester was the best time for the abortion yet somehow she failed to show up for the scheduled appointment. Instead, she'd concealed her morning sickness with complaints about the flu and lay in bed for over a week listening to Anthony cough in the next bedroom and avoiding conversation with her father. Certainly Ian would call, she believed. He'd realize he had chosen the wrong girl and remember all the things they had in common: an adopted sibling, an intense love for the ocean, and eating Indian food. Not to mention a baby. Surely those things meant something. He would miss her and know, in the way all lovers *knew*, that they were meant to be together.

At week thirteen Taylor got out of bed and opened her underwear drawer. She dug under the bras for the dirty wad of bills kept together by an elastic band. Ian's goodbye gift. She called the clinic in a sudden panic, afraid that it was too late.

"We can't get you in again until next week, which puts you," the receptionist rustled some papers, "at week fourteen."

"Can you still do it?"

"Terminate the pregnancy? Of course. It's a common procedure called a 'D and E'—dilation and evacuation. We have to do it in two steps now, though. You'll need to come in prior to the actual procedure."

The word *procedure* seemed so mild and ordinary. Lots of things were procedures: getting braces, a real estate license, making a perfect latte. The tiny fetus with movement, fingers, and a gender portrayed on

Jennie's full color poster did not strike Taylor as part of any common procedure.

"Are you paying attention? When we get to the breathing/coaching part in a few months you better be taking some serious notes."

"I'm not feeling so well … I gotta go." Taylor rose from the chair and threaded her way to the front of the room.

"Everything okay?" Jennie paused in the middle of answering a question about ultrasound safety.

"Not really," Taylor grasped the cool metal of the door knob and steadied herself. "I don't feel well. Something I ate … "

"Sorry. See you next month then?"

Taylor didn't answer. She stumbled out of the classroom and nearly ran to her car.

All the way home emotions gained momentum, swirling into a tornado that instantly transported her to the past. Before Ian, before the abortion, she prided herself on being a girl without drama. Not like so many girls she knew who were addicted to the details of romance and jealous friendships and seemed to enjoy navigating life like it was a stupid reality show. She'd learned her mother's lessons well: feelings were a private matter and their display a shameful thing. No tears. Not even when she'd fallen, face down, on a concrete sidewalk outside the condo when she was five years old.

It had been a cold day. Taylor could still remember the circumstances in detail. Instead of holding her mother's hand, she'd stuffed her hands inside her coat pockets for warmth. She scuffed at the slick winter crystals that sparkled over the sidewalk's hard surface, oblivious to her mother's quick steps in front of her. The ripple of broken concrete ahead had escaped her, its edge catching her toe as she shuffled along, lost in a crisp winter wonderland. With her hands secured deep inside fleece pockets, nothing stopped the forward sprawl when she tripped. She still remembered her front teeth driving into her lower lip as her chin hit the unforgiving gritty, cold surface, and the salty metallic taste of blood that filled her mouth.

Even with blood spilling from a split lip and broken nose it had not occurred to her to cry. *No sense in crying over what's already been done.* Calmly she accepted her mother's hand and the cloth held to her face as onlookers gasped.

"Not even a tear," her mother said. And Taylor felt pride, warm as an embrace, wrap around her.

Since the abortion something had happened. Something unsettling. It reminded Taylor of a certain movie that depicted a broken submarine and crew of men trapped at the bottom of the ocean. As the men watched in agony, screws on the bulging metal ceiling of the leaking vessel began to loosen from the pressure outside. The cameras focused, close-up, on a thin trickle of water that leaked around the screw heads. Dramatic music built into a crescendo as the water turned into a steady stream and the metal gave way in a screeching rush.

That's what she was doing, giving way. What began as a trickle with her arrival in Washington turned into a stream when Melissa became pregnant. Her metal could not hold on much longer.

# Chapter 35

Instead of drowning the feelings with several beers, Taylor walked outside the cottage and across the street to the cemetery. She meandered a path around the grave sites, pausing to read the inscriptions, examine the flower vases and balloons adorning specific headstones, and ponder dates of death. Many had been pioneers to the area, their names etched into history by the naming of nearby county roads: Bowerson, Steadman, Olesen.

Taylor continued her stroll through the cemetery and silently figured up the ages of the deceased—ten, thirty-one, eighty-nine, two, seventeen. She saw graves with pictures, and homemade markers, graves planted with rose bushes, peonies, and lilacs. Some had special verses or phrases. Her favorite was written under the photo of a portly grandfather wearing a baseball cap and a warm smile. His hand rested on the head of a black Lab. *Husband, father, grandfather, friend. You are deeply loved and greatly missed.*

The graves of children were equally scattered among those of adults and the elderly. One simply read "Baby" on a small headstone dwarfed next to a huge stone marking a family plot as "Roman." Taylor touched the crumbling stone, picking at the moss imbedded in the crevasses, and tried in vain to make out the dates of birth and death.

In the few months she'd lived in the cottage, Taylor had watched the practice of grieving with a growing interest. Some people knelt by the graves, others sat in cars, some released balloons on important anniversaries, some came and left quickly leaving behind small tokens of their thoughts: shells, stones, coins. A key chain with a football. Rituals and gifts meant to honor the lives and spirits of the dead. What did the living hope to get by returning to the past? Closeness? A whispered message they prayed God would deliver to their loved one?

Near the back Taylor paused at a newer headstone and read the inscription: *Jack Colton Smith, lived and died on May 1, 2010. At rest in the Lord's arms.*

No matter the length of Jack's small life he had been given a name. And a tiny toy fire truck. Taylor picked up the small vehicle perched under the stone and just as quickly replaced it fearing her touch violated something private and deeply personal. Remembrance was a powerful thing, honoring and sacred.

She thought of her father visiting Anthony's grave, each side guarded by a newly planted Mister Lincoln. The roses would bloom every year, delicate crimson velvet unfolding in a wave of perfume, each blossom as sweet and fragile as the boy they remembered.

In a sudden rush her deepest emotions broke free and tears flooded Taylor's eyes. She fell to her knees beside little Jack's grave and for the first time allowed herself to imagine the daughter she would never know. She would have been dark-haired, Taylor felt certain, and perhaps have inherited Ian's cleft in the chin and her own smallish ears. She would love horses. Taylor lay on her back, grass tickling her neck, and stared into the cloudless sky overhead.

*Savannah.*

The name came to her clearly as if spoken out loud in a mysterious eternity. It whispered of sun and smiles and tall grasses dancing in warm summer breezes. Taylor nodded silently and bit her lip until she tasted blood.

At that moment the crunch of tires on gravel brought her back to the present. Taylor at once rolled to her side and sat up. She brushed her hair back and wiped the tears racing past her cheek bones. The car parked and two women got out. They began walking her way and Taylor's heart thumped in her chest. Jack's mother, perhaps? What would they think of a stranger sitting by his grave crying like a fool? She scrambled to her feet just as the women gave her a curious stare and turned in the opposite direction. They approached another grave and stood with their backs to her.

Taylor relaxed. She picked at the grass and dirt on her knees while observing the strangers. She heard soft voices. One of the women bent over and deposited something near the stone. When she stood her companion put an arm around her and they stood in silence, heads bowed and touching in shared sorrow. Were they praying?

As she watched Taylor felt the strong fingers of guilt squeeze what was left of her heart. She didn't deserve comfort or even the solitary rituals of grief. Not for a child for whom there were no memories.

*You are deeply loved and greatly missed.* Taylor hoped that, somehow, Savannah was "at rest in the Lord's arms."

Overhead an eagle floated on an up current, its bald head clearly visible against a backdrop of cloudless sky. As she left the cemetery, Taylor watched the bird drift effortlessly over the pine trees toward the snowy peak of Mt. Baker and disappear into an endless blue horizon.

~ ~ ~

Rain watched, head over the gate, as Taylor walked toward the cottage. Instead of turning the door knob and disappearing into the bliss of a six pack of beer, she went to the horse.

Taylor stroked the mare's face, fingers tracing the long scar over her eye socket. She felt her breaths coming fast and shallow as she waged an internal battle for self control. Rain shifted and bumped Taylor's arm. She bobbed her head and moved off, stopping a few feet away to observe from a distance.

"*Horses value congruency.*"

"I'm no good to be around right now, Rain, I know. There's nothing anyone can do for me."

At that moment her cell phone buzzed in a back pocket. Without thinking, Taylor picked it up.

"Hello?"

"Are you okay?"

Melissa's voice sounded husky and concerned. Taylor's response was automatic. "I'm fine."

"What are you doing?"

"Uh … " Taylor glanced at Rain, "just taking my horse for a little ride. Nice day and all."

"I thought you were sick."

Taylor felt her face flush even though no one was around to see her caught in a lie. In the space of a couple hours she'd blanked out the birthing class entirely. Her frazzled mind scrambled at an explanation.

"I … "

Melissa spoke softly, "You lied to me. Why?"

A tingling sensation spread through Taylor's limbs as her heart began to pound. She felt like a confused rabbit that had been chased inside the fence and found there were no places left to run.

"I had an abortion at fourteen weeks, Melissa." Taylor clenched the phone and listened to the silence on the other end. "I know you must think I'm a hypocrite with all my advice. I'm not a very good example, or friend." Her chin began to tremble. "Maybe you need someone else to help you through this pregnancy."

"Why didn't you tell me?"

"I couldn't. Can't you see why after today? I don't want to talk about it. I gotta go … ride."

"Taylor!"

"I'll call you later, bye."

Taylor clicked the phone shut and pressed the power button.

It only took a few minutes to tack up Rain. She swung her leg over the mare and settled into the seat of the saddle. Clucking to the horse Taylor guided her out of the driveway and toward the trail head a short mile away.

# Chapter 36

No one watched her clip-clopping down the road already darkening with shadows. The towering pines edging the roadway seemed to be pushing the light to the other side of the valley. It glowed golden in the late afternoon sun. Taylor reached down to pat the mare.

"We won't go too far, Rain. Just need to clear my head."

Rain picked her way easily over the large rocks blocking the entrance to the maze of logging roads and trails that constituted their training ground for Ride and Tie. Logging roads eventually gave way to hundreds of miles of Department of Natural Resources acreage. The landscape was an undulating tapestry of color and texture: evergreen trees of every hue and type; rocky granite cliffs accentuated by the occasional hunk of emerald olivine—chunky jewels from the foothills of the Twin Sisters; huckleberry and salmon berry bushes; and the occasional stream or waterfall that meandered its way to the nearby Nooksack River.

As she rode, Taylor felt her body relax into a simple primitive rhythm of shared energy. She felt proud that the girl who could barely mount a horse unaided six months before now navigated uneven and challenging terrain with ease. She thought of Jacob and the previous months of training with him and Rain. She'd given up smoking and exchanged a few pounds of fat for muscle. When jogging her portion of a race or flying along the trail on the back of a hairy angel, she felt connected to life and engaged in the present.

Guiding Rain to a narrow dirt trail off the logging road, they made their way into the trees. The air was moist and soft. Taylor slapped at a mosquito as a huge oak leaf brushed her shoulder. Even in the waning light the nearly chartreuse foliage glowed with spring life. Moisture from a recent shower dripped down through the rain forest-like canopy overhead. Taylor felt as if she could disappear into the woods and never come back.

"Just a short loop, girl."

Taylor stroked Rain's neck and listened to the mare's even breathing as she negotiated an incline. It occurred to her that she hadn't left a note about her whereabouts. She always made a point, when riding, to leave a note in the kitchen about where she'd gone and when she expected to return. It was a deal made with Rowan—"I worry about you out there alone"—who had important phone numbers in case of emergency: her mother, father, Liz, and Melissa.

"Things happen, you know. And there is wildlife on those trails, cougar, bear … "

If Rowan meant to scare her it didn't work. Nature was her friend. Taylor felt much more anxious about people and their ability to harm her.

Taylor pushed Rain into a trot after cresting a hill. The trail meandered through a stand of poplars along even terrain, a perfect place to enjoy the horse's steady extended gait. Jacob had discovered that on level ground Rain could trot at an astonishing clip of 17 miles per hour. The mare had long since surrendered her blind side to Taylor, trusting that her rider would be the measure of sight she was missing.

Rain snorted and shook her head as they flew through the trees, happy to move out and leave the bugs behind. The warm early evening air caressed their faces and Taylor breathed in the tell-tale aroma of the river rushing nearby, a mixture of fish, dead leaves and moist soil. Soon they would come to a fork in the trail and begin the journey back home.

Suddenly Rain's neck tensed. She slowed to a walk and then stopped altogether. Taylor peered into the shadows at the trail's edge but saw nothing.

"What's wrong, sweetie?"

Rain's neck remained rigid. Taylor felt the horse's heart begin to pound under her legs and instinctively gathered up the reins. Forcing herself to breathe slow and deep she laid a hand on Rain's shoulder.

"Easy."

The mare would accept no comfort. She snorted again and swung her head around to examine the trail on her blind side. Something moved in the bushes. Taylor heard a branch snap.

"It's probably just a deer, Rain, lets move along and let it go its way. Maybe a mother and her baby are in there."

It was spring, after all. Taylor tried to imagine the innocent spotted shape of a fawn. Instead, her heart raced along with the horse's. Rain ignored her squeezing calves and continued staring into the woods as if frozen to the spot. Something was definitely in the bushes and it would likely come out at any second.

The cougar stepped onto the trail with measured dignity, the tip of a very long tail curling into a half circle. It paused and stared at them, green eyes intense and glowing, a vision of wild beauty and terrifying power.

Rain did not wait for a cue. She whirled and leapt into a gallop in one stride. They flew down the trail in a crazy zig-zag, dodging slender trees and low hanging branches along the way. Taylor simply hung on, reins slack, and let the mare go where she would. At a bend in the road Rain gave a mighty leap and cleared a downed tree, landing off trail. Taylor lost a stirrup and slipped to the side. Grasping a hunk of mane hair she righted herself and groped for the stirrup as the mare continued running madly through the slash and undergrowth of a slowly maturing clear cut.

On and on she ran, the crackle of brush and snap of branches obscuring any clues that would signal the cat had followed.

"Easy Rain, EASY."

They might get eaten, but if Rain didn't stop she would certainly break a leg in a slash pile. It took several minutes for the mare to respond as Taylor pumped the reins and called her name repeatedly. She slowed to a trot, then a walk, and finally stopped altogether, her chest heaving.

Taylor waited for the thud of velvet paws on her back, movie-style. At least she would die in a majestic way worthy of the nature channel, she thought, not fade away in the slow death of a bottle of booze. The circle of life, that's what it would be.

When nothing happened she turned around and considered the path they had come. Rain's haunches were shaking from terror and exertion, but the clear cut looked empty. As suddenly as it had appeared, the cougar melted back into the landscape. Taylor dismounted and examined Rain's legs. Sweat dripped from her chest and foam flecked her neck. She hung her head in exhaustion and, it seemed, embarrassment at letting her emotions get the better of her.

"It's okay, girl. Trust me, I freaked out too."

Outside of a few shallow cuts on her legs, the mare seemed okay. While the horse rested, Taylor sat on a stump and considered their location. Nothing looked familiar.

"The trail has gotta be back there not far … " Taylor chewed her lip and massaged Rain's withers as she continued looking around for a point of reference. She'd ridden the trails dozens of times but stuck to known routes she had mapped with Jacob and Liz. The terrain had gotten as familiar as Rowan's back yard. This made it easy to forget that DNR land was wild and extended for miles in every direction.

She looked at her watch, eight o'clock. She'd completely lost track of time. When had they left? The day faded and reappeared in Taylor's memory in snap shots: listening to Jennie at the childbirth classes, the cemetery, Melissa's phone call, the adrenaline rush of seeing her pathetic life end in the jaws of a big cat. Time had long since ceased to exist in any sort of recognizable pattern. Her stomach growled. When had she last eaten?

"Well, all we can do is go back in the direction we came. I'm sure it isn't far." Taylor tried to sound confident as she remounted.

The night air remained warm but she shivered and peered into a sky of deep purples. The evergreens all around formed a wall of black sentries. Overhead the moon hid behind cloud cover, its edges blurring as if a giant eraser was working to extinguish the light. Rain picked her way back through the slash in a direction that felt like home. Taylor sighed in relief when, a few minutes later, they stepped onto a dirt track.

"Good girl, Rain."

The mare moved to the left.

"No, that's not it. Let's go right." Taylor squeezed the mare, kicking her when she refused to move. "Left doesn't feel right so ... lets go *right*." She giggled with relief at her own turn-a-phrase and, ignoring the horse, kicked her again.

Rain tightened her body in resistance, but when Taylor continued she finally moved forward, plodding down the trail in defeat.

"Don't pout. Sometimes I have to be the boss you know."

Taylor continued talking to the horse as they walked the darkened trail. Owls hooted in the distance and the mosquitoes attacked with a vengeance as she struggled to keep the fears at bay. She wasn't sure of the direction at all.

Minutes turned into hours as Rain walked on. Dark shapes in the surrounding forest appeared and disappeared like ghosts and the noises of awakened night life became deafening, shredding what was left of her nerves. Every time she thought of the cougar returning Taylor's breathing became fast and shallow and she fought back the panic attack. Big cats hunted at night, everyone knew that. It might smell them, smell their fear and vulnerability, and return to take them down.

Her mind did not seem capable of rational thinking as Taylor strained to see through the pitch black. She had long since let Rain go where she would. They were lost so it didn't really matter. The horse had probably known how to get home at the fork in the trail, but Taylor hadn't listened. She'd taken the wrong path. It seemed as if her life had been pointing to this last desperate journey all along. A meandering road of wrong decisions had taken her to a wilderness and she was now lost beyond hope. All she could wonder now was if being eaten by a cougar would be extremely painful. Hopefully it would bite her jugular vein and she would bleed out before the eating began.

After what seemed like hours Taylor heard the splashing of the river and smelled its peculiar wet dog aroma. It jogged her back to the present and she spoke to the horse under her. "The river—Rain you got us back! I think all we need to do now is follow it south." She squeezed the reins and pulled Rain to a stop, then patted the horse's neck crusty with dried sweat. "Good girl. I probably should have listened to you way back there."

Taylor looked up. The moon and constellations were hidden behind a curtain of clouds. "Not much light, Rain. Let's stay close to the river."

Maneuvering the horse down a shallow embankment, Taylor found what looked to be an animal trail that closely followed the glinting ribbon of water in the right direction. Rain willingly walked on, her hooves sinking periodically in the muddy trail. Lazy and shallow in summer, the river now rushed, swollen with spring rain.

The sound of the water was soothing and drowned out the forest noises that kept Taylor's nerves on edge. If the cougar was following them she couldn't hear it approach and the attack would come as a surprise. Somehow that seemed better. Ignorance *was* bliss. There were so many things Taylor wished she could still be ignorant of.

The spot on the trail appeared at first to be a puddle. Straining to see it in the dark, Taylor could only be sure of a stump on one side and a good deal of mud. It appeared as an extra dark place on a barely visible track. Rain balked and tried to see it with her blind eye.

"Just a bit of mud, walk on."

At Taylor's urging the mare took one hesitating step, then another. Suddenly Taylor felt them both sink and move forward in what felt like slow motion. Rain tried to leap out of the bog as her back end sank, the stump at her side a solid barrier. The mud grasped at the horse like quick sand. One moment Taylor sat solid in the saddle, the next she tottered off the side, falling onto the trail as Rain went down.

Jumping to her feet Taylor kept a hold on the reins but stepped out of the way as the horse thrashed to free herself. When she failed to make progress Rain finally stopped and lay her head back. Mud covered her hind end up to the haunches and her front end slowly sank level with the back. It seemed to hold her in place as if she'd been super-glued to the spot.

"What do I do now?" Taylor spoke out loud, cursing repeatedly, and began a meaningless check of Rain's tack. She had no rope and no strength to pull the horse out even if rope was available. She pulled her cell phone out of a filthy jean pocket and turned it on. No service. Her hands began to shake as she watched the device roaming for a signal. Rain was stuck and nobody knew where they were.

Sinking to the trail, Taylor felt her ankle begin to throb. She must have twisted it during the crazy dismount. Ignoring the pain, she cradled Rain's jaw in her hand. The horse blinked a lone eye and looked up at her, an expression of complete surrender on her gentle face.

"Oh Rain ... " Taylor began to weep and shiver uncontrollably. She put the mare's head in her lap and caressed her velvet muzzle. Rain closed her eye and sighed deeply. She didn't seem bothered that Taylor could not help but, rather, relieved someone was near in her hour of trouble. The horse appeared to be at peace with whatever might happen next.

With nothing left to do Taylor tried to remember how to pray to Mary. In her current state of mind the words she'd once known by rote failed to continue beyond, 'Hail Mary full of Grace.' A much simpler prayer tumbled out in its place as the tears fell. "God, please help me, please help me."

Though she felt certain she needed more formality, more poetry, the plea continued, punctuated by thoughts that filtered into the night air and, she hoped, to the ears of the Almighty.

"I'm sorry, God; please hear me, please help me."

There was nothing left to hide or avoid in the midst of the insurmountable situation on a muddy trail by a lonely river. Even if God didn't hear it felt strangely good to talk to Him honestly. For once. And so she told Him about Savannah, and Ian, and Melissa. She told Him about her broken heart and resisted the urge to bargain for favors as she might have in the past. There was nothing to give, not even good behavior. Instead she pleaded for the future of Melissa and her unborn baby and for the kind-hearted mare that lay listening in her lap.

When the words had all come out a strange feeling of peace came over Taylor. She had not utterly disintegrated from the pain of remembering. The heavens had not beamed her with a bolt of lightening or the cougar returned to kill her for sins confessed. Like Rain, she felt okay with whatever might happen next. Even if a big cat was involved she felt freakishly calm about it all. The panic induced shivering had ceased without her realizing it and Taylor lay her back against the stump and looked into the sky.

As she watched, the clouds slowly moved from the face of a full moon so bright she could make out the craters on its surface. Silver light beamed down, illuminating the surface of the river, the trail, and Rain's pale face. The air seemed to thicken and warm, as if someone had thrown a blanket over her shoulders. At that moment, the mare opened her eye. Instinctively, Taylor rose to her feet and moved to the front of the horse.

Rain seemed to gather all her strength and with a mighty heave she rose up out of the bog and scrambled onto solid ground. Sticky mud dripped off the saddle and every part of the horse's body. Her tail hung in a single black rope. Outside of her head and neck she was completely covered in ooze.

Taylor looked at the horse in amazement. "You okay?" She held the mare's face in both hands and spoke to her as if she could understand completely. Rain nuzzled her arm. "Okay. I'm going to mount up. Maybe … "

Her ankle throbbed, pulsing with an unrelenting fire. Taylor limped to the off side of the horse so she could mount with the good leg. Moaning with every movement, she slowly settled herself in the saddle and let her legs hang limply out of the stirrups.

The earliest light illuminated the edges of the horizon as Rain made her way, unguided, to the trail head. Dreams of a terrifying cougar blocking the way, of penetrating cat eyes hypnotizing her, slipped in and out of Taylor's consciousness as she dozed fitfully in the saddle, her body rocking like a rag doll with every step of the mare. In each dream a pale horse and its wounded warrior rescued her. He smiled and called her "*Bellissima,*" scooping her from the trail with otherworldly strength and placing her behind him as they galloped away.

It took Taylor a few foggy minutes to shake off the dreamy images and realize their location. When Rain stopped at the metal gate that opened toward home Taylor leaned forward and wrapped her arms around the mare's neck. She lay there for a moment and contemplated how to dismount. Her ankle seemed to have lost all feeling and become part of the leather boot. When she attempted to move it she nearly screamed out in pain. At that moment she saw the truck and trailer.

## Chapter 37

"Taylor! Oh my God!" Melissa was running toward her with Liz hobbling close behind. Too exhausted to answer, Taylor simply dropped the reins and allowed the women to ease her from the saddle. She put her arms around their shoulders and limped toward the truck, the mare following like a dog behind them. Easing Taylor to a spot on the wheel well of the trailer, Melissa bent down with difficulty to examine her friend.

"I'm all about mud beauty treatments, but this is a little ridiculous don't you think?" She tried to smile and fingered a lock of Taylor's dirt encrusted hair.

Taylor opened then shut her mouth. She stared into Melissa's make-up-less eyes and felt a tear dribble down her cheek.

Melissa's chin trembled. "Why didn't you tell me?" She wrapped her arms around Taylor and burst into tears. They leaned into each other and hugged for a long moment.

"We need to get her to the hospital."

Ever the picture of efficiency, Liz had already untacked Rain and loaded her into the horse trailer. She bent down and lifted the edge of Taylor's jeans. "Looks like you did something nasty to your ankle. Can you move it?"

Taylor simply shook her head and tried to wipe her moist muddy face with an equally filthy shirt sleeve. "Is Rain okay?"

"Seems to be." Liz stared at Taylor, her eyes and mouth twitching. "I'm not concerned about Rain, I'm concerned about you."

"It's just my ankle. I'm okay otherwise."

"Hmm," Liz looked unconvinced. She straightened and hitched up her leg. "Well, lets get you inside the truck and to a doctor."

~ ~ ~

The ringing of her cell phone awoke Taylor from a drug induced sleep. Willing her mind to engage in reality, she reached for it and punched 'talk.'

"Yeah."

"Taylor Ann! It's your mother. My God, I've been worried sick. Your landlady called me, what's her name?"

"Rowan," Taylor rubbed her itchy eyes that felt too heavy to open. "Her name's Rowan."

"What on earth happened? I might have known you'd have a serious accident riding that horse of yours."

"It wasn't Rain's fault, Mom, it was mine. *I* took her out without telling anyone, *I* pushed her to take the wrong trails. She didn't choose to fall into a bog. Or run into a cougar, I might add."

Simply saying the words sapped her strength. She was in no shape to argue with her mother.

"Does Jacob know?"

Since Minnie's accident, Taylor's mother had become the veterinarian's number one fan. Regular check ups to monitor the dog's recovery had endeared Jacob to her mother's heart, a place few men had ever occupied. In no time at all they were on a first name basis and she blogged about Minnie's "Favorite Uncle" more than once. The fact he had also rescued Rain from certain death seemed to give the horse a measure of value, even though she refused to support Taylor's interest in the sport of Ride and Tie—"Too dirty and dangerous for a woman."

"No, I haven't called him yet. I've been sleeping off my pain medicine. My friends have been taking care of everything."

She emphasized the word 'friends.' It would be nice to see her mother's face and know she cared more about her daughter than a tiny dog.

"Well, not *everything*. Seems you let that sale get away—the coffee stand. Steve has a buyer, though, and they've put in an offer. Owner just signed the contract to accept it if no better offers come in the next seven days."

"Thanks for kicking me when I'm down, Mom, appreciate that." Taylor felt the tears rise, hating that her mother could always get to her.

"Sweetie, I'm not trying to kick you when you're down!" The voice turned soothing but, as always, disapproval leaked through. "*Your* buyer couldn't get financing. It happens."

Taylor gritted her teeth. The thought of Steve striking before Melissa could try again for loan approval made her want to scream. Instead, she sighed deeply. "Mother, this conversation has been ever so uplifting, but me and my seriously sprained ankle need rest."

"Of course. Just one thing before I go … something's to be delivered today."

"Something?"

"A gift."

"What for?"

Her mother was quiet for a moment.

"I wanted to thank you for taking such good care of Minnie."

"She broke her leg at my house."

"I know. But she was so happy with you. I could tell." Her mother spoke in a peculiar voice. "It wasn't your fault she got hit by a car."

"And that deserves a gift?"

Taylor felt confused. Praise of any sort was not her mother's specialty.

"It's not just Minnie. This is something that should go to you now; I want you to have it. That's all I'm going to say."

"Okay."

Curious and more confused than before, Taylor snapped the cell phone shut and closed her eyes.

# Chapter 38

When Taylor awoke the second time it was nearly four. To be still in bed, on a weekday, felt odd. And completely wonderful. Liz would be arriving soon to visit and take care of Rain. As she slowly sat up and maneuvered her way out of the bedroom with a pair of crutches, Taylor heard a knocking on the door. Assuming it was Liz, she opened it immediately.

"Delivery for Taylor Ann Reed?"

Two men stood on the small porch. A large box van with the slogan *Move It!* on the side was parked in her driveway.

"Uh, yeah, that's me."

"Sign here." The older of the two pushed a double-sided paper on a clipboard at her.

"What is it?"

The men moved to the back of the van and released a roll-up door. "Piano," said the younger, his back to her, "and it's a bitch to move."

The older man shot his companion a meaningful look.

"Sorry."

Taylor's mouth dropped open in amazement as she watched them struggle to remove a huge wooden piano strapped inside the interior of the van. Even with nearly every surface wrapped to prevent scratching during the journey from Seattle she recognized the instrument immediately.

*The piano.*

It took nearly an hour for the movers to get her mother's piano out of the van and safely to a spot in Taylor's living room. When they finally left she immediately removed the blankets and bubble wrap, excited as a child on Christmas morning. She didn't care that the piano dwarfed everything else in her small cottage or that she didn't know how to play it. Sinking to the futon she stared at the carved flute-playing maiden as joy bubbled inside. Grabbing her cell phone she punched at the numbers.

"Mom! You gave me the piano?"

Her mother chuckled, obviously pleased at Taylor's surprise and delight. "It was time for you to have it."

"But I can't play and you *do*."

"Taylor," her mother paused to measure the words, "playing the piano has never been my passion. Sure it was an outlet at times, but the truth is Grandma and Grandpa *made* me play. When I got to the point in my life where I could choose the piano playing went by the wayside. You are the one who loved the music. You and your dad."

Taylor could count on one hand the number of times her mother had said '*your dad.*' If she had to refer to him in conversation he was simply 'Neal." Sometimes Taylor thought she believed her daughter to be the product of immaculate conception.

"Maybe I'll get lessons."

"Yes, that's exactly what I was thinking."

"Really?"

"You should do what makes you happy, Taylor, whatever it is."

The words felt like a blessing—one late in coming, but cherished just the same.

"Thanks, Mom."

"Talk to you next week when you're back at the office, okay?"

A brisk efficiency obliterated the emotion between them. Taylor knew the office—and related career—was a conversation they'd be returning to. Soon. Something had to change.

"Okay. Bye, Mom."

Clicking the phone shut Taylor continued to feast her eyes on the wooden majesty of the instrument. She thought of her mother's words: *Do what makes you happy.* Real estate did not make her happy and she doubted it ever would. What made her happy was a simple barista job, music, and riding a beautiful grey mare. Giving words to the pain of the past on a terrible night *had* created something inside her, but it wasn't what she'd expected. Instead of devastation, a tiny flame of hope flickered within. The flame said she was worthy of love, forgiveness, and a new beginning.

Taylor hobbled to the piano and lifted the cover on the keys. She'd love to learn to play it like Jacob did, caressing a melody from compliant black and white keys. But there was another sort of music the piano could create. She touched a key and listened to the tone reverberate in the small space—the opening note to a new beginning. She had never felt so certain of the move she needed to make next.

☙

## Chapter 39

"You say this is an antique?"

"Yes, it was built in 1892. I have the original sales slip."

The pencil-thin man in black slacks and loafers looked at her quickly and smoothed down wiry sprigs of greying hair. "That's hard to believe."

Taylor shrugged, "Believe it. This piano has been cherished like a human being. I have a folder of records on it: restoration information, tuning over the years, the original sales receipt. It's appreciated quite a bit since that purchase."

"Hmm."

Mr. Simms, of Simms Piano and Music Studio, walked slowly around the instrument, considering it from every angle. He paused and crossed his arms.

"It's a beauty. And the carving is unusual. But the market is narrow for this sort of thing. Only a collector would give you top dollar."

Taylor wanted to roll her eyes. What did this guy think? That she was born yesterday? He'd been unable to hide his surprise at finding a piano of such quality in a small cottage tucked away in Redneckville. She'd recognized the love in his slender musician fingers the moment they brushed the ivory keys and examined the interior of the instrument. He was trying to play it cool, but it was obvious this man either wanted the piano for himself or knew someone who did. She wasn't about to let him swindle her out of the full value.

"I love this piano, Mr. Simms. I will not sell it for less than the appraised price of $17,000."

"I don't know *who* would appraise it for such a price. I can't give you more than $15,000."

"Lervicks Pianos in Seattle gave the appraisal." Taylor waited for Mr. Simms to make eye contact. "They told me there is a standing offer of $17,000 on this piano, should I ever want to sell. For an extra $500 I'll *let* you buy it instead."

"That's an outrageous price!"

"Then don't buy it." Taylor looked at him calmly. "I wanted to keep the piano local, for sentimental reasons. That's the only reason I called your store."

She watched Simms walk unhappily up and down her small living room. He appeared to be losing an intense battle with his desires.

"Should I leave you for few minutes so you can play some more?"

The man nodded, relieved to have extra time to struggle with his decision. He sat down on the bench and without a sheet of music put on an extraordinary 15 minute concert while Taylor listened outside. It very nearly made her change her mind. When he was finished, he pressed a check in her hand.

"I'll make arrangements to pick up the piano tomorrow."

With check in hand, Taylor was ready to make the next move. Easing herself onto the futon, she punched Melissa's number.

~ ~ ~

"There is no way I can take that kind of money from you," Melissa's blue eyes looked like marbles as she peered at the face of the $17,500 check. "No way."

Taylor looked around the studio apartment Melissa had once shared with Peter. Books on pregnancy and adoption where stacked on the table next to a bag of fresh roasted coffee beans.

"Why not?"

"Because," Melissa picked up the coffee beans and inhaled the roasty aroma that leaked out, "my life isn't your problem."

"Uh, excuse me! You insisted the adoptive parents name the baby after me; I thought I was part of this whole process."

"You are. I'm just worried," Melissa fidgeted in her seat and looked away, "that you feel like you have to make up for something. You know … " Her eyes glistened.

"Atone for my own choice by helping you with yours?" Taylor's voice was soft.

"Yeah," Melissa looked down. "I feel bad for asking for your help during this pregnancy. I had no idea … "

Taylor leaned over and squeezed her friend's shoulder. "I know, but know what? You made me face it and it helped me begin to heal. You don't have to be afraid *for* me … like I might freak out or something. I'll still get sad, but I need to talk about it. I can see that now. I only have one stipulation on the money: you have to use it to buy a coffee stand and you must hire me as barista."

Melissa squealed, "No way! What about real estate?"

"I'm quitting. Can't take the crap coffee everyday."

"Woohoo!"

Melissa eased her swollen belly from behind the table and held out her arm. Taylor took it and limped along with her as they danced around the small room. Afterward, they sat down to discuss strategy.

"Now, I know Steve got another buyer for Holy Grounds, but maybe there's some way to approach the owner before the existing offer deadline." Taylor bit the end of a pencil while she thought. "We could offer full price and maybe squeeze Steve out."

*Unlikely, but possible.*

Taylor felt defeated even with the fat check sitting on the table between them. Melissa didn't seem to notice.

"I could care less what he thinks or does cause guess what?" She clasped her hands together.

Taylor stared at her friend.

"I found out I'm eligible for a special grant. I got *all* the goods, baby." Her eyes sparkled.

"What goods?"

"I'm one quarter Native American. And a woman, in case you hadn't noticed." Melissa giggled, then sighed. "I knew my dad would be good for something one day."

"So you can get a loan?"

"Yep, I'm a minority. And with your check as down payment we can buy a great coffee stand. It doesn't have to be Holy Grounds." Melissa grabbed Taylor's hand across the table and squeezed it. "We'll be partners."

Life was strange. When dreams were shattered and the future seemed hopeless, a second chance could bloom like a dandelion in summer—persistent and irrepressible. Taylor thought of her lonely dialogue with God as Rain rested in surrender in the middle of the bog. She'd gotten it all wrong. God didn't wait to pounce, stern-faced and unyielding, from the shadows of a confessional. He offered a field of dandelions.

༄

# Chapter 40

Taylor sat up and swung her bandaged ankle off the couch. "Who could be here?"

Melissa continued to chop vegetables, but Liz turned around and jerked her head toward the door. She raised one eyebrow, a smile twitching at the corners of her mouth. "You better find out."

Taylor heard whispered murmurings behind her and a soft chuckle as she hobbled toward the door and opened it.

Jacob stood on the small porch, a bouquet of wild flowers in one hand. Kreed whined at his side, black tail waving. He looked down at her for a long moment, his hazel eyes intense, and drew her to himself without a word. Taylor laid her head on his shoulder and a sob caught in her throat as she spoke into the faded material of his denim shirt.

"There's so much I need to tell you."

"I know."

Jacob cupped his hand around the back of her head and pressed it into his chest, his fingers catching in the long strands of Taylor's hair. If not for the electricity between them she would have felt like a child.

"You're okay; that's all that matters now." He spoke into her hair and she shivered from the warmth of his breath. She could have disappeared into the safety of his arms forever had a husky voice not interrupted.

"Ah, hello! Dinner's ready you love birds."

Jacob released Taylor and they turned to acknowledge Melissa who stood with one hand on what was left of her waist, a mound of pregnant stomach swelling beyond her finger tips.

"Nice to see you, *Dr. Wilson*."

"I told you not to call me that." Jacob wagged a finger at her.

"I'm not good at doing what I'm told. Now sit down and enjoy a feast."

As they ate and chatted about babies, coffee, and horses, Taylor looked from the twitching eyes of Liz, to the pierced brows of Melissa, to the stubble sprouting on Jacob's chin. In some strange way they had become a family. Even as her ankle began to throb in earnest, Taylor relaxed into a feeling of well-being like she had never known. The pain of the past was slowly releasing. It flowed into the present and mixed with the incredible sweetness that existed there.

"Hey guys, I gotta go lay down."

"Let me get you some more drugs." Melissa frowned and pushed back her chair.

"No, no," Taylor raised her hand, "I want to feel everything right now. You all go ahead and finish."

She lay on the couch, pain pulsing through her leg, and pondered the curious new feelings of congruency in her life. Outside the day faded. Shafts of light slanted through a window, illuminating particles in the air until they glittered like fairy dust. Across the room Kreed dozed on the floor, his body stretched out nearly six feet in length. He lifted his head, eyes looking deep into hers, and thumped his tail in agreement.

Taylor looked at the place where the piano had stood. Indentations still marked the carpet from the instrument's tremendous weight. She listened to Jacob hum a familiar tune from the kitchen as he helped clear the table, the song's lyrics penetrating her heart:

> *Through many dangers toils and snares*
> *I have already come,*
> *Tis grace has brought me safe thus far,*
> *and grace will lead me home.*

The piano was gone but the music remained, deeper and richer, a new song of redeeming love.

## **The End**

## Acknowledgments

Many people ultimately contributed to this story, some unknowingly. I would like to formally acknowledge the following, with deepest gratitude: My parents, Dan and Sheryl Bettle, true bibliophiles who instilled in me a great respect for the power of words and laid the foundations of my writing life long before it became a dream. I am especially thankful for my father's valuable contributions to editing and natural ear for language. To Ruth Harms, your keen eye and feedback on the early manuscript was a great blessing. Leigh Shambo, your wise insight into both horse and human nature and commitment to honor everyone, regardless of mental or emotional handicap, remains an inspiration to me. To Karen Bacon, who wore many hats in the process of creating this book—editor, reader, designer, and encouraging friend. I could not have finished this without you.

I am thankful to the following people for supplying key details, allowing my use of their work, and/or general support: Joe Wilkinson, Emily Green, Kim Meeder, David Young, Helena Cavan, Sage Hollins, BJ Taylor, Julie Garmon, Sibella Giorello, CJ Darlington, and Karen Pickering, publisher of the *Northwest Horse Source*. I am also forever indebted to my *Guideposts Magazine* family, especially editor's Jim McDermott, Rick Hamlin, Amy Wong, and Edward Grinnan. Thank you for seeing the heart behind those first clumsy sentences and shaping me into a writer.

For the young women I met while working at the Whatcom County Pregnancy Clinic: I have forgotten most of your names, but your stories changed me forever.

Last, but never least, to my family: My husband, Mark, who inspires the good traits in every male character I create and loves me despite the inconvenience of a writing wife, and my children Nicholas and Haley. Being your mother renovated my life and heart in beautiful ways. I love you all.

## NOTE TO READERS

While this is a work of fiction, the character of Rain and certain plot details were inspired by a true story. In the fall of 2009, an Arabian gelding was taken into the Cascade Mountains of Oregon, shot twice in the head, and left for dead. There is no medical explanation for his survival. Like Rain, he has a special ability to minister to those who are hurting. To learn more about a horse named Hero please visit Crystal Peaks Youth Ranch: www.cpyr.org.

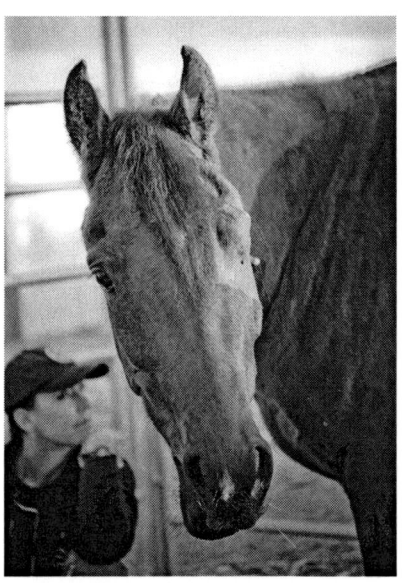

Hero with Crystal Peaks co-founder Kim Meeder.

Photo courtesy of Emily Green: http://www.shadesofgreenphotography.com

> *...God has chosen the weak things of the world*
> *to put to shame the things which are mighty,*
> *and the insignificant things ...*
> *and the things which are despised God has chosen.*
>
> 1 Corinthians 1:27-28

# Reader Guide

**Rain in Real Life: Treating Trauma with Horses**
Insight into the growing field of Equine Facilitated Psychotherapy from author and licensed mental health counselor Leigh Shambo.

### *How do therapists define and categorize trauma?*

As a mental health therapist I am trained to help people recover from the emotional aspects of trauma. Trauma begins with an event in which the person experienced or witnessed actual or threatened death or serious injury, or a threat to the physical integrity of self or others. The response to trauma is very subjective. For instance, a parent's highly emotional outburst may be emotionally traumatic to a child, although it did not involve a real threat of physical harm. In some cases trauma is repetitive, such as abuse that occurs over a number of years. This is more serious than a one-time episode, especially when this prolonged trauma occurs during developmental periods such as early childhood or puberty. Therapists who specialize in trauma recognize many factors: the severity of the experience, whether it was a single episode or prolonged, the age at which it occurred, the nature of the events and reactions of other people who were involved. One of the most important factors has to do with trauma resilience—has the person had a chance to develop the healthy coping strategies and strong relationships that help us recover more easily from life's traumatic experiences?

### *What is the difference between Acute Stress Reaction and Post-Traumatic Stress Disorder?*

Trauma affects people differently. It is expected that a truly traumatic experience will have lingering effects. These may involve flashbacks, nightmares, hyper-vigilance, emotional numbing or avoidance of any reminders of the trauma. These effects should diminish over time; typically they should diminish over a period of 3 months or so. During this time a person is said to be experiencing Post-Traumatic Stress or Acute Stress Reaction. It is when the effects of traumatic stress do not diminish naturally, leaving the person unable to resume their previous state of normal functioning, that the person is said to have Post-Traumatic

Stress *Disorder*. Traumatic experiences do not always lead to PTSD; many people recover quite quickly due to strong resilience factors—productive ways of coping including the healthy expression of emotions and strong social support from family and friends.

Post-traumatic stress disorder generally does not resolve on its own, with quite serious symptoms including flashbacks, nightmares and sleep disturbances, mood and anxiety symptoms which may go on for years, significantly interfering with life functioning and negatively impacting the person's family and professional relationships. This is where professional help from a therapist is indicated.

Reactions similar to PTSD may be caused by conditions that resemble trauma. The effects of a hostile divorce, chronic family dysfunction such as toxic anger, addictions, or emotional abuse in the family can impact one's ability to thrive as well. If you feel that you are stuck in unhealthy patterns that have their origin in an experience that is past, a mental health therapist may be able to help you.

### *What sorts of situations benefit from EFP?*

EFP—Equine-Facilitated Psychotherapy—is a targeted intervention applied by a trained psychotherapist. Carefully designed exercises with horses allow for emotional growth and learning in participants. The focus of EFP/L programs is not recreational riding, but the moment-to-moment opportunities to practice self-awareness, emotional honesty, and constructive relationship skills. The abilities developed translate readily to human relationships and environments. EFP/L can be especially effective for participants who have difficulty engaging in traditional office therapy. Office therapy is often more cognitively or thinking based, while EFP is more feeling and experience based. In this type of therapy, horses are employed to help people resolve the symptoms of post-traumatic stress or post-traumatic stress disorder. This involves helping the person process the traumatic incident and understand how and why it continues to impact life in the here and now. The person often has to build new, more appropriate responses instead of relying on the "survival reactions" that may have carried the person through the traumatic episode or time.

***In a nutshell, what do horses bring to the process of trauma recovery?***

Horses possess keen intuition regarding human emotional states and are exceedingly responsive to the level of self-awareness and emotional congruence of people. Their imposing size and tremendous strength require respect, attention to safety and a great deal of sensitivity. Once a good relationship is established with a horse, the interactions are exhilarating and liberating—engaging the mind, body and spirit in ways that are profoundly transformative.

Horses display unparalleled sensitivity to non-verbal communication and behavioral consistency. They display confusion in the face of incongruities in thought, feeling and behavior, and they are incapable of masking emotion or lying, making them powerful therapeutic mirrors. As the person sorts out feelings and learns to express them appropriately the horse responds with cooperation and generosity, providing immediate reinforcement for positive changes in affect, cognition and behavior.

~ ~ ~

**Leigh Shambo** has her Masters in social work and maintains a private practice counseling both children and adults at her ranch, Human Equine Alliances for Learning (HEAL). She is the first person to formally study the long term results of using horses to treat those suffering from PTSD and currently teaches on this topic in the United States and England. She lives in Washington State with her husband, David Young, and a small herd of horses. To learn more about this work and Leigh's book on the subject, please visit: www.humanequinealliance.org.

**Catherine Madera** writes and rides in the Pacific Northwest where she lives with her family and a trio of horses. She is the author of *Rodeo Dreams*, editor of the *Northwest Horse Source* and the recipient of the Merial Human-Animal Bond award, given by American Horse Publications for "A Hero's Work," the true story behind *Rain Shadow*. To read the story and for more information, visit: www.catherinemadera.com.

CPSIA information can be obtained at www.ICGtesting.com
Printed in the USA
BVOW081037040313

314594BV00001B/1/P